Cowboys of the Butterfly Ranch

Jessie and James

JEN SPENCER

Jessie and James
Copyright © 2019 by Jennifer Beckstrand
All rights reserved

This book is a work of fiction. Any references to historical events, real people, or real places are used fictitiously.

First Edition July 19, 2019

Printed and bound in the United States of America

ISBN: 978-1-079772-90-6
ASIN: B07R77G9HH (ebook)

Dedication

To my eight beautiful grandchildren.
You give so much meaning to my life.

One

Spring 1885

James Kelsey reined in his horse, took off his hat, and swiped his bandanna at the beads of sweat that trickled down the back of his neck. It was only early May, but the five-hour ride from Santaquin had been unseasonably warm. And dry.

He breathed in the fresh desert air. This land of big sky and bigger dreams felt like home. He'd been away a very long time, but he'd never forgotten.

James dismounted, fed the horse a carrot from his saddlebag, and squinted into the afternoon sun. A jagged outcropping of rocks in the distance told him he was getting close to gold country. From what he'd been told, there was enough gold, silver, and copper in those hills to make a hundred men richer than kings. James was going to find it.

And finally make Father proud.

    Staked in the ground, hiding behind a juniper, a road marker leaned precariously to the right. "Eureka 2 miles," it said. James mounted his patient horse. The hard part of the journey was over. He clicked his tongue and prodded his horse forward. The promise of a hot meal and a soft bed was all he needed to keep going.

    It wasn't long before he saw more signs of civilization. A weathered log cabin stood just outside of town, next to a house built of stone. Homes got closer together. Several tents—permanent housing for miners—crouched along both sides of the road.

    In the distance, James could make out the massive timberworks of a mine, with stairs and chutes and lumber clinging to the hillside on a framework of timber that looked as if it would easily topple in the face of a stiff wind. Higher up in a patch of leftover snow, a single headframe stood sentinel over the town, a monument to men's unrelenting hunger for gold.

    A two-story hotel and a livery stable were sure signs that James had reached his destination. New mining towns like Eureka were nothing compared to cities like Boston or Chicago, but James counted three hotels, a saloon, a barbershop, a blacksmith shop, and several modest homes along the main street. A hard rain some time in the past had carved a gully out of the dirt down the center of the street. At almost a foot deep, the gully would give a teamster trouble if he was ever unfortunate enough to get a wheel stuck in it.

James scanned the main street for the boarding house where he was supposed to be staying, but he didn't see it. He'd have to ask directions. Spying a water trough, James guided his horse to the west side of the mercantile. After dismounting, he tied up his horse so she could drink. James had bought the mare in Provo, so he didn't know her personally yet, but so far, she seemed as mild-mannered and gentle as a nun—just the kind of horse he needed. They'd be spending the next few weeks together roaming the foothills of Eureka. There wouldn't be any excitement for a horse that wanted to run.

James walked around the corner to the front of the mercantile just as a loud crash came from inside. A loud crash, a clatter, and a shout. James jumped as a miner, who looked like he'd just emerged from below ground, shot out of the store, both hands pulling at the hat on his head as if he was trying to keep it from blowing away in the wind. And maybe he was, because a purple whirlwind blew out the door behind him. A young woman, with a shotgun hanging over her shoulder by a strap and murder in her eyes, stormed out of the mercantile with a flour sack clutched in one arm like a baby. Her chestnut hair tumbled around her shoulders like the unruly branches of a juniper bush, and her brown eyes flashed like two hot coals in the fire. James had never seen anyone look quite so fierce.

"I didn't mean anything by it, Miss Jessie," the miner said, backing away from the woman as if she was a mother bear and he'd gotten in the way of her cubs. It didn't take a keen observer to see that the man was two sheets to the wind and that Miss Jessie would have no mercy.

Miss Jessie dropped her flour sack, pulled her shotgun off her shoulder, and pointed it at the drunken miner, who backpedaled so fast he lost his balance and fell to the ground. "You meant it, sure enough," Miss Jessie said. "Just like the last four times you meant it. I should shoot you just for being thickheaded."

James didn't know if he should help the miner off the ground, stand between the poor man and that shotgun, or give him a swift right hook to the jaw. But whatever the miner had done to earn the wrath of Miss Jessie, James was pretty sure he didn't deserve to get shot for it.

"I can't resist, Miss Jessie. Your hair is like my Abilene's, and I miss her so much."

Miss Jessie showed no signs of relaxing her grip on that shotgun. "Your Abilene left because you take liberties with other women. You have no one to blame but yourself."

The miner knew better than to be anything but contrite. "I know it. I know it, Miss Jessie. But you should feel sorry for me instead of trying to kill me. They'll send you to prison."

Miss Jessie grunted her disgust, but the barrel

of the shotgun drooped to a forty-five degree angle. "They'll give me a medal for ridding the town of a menace."

By this time, a few people had gathered to watch the spectacle. Two men poked their heads out from the mercantile door. Two more stood at the opposite corner of the mercantile, probably so they could duck behind the building if there was any shooting. Another man watched from across the street, leaning against the wall of the barbershop and smiling as if this was the most entertainment he'd had in months. It probably was. None but James was close enough to actually get shot.

"Miss Jessie, let old Petty be," said one of the men standing inside the mercantile door. "You can see how regretful he is."

Miss Jessie's gaze flicked in the direction of the mercantile, but she made no other sign she'd heard the man. She motioned to her right with the barrel of the shotgun. "Go home, Petty."

Petty jumped to his feet and ran down the road so fast, he could have outrun a horse. Miss Jessie lowered her shotgun, propped the barrel on her forearm, and huffed out an exasperated breath. "Everybody can quit staring," she said to no one in particular. "It's nothing you ain't seen before."

James cocked an eyebrow. How many times had Miss Jessie tried to shoot someone at the mercantile?

He bent over and picked up Miss Jessie's flour

sack and flung it over his shoulder. It was heavy. He should probably offer to carry it home for her. As he stood up straight, he found himself staring down the barrel of Miss Jessie's shotgun, and unlike Petty, James had nowhere to run. His heart leapt into his throat.

"You trying to steal my flour?" Miss Jessie said, staring down the barrel of the shotgun like a seasoned killer.

James wasn't one to get easily rattled, but being mere inches from death made him a little bit testy. In a lightning swift motion, he shot out his free hand, wrapped his fingers around the barrel of the gun, and shoved it upward so the shotgun pointed at the sky. Miss Jessie gasped as the movement wrenched her arm and the butt of the shotgun dug into her shoulder, but she didn't release her grip or disintegrate like a pile of sand. "I apologize for hurting you, ma'am, but I rather not get shot today. This is a new shirt."

Scowling, she leaned back, straining to pull the barrel of the gun from his grasp, but she couldn't have known how useless she was against him. "We hang thieves around here."

He held strong to the barrel of the gun. He didn't want to fight her, but he also didn't want to get shot. "I'm not trying to steal your flour, ma'am. I was picking it up for you. I might even offer to carry it home for you if you promise not to shoot me."

"I don't need your help," she said, still

struggling for the gun. With her tight grip, it was a wonder it hadn't already gone off.

He pulled the gun closer, and since she wasn't about to relax her grip, she came with it. That close, her cheeks looked as smooth and as soft as kid gloves, and she smelled faintly of vanilla and cherry blossoms. James' stomach clenched. Her smell, her tumbling hair, her reckless determination attacked his reason and sent him reeling like a drunk. Fortunately, he had enough of his wits about him to keep tight hold on that gun. His grip was the only thing between him and certain death.

The man at the mercantile door must have been used to coming to the defense of Miss Jessie's victims. "Jessie, leave the fellow be."

Jessie glared at James with all the rage of a forest fire. "Let go of my gun," she hissed.

"I'll let go if you promise not to shoot me."

"I'll promise not to shoot you right now, but that doesn't mean I won't shoot you later."

"If I ever touch your hair like that Petty fellow did or take liberties or do anything to disrespect you, ma'am, you have my permission to shoot me."

A ghost of a smile tugged at her mouth, but it was gone so fast, he might have imagined it. "I don't need your permission."

"I suppose you don't." He slowly relaxed his grip on the gun barrel, because if he let go while she pulled so hard, he'd send her toppling to the ground, and he'd rather not cause more trouble.

As soon as he let go, Miss Jessie gave him the evil eye, slung her shotgun over her shoulder, and snatched the flour sack from his grasp. She winced when she moved her arm, and James felt sorry that she'd probably have a bruise, but he couldn't regret trying to keep her from putting a hole in his chest.

"I meant what I said, ma'am. I'd be honored to carry the flour to your house."

She narrowed her eyes. "You're not from around here."

"But I'd still be happy to help, even though you recently tried to kill me."

Glaring at him, she hoisted the flour sack more securely into her arms. "I don't need your help and neither does this town. You can just go right back to wherever it is you came from and leave us alone."

James wasn't quite sure how to respond to such a welcome. Miss Jessie stepped around him and disappeared around the corner of the mercantile. A few seconds later, she emerged at the reins of a flatbed wagon pulled by two horses.

"I'll put it on your tab," the man at the door of the mercantile called.

Miss Jessie didn't acknowledge that she'd heard him. She turned onto the road and drove away, her flour sack the only load in her wagon. James didn't know whether to feel relief that she hadn't shot him or regret that they'd parted on bad terms. For better or worse, Miss Jessie was the most fascinating woman he'd ever encountered.

The two men stood at the door of the mercantile watching Miss Jessie's wagon, as if to make absolutely certain she wouldn't change her mind and come back. James stuck out his hand.

"I'm James Kelsey," he said, shaking hands with the older man, then the younger.

The older man had a shock of white hair that floated about his head with the aid of static electricity. The younger man's black hair was slicked back so not a strand was out of place, making it look like his hair was painted onto his head instead of combed there.

"I'm Lou Johns," the older man said. "This is my son Hubert. We own the place and live upstairs. I'm sorry our Jessie didn't give you a warmer welcome. She's usually real sweet."

Hubert let out a high-pitched laugh. "About as sweet as a rattler."

Lou shook his head. "It ain't easy being pretty and single in a town of slommacky miners. Petty come in here and pulled the pins out of her hair. Of course she got mad. That's why she carries her shotgun wherever she goes. She's got a right to defend herself."

"Yes, she does," James said, suddenly feeling protective of the woman who'd just tried to kill him. Miners could be a rough sort, and Miss Jessie didn't deserve to be accosted every time she went out.

And she wasn't married.

James bit down on his tongue and tamped down his sudden enthusiasm. He was already on her bad side. He should definitely steer clear. Steering clear wouldn't be too hard. He wouldn't be in town long, and most of the time he'd be roaming the hills looking for promising veins of ore.

"You sound like you're from parts east," Lou said. "You looking for gold?"

"I'm here looking for a claim for the London Mining and Ore Company. Silver, gold, copper, it doesn't matter which. I hope I'm not unwelcome."

Lou swiped his hand across his mouth. "Nah, a new mine means more money and work for everybody. Jessie's just wary of new folks, and she doesn't much like the mining business to begin with. Too many shysters looking for easy money and too many hard men who don't know how to behave themselves." Lou studied James' face. "You need a different hat, but you have an honest face. Now, that Frank Roberts, I don't trust him as far as I can throw him, but I reckon time will tell with you."

Hubert pulled a handkerchief from his pocket and wiped his hands. "You got a place to stay, Mister Kelsey?"

James nodded, wondering what was wrong with his hat. "I'm expected at the Madsen House. Can you tell me how to get there?"

Hubert threw back his head and laughed. "Well, if that ain't the best joke I've heard all day."

Two

Jessie didn't have an angry disposition. It wasn't even particularly easy to irritate her, but there was so much to be angry about and so many men who liked to irritate her that she was angry most of the time. Angry, defensive, and ready for a fight.

She hadn't even picked up half of what she needed at the mercantile, but after Petty had ruined her hair and that uppity Easterner had injured her shoulder, she hadn't had the gumption to go back in and finish her shopping. She'd have to go back tomorrow. Alice still needed cornmeal, soda, sugar, and about ten other things, and Jessie was the one who ran the errands. With her shotgun.

Jessie peered at herself in the mirror as she stuck a hairpin into her bun. The mirror was so small, she couldn't see her whole face, but it was sufficient for seeing the top of her head when she put her hair up in the morning and on days like today when she needed to do it twice. They were expecting a new boarder, and she wanted to look respectable. He'd specifically mentioned in his letter that he wanted a reputable place to stay. That was enough to make Jessie like him already. There were plenty of the other kind of places to stay, but a fellow didn't stay at a saloon unless he was looking for easy sin.

Jessie had driven home from the mercantile, unhitched the horse, and tried to explain to Alice why she'd brought nothing but flour home from the store. She left out the part about the shotgun and the Easterner because Alice always insisted that proper young ladies did not carry shotguns to run errands.

Then she'd hurriedly fashioned her hair into a bun at the back of her head, even though it was never an easy or a fast job. Her hair fell nearly to her waist, and getting it to behave was a fifteen-minute task every morning. Petty's obsession with her hair was, at best, an aggravating inconvenience.

Today, it was also a painful task. When that Easterner had grabbed the barrel of her shotgun, he'd rammed the butt of the gun into her shoulder, and she was sore up the side of her neck and clear down to her ribcage. That man had a strong arm and a powerful grip—not that she could blame him for being rough. She'd pointed her gun at him.

He had lashed out like a cougar in a trap.

But he didn't have to be so aggravatingly smug about it. *It would be my honor to carry your flour, Miss Jessie, even though you tried to kill me.*

She growled at the ceiling. *Don't patronize me, Mr. Fancy Pants. I know your type well enough.*

Jessie finished her hair and headed for Scully's livery stable to see to Red and Jerry Boy before she helped Alice with dinner. They saved money by feeding and caring for their horses themselves instead of paying Scully to do it. The price to board the horses was high enough. Jessie cared for the horses, and Papa paid for their stabling. Papa just couldn't do the hard labor.

Scully's livery stable was small and in serious disrepair, but it was also a stone's throw from the boarding house, and the cheapest livery stable in town. Being an old wrangler, Scully took great pride in caring for the horses, but the stable walls were rotting and the roof leaked, even with the three tarps tied over the top. Scully couldn't charge a premium for boarding horses. He was old and blind in one eye and never had two nickels to rub together. He hadn't the money to buy materials for repairs, and neither could he pay someone to do them.

Jessie retrieved two galvanized metal buckets hanging on nails just inside the stable door then went out back to the pump to fetch water to fill the drinking buckets. The chore went faster when she carried two full buckets to the stall at once. Full buckets were always staggeringly heavy, but when she took two at a time, she could balance herself out, making the job a tiny bit easier. Still favoring her right side, she worked the pump with her left arm. It went slower than usual, but Jessie was nothing if not stubborn. She had to be. The farm wasn't going to take care of itself.

When she tried to pick up the first bucket with her right hand, pain shot from her shoulder down to the tips of her fingers. She gasped, let go of the handle, and thought of about ten cuss words she wanted to say to that Easterner.

But then, speak of the devil, she heard his voice. Or what sounded an awful lot like his voice, with that clipped northeastern pronunciation of long, drawn-out A's and missing R sounds. Jessie left her buckets by the pump and peeked around the corner of the stable.

Jessie stopped breathing, and her throat tightened as if someone was strangling her. The gall of that man to show up on her side of town!

His saddlebag was slung over his shoulder and his back was turned, so Jessie wasn't in much danger of being discovered. But she didn't have to see his face to remember those eyes, the color of the sky on a warm spring day, studying her face like he could discern all her secrets by just looking. Her mouth went dry. She wasn't ever going to let him look that close again. She'd already made that mistake once.

He wore tan trousers and sturdy work boots,

Jessie and James

not ideal for riding a horse, but adequate for just about any job in a mining town. His dark brown jacket hung midway down his thighs, over a cream shirt and tie and navy blue button-up vest. He was dressed like an educated, sensible man who wasn't afraid of work. The only thing not quite right was his bowler hat—likely the style back East, but wildly out of place in a western mining town.

The Easterner and Scully seemed to be having a disagreement, but it couldn't have been a fair fight. The Easterner was a good foot taller than Scully, and he looked as if he ate stable hands for breakfast. And Jessie knew from very personal experience how strong those arms were.

Scully squinted with his good eye. "Cost is twenty dollars a week for full board and fifteen for partial board."

Jessie raised an eyebrow. Twenty dollars a week? It was an indecent price, double what Scully usually charged to full board a horse. Scully was blind in one eye, but it was obvious he knew a golden opportunity when he saw one. No doubt the Easterner could afford to pay, and Scully wasn't above fleecing a sheep for drinking money.

"I only need partial board," the Easterner said. "I can clean out my own stall and exercise my horse. And I'll pay seven dollars a week."

"Seven dollars?" Scully said, making a decent show of utter distress. "That's highway robbery. I can't do it for less than fourteen, but that's as low as I'll go."

The Easterner shrugged. "Your roof is covered with tarps and looks like it might collapse with the next storm. I won't pay fourteen dollars for a wet horse. And how sturdy are your walls against the wind?"

"It never rains here," Scully said, trying to bolster his argument, but he couldn't contradict the Easterner about the condition of the stable.

"I'll pay seven dollars a week or go elsewhere."

Jessie pressed her lips into a hard line. Scully was asking too much, but couldn't the man have a little compassion? It was plain to see how badly Scully needed the money, and the Easterner obviously had deep pockets. They all did.

"Okay, okay," Scully said, stepping into the Easterner's path when he started to walk away. "Seven a week partial board. Paid in advance."

The Easterner nodded. "In advance." He pulled a pouch from his saddlebag and handed some money to Scully. "Which stall?" he said.

Jessie jumped like a spooked horse and quickly ducked out of sight. This wasn't good. Not good at all. How long would that horrible man be in town? And how would she avoid him when their horses shared a stable? She took a deep breath and squared her shoulders. Why did *she* need to avoid *him*? He was the one who had nearly torn her arm off with sheer brute force. She had nothing to be ashamed of.

Except for that little matter of trying to kill

him.

She pressed her palm into the sorest spot on her shoulder. Red and Jerry Boy needed to be watered, and she couldn't hide out here in the back until the Easterner went away, especially since he was bound to find her when he came to fetch water for his own horse. She'd just have to ignore the man. Surely he wanted to avoid her as badly as she wanted to avoid him.

"Pleased to see you again, Miss Jessie."

Jessie jumped out of her skin at the sound of that low, husky voice. She turned to see the Easterner leaning against the wall of the stable with his arms folded across his wide chest and a casual smile on his lips. He tipped his hat, and her pulse sped to a gallop but only because he seemed so aggravatingly nonchalant. "I wish I could say the same," she said, bending over to pick up her full water buckets. No need to lollygag when there were chores to be done. She stifled a groan as pain shot up her arm. There was nothing she could do. She'd have to take the buckets one at a time.

Before she could even blink, Mr. Fancy Pants snatched up both her buckets like they were filled with bubbles. "Allow me," he said.

She tried to take her buckets back. "I don't need your help."

He was already halfway to the stable. "What kind of man would I be if I let a woman heft her own water?"

Jessie had no choice but to follow, but she still

felt the need to protest. "I can carry it."

"But you shouldn't have to. Not when a man is present."

"I don't need a man."

"I know," he said, flashing her a half smile. "You are perfectly capable of taking care of yourself."

She gave him a sharp look, but he wasn't teasing or scolding her, but she was still irritated with him. "Scully is dirt poor," she said, hoping he heard the chastisement in her voice. "If you had any goodness in your heart, you would have agreed to the fourteen dollars. I dare say you can afford it."

The Easterner seemed more amused than offended. He cocked an eyebrow. "You are a woman of many talents, Miss Jessie. You know how to hold a shotgun, and you're an excellent spy. But perhaps you shouldn't presume to know how much I can afford."

Jessie felt her face get warm, but she wasn't about to back down, even though he was right about her being presumptuous. "You have a two-hundred-and-fifty-dollar horse and a fancy hat. Even if you're not rich, you have big money backing you up."

The Easterner lost his smile and drew his brows together. "I should have brought a different hat." He poured the water into the two buckets in Jerry Boy's stall then headed back outside for more. She followed him to make sure he didn't steal her buckets. He worked the pump as easy as you please and filled the buckets far faster than she had. Again, he refused to let her carry them. Such an irritating man. "Miss Jessie, I know you're mad, but I did what I did at the mercantile because I didn't want to die."

She made a sour face, but he was pouring water and didn't see it. "I wouldn't have shot you."

"That thought brings me great comfort." He emptied the second bucket. "I'm sure you don't think I have an ounce of compassion, Miss Jessie, but if I had agreed to Scully's boarding price, I would have been marked as a fool on my first day in town. Men of honor won't trust me if they think I'm an ignorant man, and unscrupulous men would try to cheat me in all future business I do here. They have to see that I am smart enough to know what it costs to board a horse."

It was annoying that he was talking complete sense. "But what about Scully?"

"Scully might get a big tip from me when I leave town." He turned and gave her a smile that nearly knocked her over. "That is, if I can afford it."

"You can afford it," she said, scowling at him. He was deliberately trying to provoke her. It was working. She cleared her throat and reminded herself that she had vowed never to believe a handsome-faced, smooth talker again. "You're here looking for gold, aren't you?"

He studied her face. "Nothing wrong with

that."

"Everything's wrong with that. You get people all worked up over the promise of gold."

"I've never personally gotten anyone worked up over anything."

Jessie glared at him. "Men sell everything they have and move here to live like animals in tents. They behave like animals too, getting drunk every night, starting fights, harassing decent people."

The Easterner gave Red a pat on the neck. "Miss Jessie, I don't want to contradict a lady, but that seems more like a man problem than a mining problem." One side of his mouth curled upward. "Do you have a man problem?"

Ignoring the pain that stabbed her right between her ribs, she narrowed her eyes. She would have smacked him upside the head with the butt of her shotgun, but she'd left it sitting on her bed. "Oh, yes, I have a very serious man problem, and he'd better hightail it on out of here before I pull my jackknife on him." She didn't really have a jackknife hidden anywhere on her person, but he didn't need to know that.

He held up his hands and took a step backward. "This is a new shirt. I'd rather not—"

"Blood washes out," she snapped. He was a fancy-pants Easterner, all right. Nobody around here cared about getting their clothes dirty. Most of them never even bathed. Jessie'd had enough with this one. Now that the horses were watered, she didn't have to spend another minute in the stable. She turned on her heels and headed for the closest way out.

"Miss Jessie," he said, bidding her to turn with the mere attraction of his voice. "You have the most beautiful hair I've ever seen."

She didn't even respond. He was trying to wheedle her, and she wasn't about to give him the satisfaction of thinking he'd succeeded. She stormed out of the stable and up the hill to the boarding house. Even though Eureka was a small town, she hoped to never run into the Easterner or his shocking blues eyes again. Maybe she'd stay at home and offer to do the cooking and let Alice run the errands until they all saw the welcome sight of that man's horse riding out of town.

Jessie gasped and stopped in her tracks. Balling her hands into fists, she turned her face to the sky and growled.

That Easterner was the new boarder.

Three

Jessie marched out of the stable as if it was on fire.

James met eyes with one of her horses. The horse glared back in disgust. "That didn't come out the way I wanted it to," James said. Not the part about her hair, but the part about Jessie having man problems. What James had meant to say was, "Do you have a beau? Because if you don't, I'm interested."

He shouldn't be interested. He was only going to be here until he found a claim, then he'd be assigned to go somewhere else, maybe Idaho or Colorado, to look for another mine and another way to earn his father's approval. But a girl like Jessie made him momentarily forget about any other dream he had. That hair and those big brown eyes were downright irresistible. Even the way she scowled at him was appealing, like she thought he was the biggest fool in the entire world.

He slipped the saddle and pack off his horse and brushed her down. Maybe he'd name his horse Jessie, to help him remember her when he was far away from Eureka. And maybe he wouldn't. Something told him Jessie would be insulted to have a horse named after her. But it might be fun, just to see those brown eyes flash with righteous indignation.

He had a feeling she was going to be very surprised when he showed up at the boarding house. The company was paying the Madsens handsomely for his board, and she probably wouldn't have been quite so sharp with him if she'd known who he was. But he wouldn't have changed either of their encounters for a barrel full of politeness. He'd seen the real Jessie Madsen, and his heart pounded against his chest just thinking about her wild, flying hair and the fierce, determined look on her face.

Nope. He wasn't interested. Couldn't be interested. He had places to go and people to impress. Eureka was next door to nowhere important, and he'd be a fool to forget it.

With his pack in one hand and his saddlebags over his shoulder, James climbed the gentle slope to the boarding house. A young, blossoming cherry tree spread its branches in the front yard. It was already losing petals, and they fell to the ground like snowflakes. There was little other growth in the yard. Eureka was on the edge of a desert. Just how did they water that tree? James winced at the thought of Jessie carrying bucket after bucket to keep that cherry tree alive.

The Madsen House wasn't impressive by any standard in Boston, but for Eureka, it was substantial enough. The walls of the first floor were built of stone in plaster, and it looked as if it had been standing for many years. The second floor was shiny white clapboard, obviously added to the original structure to expand the house. It was an odd combination of old and new, but well-kept and more-than-adequately maintained. James smiled. He'd be comfortable here.

Every boarding house had its own customs, so he knocked on the door then let himself in. The door opened to a large room with planed wood floors and a coal-burning stove to his left. Four sturdy tables filled the space with six chairs around each table. This was the common room where boarders took their meals.

They had been expecting his arrival. A man with salt-and-pepper gray hair sat on a chair facing the door with two canes in one fist and a kind, fatherly sort of smile on his face. A fresh-faced woman with light hair stood behind the man to his right, and Miss Jessie, with a pained smile on her lips and a dot of flour on her cheek, stood next to the woman. Miss Jessie looked more irritated than surprised. James smiled to himself. Irritation was better than downright hostility.

There was also something else in her

expression, like maybe she didn't trust him. Or maybe she hated his guts.

The man in the chair didn't stand up, but he reached out his hand. "Mr. James Kelsey?"

James set down his pack and gave the man a firm handshake. "Yes, sir. London Mining and Ore Company."

"Welcome to the Madsen House. I'm George Madsen." He motioned to the woman on his right. "This is my wife, Alice. She's the cook. And this is my daughter, Jessie. She does just about everything else around here."

"I do not, Papa."

A smile tugged at James' lips. "Miss Jessie and I have already met."

Jessie stiffened like a post and gave him a glare that could have set his hat on fire if he stood still long enough.

"You have?" Alice said.

"I encountered Miss Jessie at the stable. She gave me a warm welcome." Jessie relaxed her shoulders, but she didn't seem especially grateful that he'd kept her secret. Maybe she regretted not shooting him.

Alice offered her hand, and James gave it a light squeeze. "If you need anything, Mr. Kelsey, don't hesitate to ask. Are there foods you particularly like to eat? I can make just about anything if the ingredients are available at the mercantile. I used to cook for a family in Denver."

James hid his curiosity behind a wide smile.

Alice and Jessie looked nothing alike. Jessie was tall and wiry. Alice was short and decidedly plump, and she couldn't have been more than ten years older than Jessie. Certainly not her mother. "I'll eat just about anything you put in front of me, ma'am. I don't wonder but everything you make is fit for a king."

Alice touched her hand to the back of her head, as if checking to make sure her bun was still in place. "What a nice thing to say."

With a cane clasped tightly in each hand, George pulled himself to his feet. "I reckon you're worn out after your journey. I'll have Jessie show you to your room."

James stole a glance at George's legs. He couldn't see well beneath the baggy trousers, and George wore boots, but one of his legs looked as thin as a stick. Had George lost a leg? It was rude to ask questions, so James simply smiled and kept his mouth shut. George owned the boarding house where strangers came and went, but his business was his business.

James couldn't have been more shocked when Jessie picked up his pack as if she was going to carry it to his room for him. His shock quickly gave way to irritation. What kind of a lout did she think he was? He nearly snatched it out of her hands before thinking better of it. Instead, he winked at her as if he wasn't provoked beyond endurance. "Miss Jessie, I can't allow you to carry my pack."

She gave him a tight smile. "It's part of the

service."

He gently nudged his pack from her arms. "Not where it applies to me. What kind of a man would I be if I let you heft my pack?"

She seemed to relent reluctantly, but why she was so reluctant was anybody's guess. Perhaps she thought giving in on anything stole her power. Perhaps she was truly set against him and wanted one more reason to dislike him. Carrying his pack would have been a reason indeed. The anger simmered at the base of his throat, and he wanted to throttle every man who had ever let Miss Jessie carry his bags up the stairs.

James slung his pack over his shoulder and motioned for Jessie to lead the way. She picked up her skirts and in a show of unladylike rebellion, tromped up the steps without looking back. On the second floor, he followed her to the end of a long hall with three closed doors on the left. At the end of the hall, a knotted rope hung from the ceiling. Jessie pulled on the rope and a ladder descended from the ceiling. A hidden passageway to the attic.

He was sleeping in the attic? Maybe his company hadn't paid as much as he thought.

Jessie pointed at the ladder. "You first."

She probably didn't realize what a very good idea that was. Had she gone up first, he would have been forced to avert his eyes from her graceful hips swaying beneath her light purple calico dress as she climbed. Much better to avoid the enticing temptation.

With not the greatest of expectations, James climbed the ladder to his room. The attic itself stretched the entire footprint of the house, making it the biggest room, even though much of the space was unusable. At its highest point, the upside-down V of the roof was probably just shy of seven feet high. If James wanted to stand up straight without hitting his head, he'd have to stay in the center four feet of the room.

The floors were wood planks, sanded smooth and varnished, but weathered as if they'd been stripped from an ancient barn. What the room lacked in height, it made up for in other comforts. A cabinet with a washbasin and mirror stood at the far end of the room, along with a chamber pot and a dowager chest tucked to one side. There were two small windows, one facing the front of the house and one facing the back, letting in good, bright light to make the slanted space feel less like a dungeon. Both windows were open, no doubt to invite a cross breeze in.

The best thing about the room was the bed. It was massive, at least six feet by seven feet. James had never slept in a bed where his feet didn't hang over the edge.

"How did you get this bed in here?" he asked, when Jessie finally made it up the ladder.

"We brought up the parts, and Papa built it in here." She folded her arms. "It's meant to make up for the low ceilings."

"I suppose it does," James said, not altogether

Jessie and James

certain he wouldn't smack his head a hundred times before the week was out.

"All the other rooms are occupied," Jessie said. He knew her well enough to know that was her version of an apology.

"It's better than sleeping on a bedroll in the rain."

She gave him a skeptical look, as if she didn't believe he'd ever actually done that. "Dinner is at five. Breakfast at six every morning but Sundays when we serve at seven. On Saturdays and Sundays, we serve breakfast for twenty-five cents to anyone in town who wants to come. Boarders are always free. It gets crowded and noisy, just so you know. Tomorrow's Sunday, so you'll see for yourself soon enough." She placed her hand on the short ladder railing, ready to climb back down. "I clean the rooms at 9:00 in the morning, so if you aren't planning on being out, tell me ahead of time so I don't catch you in a compromising position."

James didn't like her sudden formality. He'd rather she was scowling at him. And he certainly didn't want her to leave so quickly. "Aren't you going to thank me for not telling your father you tried to kill me?"

There was the indignation he was so eager to see. "I didn't try to kill you."

"Miss Jessie, I'd say that's exactly what you tried to do."

She shook her head. "Aren't you going to thank me for not telling them you tried to steal my flour?"

His lips twitched in an attempt to hold back a smile. "What would I want with a bag of flour?"

"How do I know what goes on in the mind of a thief?" She arched her eyebrows. "I mean, I can't imagine what you were thinking when you bought that hat." She cracked a smile, either because she thought his hat was funny or because she didn't dislike him as much as she wanted to. "You can open the windows whenever you want. It gets hot up here."

James nodded. "Heat rises." No one ever wanted to get stuck sleeping on the top floor in the summertime. With any luck, he'd be out of town before it got unbearably hot. He looked at Jessie, not at all put off by the stubborn set of her chin and the flame dancing in her eyes. Maybe a long summer in Eureka wouldn't be so bad.

"The heat will give you a little taste of what it will feel like in Hell for gold diggers," she said.

He was almost giddy that she cared enough to try to get under his skin. "Miss Jessie, I know you don't have a high opinion of me, but do you really think I'll burn in Hell just for looking for gold?"

She tilted her head as if to get a better look at him. "I haven't decided yet."

He chuckled. "Maybe when you know me, you can make a better assessment."

"You'll see the dregs of Eureka's mining community tomorrow. My father preaches a sermon after breakfast. Those miners come week after week but never change their ways."

"But they gather to hear the Good Word. That's something."

"What use is the Good Word if it doesn't change anybody?"

James grinned and shrugged. "That's a question too deep for me." He held her gaze until she turned away and looked out the window. It was the first time he'd been able to crack her hard shell. It was a gratifying feeling. "So your father's a preacher?"

"Of sorts. The boarding house is his church, but he doesn't ask for money. Twenty-five cents will get you breakfast and a sermon."

"A bargain."

"He cares that the miners have a little religion," Jessie said. She tapped her hand on the railing. "Thank you for not telling Alice about what happened this morning. She gets a little touchy about a lady carrying a gun." She shot him a withering look. "But don't think I'm apologizing for what I did."

He raised his hands. "I would never think any such thing."

"Good," she said. She headed backwards down the ladder. "Dinner's at five. No hats at the table. Especially not yours."

James had a hearty laugh then made a plan to buy a new hat first thing Monday morning.

Four

"Greater love hath no man than this, that a man lay down his life for his friends. Jesus is my friend. He's your friend. What a friend we have in Jesus." Jessie's father, George, nodded to Alice, who stood up and played a two-measure introduction on her concertina. James had heard a concertina on the streets of Boston where men played for a few coins in their hats, but he'd never known a concertina to be played in church. The concertina looked like a small bellows with handles and buttons on the sides. Alice pushed the buttons to play certain notes, and she was very good at it.

Of course, they wouldn't have anything as fancy as an organ. Few churches in these parts did. They had to create their own music or make do with what they had, which was a pretty good description of the whole Western movement.

Ingenuity was a way of life.

George, sitting in a chair, waved his hand to start the singing. The men and the few women sang loudly enough to lift the roof. "What a friend we have in Jesus. All our sins and griefs to bear." James smiled. What the congregation lacked in talent, they made up for in enthusiasm.

He stood leaning against the far wall because there wasn't an empty chair in the entire room. Miners sat on every available chair plus the tables and on the floor for George Madsen's worship service. There had to be forty men in attendance. Ann Whitlock, one of the Madsens' boarders, sat to James' right on one of the precious chairs, holding both her son and daughter on her lap. Another woman, who James guessed was a soiled dove from the saloon, sat in the corner by herself, singing at the top of her lungs. Jessie was on a chair at the back of the room, her arms folded, her lips pressed together, as if she was there to observe the worship service but not participate.

Since Jessie's attention was focused on her father, James took the opportunity to gaze at her. Her chestnut hair was fashioned into a plump bun at the back of her head, but the bun did nothing to conceal the curls that threatened to escape with just one pull of a hairpin. James balled his hands into fists and slid them behind his back. He understood completely why Petty was so crazy about Jessie's hair. It looked like coffee and brown sugar spun into silk.

Her eyes were the color of rich molasses, and her skin looked softer and pinker than any rose petal. He held his breath as his gaze traveled to her lips. Oh, boy. What he'd give to have a taste of those.

With his heart beating in his throat, James looked away and sang louder—nothing like a good revival song to lead a man away from temptation. No wonder Jessie was set against miners. Men with little self-control wouldn't hesitate to take what they could from a beautiful woman like Jessie. James' blood boiled at the very thought. Too few men knew how to bridle their passions. No wonder she carried a shotgun.

The service ended with a prayer by George. The miners began to file out of the room, with hats in hand and smiles on their faces. Several men shook George's hand or said goodbye by placing their hands on their hearts. Others pressed coins into George's hand, which he promptly returned. Maybe Jessie hadn't seen it, but it was obvious to James that even though the men were still hardened miners who lived hard lives, each of them left the boarding house changed—maybe determined to be a little better, maybe filled with the comfort of God's love.

George had preached his entire sermon sitting down, as if he had pulled up a chair for a personal chat with each person in attendance. He was most surely missing a leg.

Alice and Jessie stood at the door to bid

farewell to everyone who had come to the service. Alice couldn't have acted more gracious, shaking hands and giving each grungy miner a genuine smile. Jessie was also friendly, but James sensed her hesitation and maybe dislike for the miners. They were definitely an unkempt, unruly lot, with their fingernails permanently stained black and their straggly hair and soiled clothing. Water was scarce. Most of these men took a bath maybe twice a year, and it was too much of a chore to wash their clothes when they were just going to get dirty in the mines again.

The men were astonishingly well-behaved as they said goodbye to Alice and Jessie. Only one man held onto Jessie's hand too long, and Alice quickly but kindly nudged him away. James liked Alice more and more all the time.

"Did you enjoy the service?" Ann Whitlock asked.

James flinched. He'd been so focused on Jessie, he hadn't even noticed Mrs. Whitlock's approach. She held tight to both of her children's hands, and her son, who couldn't have been more than three, kept trying to pull out of her grasp. Her daughter, a few years older than the boy, stuck her thumb in her mouth and stared at James as if he was an oddity in a museum. Ann acted as if she didn't even notice her son trying to wrench her arm off.

"I liked it very much, ma'am."

"Nobody preaches Jesus like George," Ann

said, valiantly maintaining her balance while her son pulled harder on her arm. "I'll miss it when we go. I don't know that we'll find such fine sermonizing in California."

James raised his brows. "I didn't know you were leaving."

"We've been living at the Madsen House for four months since my Heber died. My brother is sending money so we can join him in San Francisco. We'll be leaving come June, I hope."

James smiled. "God speed to you."

"Thank you. I'll be glad to continue your acquaintance for another month, at any rate." Ann finally seemed to notice her son swinging back and forth like a pendulum attached to her arm. "Titus is due for a nap, but we will see you at dinner, I hope."

"I hope so too."

The last miner left, and Jessie followed him out and shut the door behind her. Alice studied James' face, looking more than a little put out with him all of a sudden. "She went to get the plate and cup from Scully. She takes him breakfast every morning."

"Does she?"

"He won't come up to the house and join us for meals, and Jessie doesn't want him to go hungry." Alice, usually so cheerful, gave James a disapproving look. "I must talk to you, Mr. Kelsey."

She pointed to the entrance to the kitchen.

Jessie and James

There was a doorframe but no door. James drew his brows together. Alice seemed irritated with him, but he didn't know what he'd done, unless she was irked that he'd eaten seven griddlecakes at breakfast.

He followed her into the kitchen. Dirty plates and cups were stacked in the deep porcelain sink. A kettle of water boiled on the cookstove. "Miss Alice," he said. "I'm sorry if I ate more than my share this morning. Your coffee was the best I've ever tasted, and your griddlecakes are like manna from heaven."

Miss Alice turned on him, agitated, upset, and a little bit angry. In a voice of perfect politeness, she said, "I like to see my boarders well fed. Eat up. If you don't get fat while you're under my roof, I'll consider it an insult. Do you understand?"

"Uh...well...yes."

She nodded curtly. "Now, Mr. Kelsey, I am a reasonable, friendly woman, but when someone harms my daughter, I get riled up."

"You mean Jessie?" he said, just to clarify that Alice considered Jessie a daughter though she was more the age of a sister.

"Of course I mean Jessie. As you've probably guessed, I'm not her natural mother, but I'm the closest thing she's got to one, and I won't stand for anyone hurting her."

"I'm glad she has you to watch out for her."

This seemed to make Alice even angrier, in a

ladylike sort of way. "She does. And if you ever hurt her again, I'll throw you out on your ear. I don't care how much the London Mining and Ore Company pays us to let you stay here."

James drew back as if she'd shoved him. "Ma'am, I apologize, but I can't begin to guess what you're accusing me of. I wouldn't consider myself any kind of man if I ever hurt a woman."

Alice sniffed as if she didn't believe it but was too polite to contradict him. "I saw the bruise. As big as an apple. She can barely move her shoulder."

Astonishment rendered James momentarily mute. A bruise? Who had given Miss Jessie a bruise? He'd teach that scoundrel a lesson he'd never forget. "I don't know what you think happened, ma'am, but I would never lay a hand on Miss Jessie." But…wait a minute…her shoulder? Maybe he would lay a hand on her gun if he was about to get shot. He ran his hand down the side of his face. "Miss Alice, what about Jessie's shoulder?"

Alice pursed her lips. "This is why I don't approve of her taking a gun into town. She said there was a misunderstanding, at which time you wrestled with her for the gun and injured her shoulder."

James felt about as low as a snake. He'd given Jessie a bruise, and according to Alice, it was a big one. Miss Jessie had tried to kill him, but he could have been gentler when wrestling with her gun.

Jessie and James 35

No wonder she hated the very sight of him. He swiped his hand across his forehead. "Miss Alice, I'm truly regretful. I thought she was going to kill me, and I reacted roughly. I didn't want to hurt her."

Alice seemed satisfied. She pulled an apron off the hook by the door and put it on. "I'm glad you didn't let her shoot you. Her father would never recover if Jessie got hanged for murder, but maybe next time you will remember that you are ten times stronger and try to be more considerate."

"Yes, ma'am," James said, a sick feeling pulling at the pit of his stomach.

"Don't tell Jessie I said anything."

James curled his lips into a half smile. "But how can I apologize if I have to keep it a secret?"

Alice stacked dishes in the sink. "You'll think of something. Now please leave my kitchen so I can finish up the breakfast dishes and start supper."

She took a dishrag and wrapped it around the kettle handle. "Please allow me," James said, grabbing the handle and lifting the kettle from the cookstove. She directed him to pour the hot water from the kettle into the sink. A water pump emptied into the sink, and James pumped cold water in after the hot so Alice wouldn't burn her hands. She picked up the rag and started washing dishes.

Jessie came into the kitchen carrying Scully's empty plate and cup. She stopped short when she saw James, then pretended he wasn't there, grabbed a dishtowel from the cupboard, and started drying dishes for Alice. James picked up another dishtowel and dried alongside her. "What are you doing?" Jessie said.

Now that he was aware of her injury, he could see how she favored her left side and tried not to move her right shoulder. He hated himself for hurting her. "The sooner we finish the dishes, the sooner you can show me around your farm, if I should be so lucky."

Jessie raised her eyebrows in sort of amused annoyance. He'd surprised her. "Boarders don't do dishes."

"I do."

She narrowed her eyes. "Why?"

"Can't you tell, Miss Jessie? I'm trying to get on your good side."

She snorted. "I don't have a good side."

He smiled at her, even though he felt terrible for hurting her shoulder. "I haven't seen a bad side yet."

"Ha. Where did you learn how to talk all fancy and charming like that?" she said, taking a wet plate from Alice and shoving it in his direction.

He swiped his towel across the plate. "I don't know what you mean, Miss Jessie. I haven't seen anything I don't like about you." He handed her his dry plate, and she stacked it on the shelf anchored to the wall.

Alice handed him another plate. "What I want

to know is where did you learn to sing? Amos Beecher sat near you during the service, and he says you've got a voice that would charm a bull."

"More like start a stampede."

Jessie propped her hand on her hip and eyed him skeptically. "Sing something for us."

James shook his head. "You'll kick me out of your kitchen."

Jessie scrunched her lips. "Only if you don't stop when we tell you to."

Alice and Jessie stared at him as if he were an exotic animal standing in their kitchen. Might as well get it over with. They'd pester him until he sang; then they'd hear he wasn't anything special and never ask him again. "O bury me not, on the lone prairie, where coyotes howl and the wind blows free, in a narrow grave just six by three. O bury me not, on the lone prairie."

Alice stared at him, mouth agape. Jessie pressed her lips into a stiff line and fingered a strand of hair at the base of her neck.

"I never heard such a voice," Alice said.

James chuckled. "I told you so. It's better for long, solitary rides on a horse."

"No," Alice said, with a hint of a scold in her voice. "I've been to real musical performances in Salt Lake and Denver. Your voice is better than anything I ever heard there."

"Well, thank you, Miss Alice." He didn't want to mention that maybe she'd been in Eureka too long if she thought his singing was anything special.

Jessie seemed to remember that she had a plate in her hand. She stacked it with the others. "That's a cowboy song," she said.

James grinned. "The cows are less fractious if you sing to them."

"But I thought you were from back east."

James dried another plate. "I am, but I was kind of reckless in my youth." A sharp pain dug into his chest. Those were heart-wrenching times at home. "I ran away at fourteen and spent a couple of years working a ranch in Colorado."

That news seemed to win Jessie's full attention. "You were a cowpuncher?"

"Don't worry. I saw the error of my ways and went home for college." Father had never forgiven him for leaving, and James had been trying to make it up to his parents ever since.

"Sing us another one," Alice said, setting another stack of plates in the sink.

"What do you want me to sing?"

Alice closed her eyes and sighed. "Anything you want."

James spent the next half hour singing cowboy songs with a few hymns mixed in. Alice sang along with the songs she knew. Jessie just listened, and she didn't seem inclined to be as prickly as she had been yesterday. Maybe James should do more singing. It might just go a long way to melting Jessie's rock hard exterior.

Once they finished the dishes, Jessie swept the

floor in the dining room while James wiped tables and put up the chairs. When Jessie propped the broom against the wall, James saw his opportunity. "Now, Miss Jessie, I would be much obliged if you'd show me around your farm. You have a nice spot of land here."

Jessie glanced in the direction of the kitchen, as if hoping Alice would run out and save her. "I don't have much time before I need to help Alice with supper."

"I won't keep you long."

"All right," she said. "Let me fetch my shawl."

There were two doors on the far side of the dining room that most likely led to the Madsens' quarters. Jessie opened the door on the left and ducked inside. She emerged wearing a knitted burgundy shawl that accented her brown eyes.

"That's a mighty pretty shawl," James said. The woman underneath was even prettier.

She gave him the stink eye. "Don't try to butter me up."

He should have known better than to say anything. He'd been acquainted with Jessie less than twenty-four hours, but it was plain she wasn't inclined to accept a compliment. She certainly wasn't inclined to believe one. She saw his sincerity as nothing more than flattery.

She led him out the front door to the cherry tree. So many blossoms had fallen, the ground around the tree looked as if it were covered with a light pink blanket. "This is the first cherry tree we planted. There's a man in Provo who'll pay a dollar a bushel for sweet cherries."

He wasn't interested in small talk. "How bad is that shoulder?" he asked, resisting the urge to smooth his hand down her injured arm.

Jessie acted as if the question took her by surprise. "It's fine."

He frowned. "It's not fine, Miss Jessie."

She drew the shawl tighter around her. "Are you calling me a liar?"

"I'm calling you stubborn." He reached out and caught one of the tassels of her shawl between his fingers. "Alice says there's a bruise. A big one."

"Alice has no call to share my private business with a stranger."

"That's why you couldn't carry two buckets at a time yesterday, isn't it?"

She lifted her chin. "I *didn't* carry those buckets because you snatched them away from me. What was I supposed to do? Challenge you to an arm wrestle?"

He tamped down his irritation. He was supposed to be apologizing, not arguing. He huffed out a breath and pinned her with a remorseful gaze. "Miss Jessie, I would never intentionally hurt you. I would never hurt any woman, and it plagues me to think I caused you pain. Will you forgive me?"

She stared into his eyes. "You really mean it, don't you?"

"I can't look at myself in the mirror knowing

you bear me ill will."

One corner of her mouth curled upward. "You don't have a mirror."

"Good thing."

She tugged her tassel from his grasp and tilted her head as if to get a better look at him. "In my experience, men don't apologize."

"I do." He was still apologizing to his father for years of childish mistakes. "Miss Jessie, I feel sick about giving you that bruise and injuring your shoulder."

She pursed her lips, thought about it for a second, then bloomed into a smile. It was the most breathtaking expression James had ever seen. "Much as I think you deserve to go on feeling rotten, I did try to kill you. You got worked up. I can't blame you for that. I tend to lash out when *I* get worked up."

"Yes, you do."

She cuffed him on the shoulder and winced. That little sign of pain sent a sliver of glass sliding down his throat. "Will you forgive me?"

"I suppose. But just because I forgive you today, doesn't mean I won't find something else to hold against you tomorrow. I might decide to shoot you anyway."

He chuckled. "As long as you give me fair warning."

She gave him a wry smile. "Where's the fun in that?"

He plucked a blossom from the cherry tree.

"Don't be mad at Alice."

Jessie strolled around the corner of the house. James followed her. "Who could be mad at Alice?" she said, a sort of breathless longing in her voice.

James studied her face. "Are you mad at her?"

"I'm mad that she isn't my mother."

It wasn't hard to hear the catch in her voice. "I'm sorry," he said softly.

"Mother died almost eight years ago. Papa married Alice not three weeks later, as if he'd never even loved my mother."

James understood that kind of loss. "I'm sure that hurt."

Jessie blinked rapidly. "Like someone digging my heart out of my chest with a spoon. But I try to remember Papa didn't do it to hurt me. He thought I needed a mother, and he needed someone to take care of him. Alice is sweet and good-natured. It can't have been easy to marry a man with no legs and take on a sixteen-year-old daughter. She was only twenty-six when they married. Papa is handsome and good. Despite their difference in age, she fell in love with him. I can't fault either of them for finding love." She sighed and smiled sadly. "Even though I want to."

James narrowed his eyes. "Your father is missing both legs?"

Jessie pressed her lips into a hard line. "Mining accident."

James' heart sank. The mountain could make a man rich. It could also crush a man to dust. No wonder Jessie hated the very thought of another mine in Eureka.

She led him to the back of the house, and James caught his breath at the sight of at least an acre of blossoming cherry trees. The trees were puffy with pinkish-white blossoms, and the ground looked as if it had been dusted with late snow. The petals on the ground were almost as thick as the petals still on the trees. And the smell was heavenly, sweet and heavy, as if he could take a bite out of the air itself.

"It's beautiful, Miss Jessie."

Her lips formed into a measured smile. "We planted all of them not long before Mama died. When I walk among the trees, it feels like she's with me."

"How do you water them? Nothing grows here but juniper and sage brush."

Jessie pointed to a small, two-wheeled wagon against the house. "I hitch up Red, fetch water from the well, and bring it to the trees."

James gazed at Jessie in astonishment. "How long does that take you?"

"I haven't had to do it yet this spring. April was nice and wet." That didn't answer the question, but it had to be several hours a day in the dry months.

James squinted at one of the trees on the edge of the orchard. "Is that a cow?"

Jessie grinned. "That's Lily Bell. She grazes in the orchard during the day, and I keep her at

Scully's at night so she doesn't wander off or fall prey to the coyotes."

"Do you milk her?" James said.

"In the morning. If Papa feels well, he milks her in the afternoon." She turned her gaze to Lily Bell sitting under one of the cherry trees chewing her cud. "I usually milk her. She can be hard for Papa to handle. She thinks she's a princess."

James laughed. "Cows have a mind of their own."

There was a wide, fenced-in area up against the house. Jessie reached for the gate, but he shot out his hand and opened it for her. She rolled her eyes as if she didn't appreciate the gesture in the least. Inside the fence, a chicken coop stood on stilts in the center of the yard and at least twenty chickens pecked the ground at James' feet. A black and white rooster with a bright red comb stood on top of the coop keeping watch.

"Papa and I built the fence to keep the coyotes out, but I close the chickens in the coop at night for extra protection. Those coyotes are clever. I shoot one or two a week."

James pointed to the three-foot-high pile of wood. "You chop the wood too?"

She shrugged. "Papa can't do it."

A lump the size of a chicken egg lodged in James' throat. From the wood neatly stacked to the rows of newly pruned cherry trees, James was beginning to comprehend just how hard Jessie worked on her farm and how difficult life must be for her. No wonder she seemed so sharp around the edges. She didn't have time to breathe, let alone be happy. The need to protect her grabbed him by the throat and stole his breath. What could he do to make Jessie's life easier?

"You raise chickens, grow cherries, milk cows, shoot coyotes, and chop wood. You're a woman of many talents, Miss Jessie."

She turned her face away as if he'd just insulted her. "Don't mock me."

He leaned his head so he was in her line of sight. "I'm serious, ma'am. Is there anything you can't do?"

She acted as if she didn't believe a word that came out of his mouth. "Plenty. I can't cook. If I don't like someone, I can't be polite just for the sake of being polite." She counted on her fingers. "I don't knit, tat, or sing, and Alice is never going to make me into a lady." She cupped both hands on the top of the fence and looked out into the orchard.

James up sidled behind her and made his voice soft and low. "It doesn't reduce your charms one bit that you can't knit, Miss Jessie. Leave the knitting to the old ladies. Your talents are more to my liking. You know how to make a miner behave himself. You take Scully breakfast every morning. You don't show weakness, even when I know that shoulder is aching something fierce. You don't back down, and you can shoot a gun with your hair up or down. Though, I prefer it down."

With her back to him, she stood as still as a deer caught in the light of the lantern, and it was all James could do not to place a kiss on the alluring curve between her neck and shoulder. But he was a gentleman first, and he didn't take liberties the way some men did. He wouldn't do anything to frighten her or risk turning her against him. Jessie would always be safe with him.

James cleared his throat and took a step away. "I very much enjoyed your father's sermon this morning."

Jessie also took a step, in the other direction, and glued her gaze to his face. Did it seem as if she couldn't catch her breath? She fingered the fine hairs at the nape of her neck. "Papa knows the Bible, but his sermons are all wrong."

"Why do you say that?"

"He always talks about how much God loves us and Jesus is our friend, but these men don't need love. They need discipline. They need the fear of God. They need hellfire and damnation, or they'll never change their ways."

A smile tugged at James' lips. "They'd stop coming to his sermons if all they got was chastisement."

"Perhaps. But it would be better if Papa told them exactly where they'll end up if they don't repent. God isn't a comfortable God. He said, 'If you love me, keep my commandments.' "

James fingered the stubble on his chin. "I believe that, but men should keep the commandments because they love God, not because they're afraid of him. Maybe your father wants to show them the love of God and change their hearts. When their hearts are changed, they'll change their ways."

She shook her head. "You have some strange notions, James Kelsey."

James only laughed. He loved that look she gave him when she thought he'd said something foolish. It was mostly how she looked at him all the time.

James peered out over the orchard then beyond to the rocky hills behind the house. Like most of the hills surrounding Eureka, they seemed like a good place to look for gold. "Has anyone laid claim to that land up there?"

Jessie transformed from friendly to cold in two second's time. "That's our claim."

James didn't know what to make of her sudden change in temperature. "Your claim? How many acres?"

"Enough."

"Have you ever prospected it?"

She turned on him so fast, she fanned up a breeze. "Mr. Kelsey, I'm fully aware that you are in town to find a hill you can tear apart using the labor of these poor slobs who think they're going to get rich. But you keep your hands off our claim."

Her reaction shouldn't have surprised him. In a mining town, everyone got hostile about claim jumpers, and the lure of riches made even the best people suspicious. He raised his hands and backed up, something he seemed to do a lot when he was in Miss Jessie's presence. "I'm not a claim jumper, Miss Jessie. I'm just saying your claim might have something that would be beneficial for both of us."

Her glare could have stripped all the petals off a cherry tree. "We're never selling our claim, and I won't be persuaded, romanced, or browbeaten into it."

"I would never browbeat you."

"You have the entire western half of the territory, Mr. Kelsey. Go find your own claim and leave us alone." Jessie opened the back door, stormed into the house, and slammed the door behind her, rattling all the windows on the north side of the house.

James was left standing with the chickens, wondering just where he'd gone wrong.

Five

Jessie glanced out the kitchen window and growled. James was out there in his rolled-up shirtsleeves chopping enough wood to last through three winters. She should have shot him a week ago when she had the chance.

That man could not take a hint. Heck, he couldn't even take a direct message. *Mr. Kelsey, boarders do not chop wood. They are not allowed to milk the cow or water my cherry trees. Boarders do not have permission to follow me around the yard and help me carry things. Boarders need to stay out of my way and quit bothering me.*

On Sunday, she had succeeded in avoiding him during and after the evening meal, and he'd left for town so early on Monday, she hadn't even seen him in the morning. He'd come back Monday night with an armful of maps and a new tan hat that suited him and the town much better. But she had still refused to talk to him. It didn't matter that he was handsome and charming and excessively polite. He was after her claim, just like everybody else, and she wouldn't be fooled by his charm or his angelic voice.

Angelic. Ha. The only angel he resembled was the Angel of Death.

On Tuesday morning, Alice had packed him some food for what must have been a long journey because he hadn't returned until Wednesday night late in the evening after Jessie and the rest of the household had gone to bed.

But since then, it seemed Mr. Kelsey didn't have anything to do but harass the staff and make Jessie's life completely miserable. He'd watered her cherry trees, milked the cow twice, and hauled wood for the fire. Alice thought he was one of the blessed saints for all the help he gave around the house. Jessie thought he might be a demon sent to torment her for all her past mistakes. Doing good wasn't the usual way with a demon, but Jessie was beginning to think that James knew being kind was the best way to make her feel testy.

Well, he'd succeeded. She was about ready to unload her shotgun on him.

Jessie started when the back door opened and James came in lugging an armload of wood. She should have been watching his movements closer. Alice was gone, and Jessie wasn't about to be alone in the same room with Mr. Kelsey. Unfortunately, her only escape was blocked by those broad shoulders. She retreated to the far side of the kitchen and rearranged plates on the shelf, hoping he'd drop his wood in the box and go away.

He dumped his load but didn't leave. She really couldn't have hoped that he would. "Miss Jessie, it's a beautiful day out."

"Yes, it is." What would they do if it weren't for the weather? Without it, most people wouldn't know how to start a conversation.

He studied her face, as if he was trying to read her thoughts. It was how he always looked at her. She hated it, and it made her insides feel like a meadow of butterflies. "Can I ask you something?"

"You can ask. I can't say as I'll feel inclined to answer."

A grin slowly grew on his face. "Fair enough. Will you come outside?"

That was what he wanted to ask? "Why?"

"I want to ask you something."

"You can ask me right here."

The smile grew wider. "I want to ask you a question and show you something at the well."

She folded her arms. He was so aggravatingly polite and so irritatingly kind that it was especially hard to dislike him, and dislike was the only defense she had. "Are you planning on murdering me and throwing my body down the well?"

This time, he laughed. What did she have to do to make James Kelsey lose his temper? "No such thing, ma'am. I just want a friendly chat."

She huffed out a breath. The dishes were done. It would be another hour before they needed to fix dinner. She really had no excuse. "Very well, Mr. Kelsey, but I can only spare a few minutes. I must work on my knitting."

She might as well have told him she was giving him a million dollars. His smile could have lit up every lantern in town. "Only a few minutes. I know how much you love your knitting."

She tried not to smile, but the way he said "knitting" and the teasing look on his face coaxed it out of her. But she would still detest him until the day she died, and she would never, ever let her guard down again.

He offered his arm but let it fall to his side when she gave him the evil eye. They were going outside for a question, not a stroll in the park. Still, he opened the door for her and waited for her to collect her shotgun before following her outside. He'd said something about the well, so she headed in that direction. Their well was a quarter mile from the house.

Jessie walked quickly, but James had no problem keeping up. "Can I at least carry your gun for you? I know it's heavy."

She didn't slow her pace. "So you *are* planning on murdering me."

He sighed. "Okay. You can carry your own gun, but if you shoot me, I'd appreciate if you didn't put any holes in my new hat."

She trained her eyes on the well in the

Jessie and James

distance. "I'll try not to. It's a nice hat."

He kicked up the dust with his sudden halt. "You like my hat?"

"Well enough."

The look on his face was pure happiness. "I tried on every hat they had."

Jessie turned her face away so he wouldn't see her smile. It was best he didn't think he'd managed to find a chink in her armor. She doubled her speed to the well. The sooner they got there, the sooner she could go back. "Here we are," she said, patting the U-shaped frame that held the pulley and bucket. "What did you want to show me?"

Now that they were here, James' excitement seemed to explode. "How old is this well?"

"Papa and some friends dug it not fifteen years ago."

"What about water rights?"

"We have water rights. The mines gobble up everything that isn't claimed."

He liked that answer. "From this well, it would be easy to run a wooden pipeline to your orchard. We could dig trenches between the trees, run the water down the pipe, and water the trees in a fraction of the time." He smiled at her as if all his hopes and dreams lived in her eyes. "What do you think?"

She drew her brows together. "I...I think it would be nice not to have to lug water for my trees, but—"

"We'd have to carry the water from the well

and pour it into the pipe, but the rest of the way is downhill."

"Mr. Kelsey—"

"Please, Miss Jessie, will you call me James?"

"It is downhill, but…you want me to call you James?"

"Please."

A warning voice sounded in her head. Calling him James would mean they were friends. How long before he used that friendship to try to take advantage of her in one way or another? "Mr. Kelsey," she repeated, emphasizing each syllable so he knew she wasn't easily manipulated. "How much would a pipeline cost?"

His face fell, but he wasn't so disappointed that he couldn't rally himself. "I don't mind if you call me Mr. Kelsey. You can call me whatever you want as long as you keep talking."

She frowned at him. "What do you mean by that?"

"You've barely said a word to me for almost a week, and I've sorely missed the sound of your voice."

She didn't want to have this conversation. She didn't want to talk to Mr. Kelsey ever again. "I know your type, Mr. Kelsey, and I'd just as soon steer clear."

Her honesty didn't seem to bother or threaten him. He brought himself closer to her by leaning against the frame. "My type? What type is that?"

She lifted her chin. "You'll say anything, make

any promise to get what you want, and you don't care how many toes you step on or how many people you hurt as long as there's gold at the end of the road."

The lines around his mouth deepened. "Miss Jessie, we don't know each other well, but does that description truly sound like me?"

No, it didn't, but she was too cross to admit it. "It sounds like every prospector or mining company representative who has ever set foot in this town."

He reached out and twisted an errant strand of her hair around his finger. Her attempts at putting her hair up this morning had been a little clumsy. Hair was probably sticking out from every side of her head. "It's so beautiful," he said, as if she hadn't just hurled some unfair accusations at him.

She should have pulled away, but her feet didn't seem to have the power to move. All she could do was stare into those blue eyes and wonder what he would say next. A ribbon of warmth traveled down her spine when his thumb grazed her cheek.

"Somebody's hurt you, Miss Jessie. I don't know who it is, but I know I want to punch him in the face."

Mr. Kelsey was too perceptive. All the more reason to stay away from him. "A woman doesn't have to be hurt to know what an unscrupulous man will do for money."

"Oh, there are plenty of unscrupulous men, and you are wise to be wary, but this is deeper. You told me you wouldn't be romanced into selling your claim, and that word struck me funny."

"You didn't laugh," she said, because she wanted to distract him from the truth. The truth made her heart ache.

He pulled away from her and shoved his hands into his pockets. "Miss Jessie, I'm a geologist. It's my job to find a claim for the London Mining and Ore Company. But you've made it clear you won't sell your claim, and I respect that. There are plenty more claims for me to explore, and I don't mind doing my job. It would be too easy if your claim was the one I came to find. I don't want you to be suspicious of me. Your claim is safe from me."

"Then why are you being so nice? Why do you care how I irrigate my cherries?"

He kicked a dirt clod at his feet. "You have a hard life here. I want to help."

She pinned him with a disapproving gaze. "You feel sorry for me."

James growled and stomped the dirt clod into dust. "For heaven's sake, woman, will you quit fighting me?"

A movement in the hills beyond James' head caught Jessie's attention. She reached behind her, grabbed the barrel of her shotgun, and slid it over her shoulder. James' eyes went wide. He probably thought he'd gone too far this time. She nudged him out of the way with the barrel of the gun and pointed it in the direction of a large boulder at the foot of one of the hills. "I see you. Come out with your hands up."

She pressed the butt of the gun into her shoulder and winced. The area was still tender. Grimacing, she pulled the strap from around her shoulder and handed her gun to James. "Take this and point it over there."

With surprise popping all over his face, James took the gun and obediently raised it in the direction of the boulder. It was plain by the way he held himself that he knew how to shoot. She liked him a little better than she had ten seconds ago. He glanced at her. "What am I pointing at?"

"Come out now," Jessie called. "Or Mr. Kelsey will start shooting."

"I will not," James whispered.

"My intentions are peaceful," called a voice behind the boulder. "Don't shoot. I'm coming out."

James lowered the gun before they even saw who it was. Maybe Mr. Kelsey was trying to be friendly, but Jessie didn't want to seem friendly. She wanted to scare the living daylights out of whoever was trespassing on her claim.

Frank Roberts inched out from behind the rock with his hands in the air and a slimy smile on his lips. Jessie snatched the gun from James' hands and aimed it straight at Frank's head. "You've been on my property one too many times, Frank."

"Jessie!" James hissed.

She ignored him. "It's within my rights to shoot you."

Frank's moustache twitched as if he found it amusing she was pointing a gun at him. "Now, Miss Jessie, you know that's not true. You can't shoot a man for taking a shortcut."

"You might think I'm a fool, Frank, but our property isn't a shortcut to anywhere."

James stepped between the shotgun and Frank. "Miss Jessie, I don't know who this man is, but you don't want to shoot him."

"Yes, I do."

He reached out his hand and gently pushed the barrel of the gun downward. If it accidentally went off, she'd hit his foot. "It's messy. His dead body would attract all sorts of critters. And this close to the house, the flies alone would drive you crazy."

Of course James was right, and not because of the flies. She would never actually shoot Frank Roberts, even though it gave her a considerable sense of satisfaction to think about shooting him. Sometimes she hated that she was so reasonable. Growling, she shoved her gun in James' direction, elbowed him out of the way, and marched toward Frank as if she was on the attack—which she was.

James followed close behind her, probably to make sure she didn't kill Frank with her bare hands.

"Frank Roberts, you're a snake. Get off my

property."

Most women couldn't resist Frank's dazzling smile. Jessie was immune. She'd known Frank for too many years to trust him or even like him. "Now, Jessie, I was just having a look around. Ain't no law against that."

"Yes, there is. It's called trespassing."

Frank tried to be charming, but he'd forgotten that his sweet talk didn't work on Jessie. "But if you've got gold here, don't you want to know it? It could make you and your papa rich. You'd never have to haul water again."

"But then all my cherry trees would die," Jessie drawled sarcastically.

Frank eyed James then reached out his hand. "I'm Frank Roberts. Pleased to meet you."

James folded his arms around the shotgun, refusing to shake Frank's hand. She liked James even better than she had one minute ago. He was obviously a good judge of character. "Miss Jessie asked you to leave. That's good advice."

Frank left his hand extended for a second too long, as if he was holding out hope that someone would be his friend. "I seen you in town couple three days ago. You're looking for a claim."

"That's my business and no one else's."

"Well, mister, there ain't a more promising vein in Eureka than Madsen's claim. You throw a little money my way, and I'll show you the best spots."

Outrage burned at the base of Jessie's throat.

Just how many times had Frank been here spying on her property? She should have brought her jackknife with her.

James was broad and thick, and even the toughest miner would be intimidated by his anger. And he *was* angry. Jessie sensed it in the tension of his shoulders and the tightening of the sinews in his neck. He let the shotgun dangle from his fingers, barrel pointing to the ground. "I don't need your help, Mr. Roberts, and I'm not interested in Miss Jessie's claim."

"You should be." Frank looked at Jessie, and his lips twitched in amusement. "Reuben Pierce always believed there was gold here. Jessie had a soft spot for him, but she wouldn't even let him look. He finally gave up and left town cuz Jessie was so stubborn."

Frank couldn't have hurt her worse if he'd lashed her across the face with a belt, but as she always did to protect herself, she let the pain explode into anger. With both hands, she shoved Frank with all the strength of her bitter memories. Frank stumbled backward but didn't fall. It took about three seconds for his surprise to wear off, and then he started laughing. "You always was a fiery one, Jessie."

He sucked in his laughter like a bellows when James thrust the barrel of the shotgun into his chest. Hard. Hard enough to make him fall over on his backside and make that moustache droop like a flower in a drought. "This is the last time I'm going to ask nice," James said, his face lined with fierce rage. "Clear off Miss Jessie's claim, or you'll be dodging buckshot till the devil won't have it."

Frank inched away from the gun, sliding his bottom along the ground until he met with the boulder at his back. "You don't have to get tetchy. I was trying to have a friendly conversation." He stood up and brushed the dust off his trousers. "Let me get my gear," he said, raising his hands in the air while walking backward. He disappeared behind the boulder and emerged with a canvas bag and a small pick ax.

"Just taking a shortcut, huh?" Jessie said.

Frank looped his bag around his shoulder and made a beeline for the shortest way off the property. When he'd put a safe distance between them, he called over his shoulder, "Watch out for that one, mister. She'd just as soon kill you in your sleep as look at you."

James pumped the gun, raised it over his head with one arm, and shot into the sky, which was a Herculean task considering how heavy that gun was. Frank jumped out of his skin and ran like a wild man.

Jessie was too rattled to laugh at the spectacle of Frank Roberts running for his life, but it was surely a pleasant sight. Her legs felt like jelly, so she plopped herself on the ground and gulped in some fresh air.

James leaned on the barrel of the gun and knelt on one knee beside her. "Are you all right?

Can I help you back to the house?"

The concern on his face was endearing, even if she didn't appreciate being treated like an invalid. She certainly couldn't be mad at him. "I want to learn that trick," she said, unable to keep herself from smiling.

"What trick?"

"The one where you shot into the air."

A smile sprouted on his face. "It's a dangerous trick. Buckshot falls everywhere."

She sighed. "It's just as well. I'd probably break my arm on the kick-back."

He gave her a look that might have set her heart all aflutter if she'd been one of those refined and dainty city girls. "Can you walk?"

"Of course I can walk. I'm angry, not crippled."

"You look a little shaken. I can carry you, if need be."

Jessie stood up faster than a coyote on a chicken. "He didn't hurt me," she said, stating the obvious. James had seen the whole thing. Frank hadn't laid a hand on her.

"Yes, he did," James said. He reached out and brushed his thumb across her cheek.

She savored the touch of his rough hand on her skin until she decided she didn't like it and smacked his hand away. "I'm not a baby, Mr. Kelsey, and I'll thank you not to treat me like one."

"I would never baby a woman who carries a shotgun and drives a team of horses."

She brushed the dust off her dress and stamped her feet for good measure. "Frank Roberts used to be nobody special. Then he found gold on his claim about six years ago."

James raised his brows. "He's got a mine?"

"He pulled enough gold to buy a house and a real nice buggy and put a little in the bank. But the mine's derelict. Now he's looking for more gold, trespassing on claims that aren't his own. He's running out of money and soon he'll have to go back to working in other people's mines. He's wanted our claim for two years. I'm not going to sell it to him."

James grinned. "I think he got the message."

"He never gets the message. I've had to run him off my property four times this year." She tucked a strand of hair behind her ear and gave James the hint of a smile. "Thank you for sending him off. I don't wonder but he'll stay away for a spell."

James frowned and studied her face. "I won't stand for him upsetting you like that."

"He didn't upset me," she lied. Mr. Kelsey was never going to know what a fool she'd been or how much her mistakes had cost her family.

"Oh, Miss Jessie," he said, as if he was about to argue. Then he cleared his throat and handed her the gun. "I'm glad to hear it."

She handed it back to him. "You shot it. You're going to have to clean it."

His mouth fell open in mock indignation.

"You're the one who wanted me to shoot him."

She narrowed her eyes. "That's another thing. When I tell somebody you're going to start shooting, I'll thank you to pretend to be happy about it."

"It was a lie. I wasn't going to start shooting anybody."

She huffed out a breath. "Well, then. I'm never letting you hold my gun again."

With her apron strings flapping in the breeze, Alice came puffing up the hill, a look of alarm on her face. "Is everybody all right? I heard a gunshot. Or it might have been an explosion at one of the mines, but it sounded closer than that."

Jessie smirked at James. "Don't worry, Alice. James just wanted some target practice."

Alice paused to catch her breath. "Well, I suppose that's all right, but always make sure there are no children or farm animals about. And never shoot when you've been drinking. And please don't hit Jessie. A gun shot is a terrible way to die."

"Yes, ma'am. I'll be careful."

Alice turned to go back to the house. "And next time you do target practice, take better aim. Frank Roberts could still walk when he passed the house just now."

Six

The sun peeked over the distant hills to the east, making everything it touched shimmer in the new sunlight. No wonder men looked for gold in these hills. The very dust at James' feet sparkled like a king's ransom.

It was moments like these that James wanted to share with Jessie, when God painted the sky blue and white with slashes of purple and dabs of gray. Maybe they would stand on the crest of a hill and look to the east, not quarreling or even talking. Just taking it in. And sharing it together.

And maybe Jessie would bring her shotgun and he would bring his songbook, and she could shoot things while he sang hymns. James smiled to himself. A relationship with Jessie was never going to run smoothly, but it was the bumpy parts that made life so exciting. If Jessie would just smile at him occasionally, he'd choose bumpy every time.

James spurred Jessie the Horse down the gentle slope to the stand of scrub oak that marked the beginning of Jean-Pierre's claim.

"Zee claim is twenty acres," Jean-Pierre said, pointing northeast across the vale where hardly anything grew but sparse sage and brilliant Indian paintbrush. "Zee connected land is not claimed. You could get it for a song." Jean-Pierre smiled. "But my claim, you vill pay top dollar. I feel in my bones, it is very rich."

Jean-Pierre Bonheur was a businessman who had staked several claims in the Tintic mining district. James had met Jean-Pierre last week at the recorder's office, and Jean-Pierre had offered to show James one of his most promising claims. In Eureka, they called Jean-Pierre "The Frenchman," mostly because that was easier to pronounce than his name.

Jean-Pierre seemed like a decent fellow, and James was inclined to be trusting of a man unless he proved otherwise. But he didn't have to rely on Jean-Pierre's assertions about his claim. James had an expensive geology degree. He could discover for himself if Jean-Pierre's claim was worth what The Frenchman said it was.

"Let's take a look," James said, clicking his tongue and spurring Jessie forward into a canter. He'd named his horse Jessie, but it wasn't to irritate the real Jessie. It was because every moment he thought of the real Jessie made him happy. What better way to keep her fresh in his mind than to name his horse after her? Of course, Jessie would never know that she was namesake for a horse. It wasn't altogether certain she'd be flattered. When James was around Jessie, he called his horse "J." Jessie never had to find out what the "J" stood for.

They rode a few hundred feet to where the rocks grew thick out of the ground like toadstools—a good place to take samples and see if anything promising cropped up. James dismounted and fed Jessie a carrot. Then he took a notebook and pencil from his bag, sat down on a boulder, and sketched a map of the area. He had a system for marking where he took samples and how those samples tested out. If he did it right the first time, he wouldn't have to do it again if and when they started digging.

If there was one thing James had learned from prospecting for gold, it was that patience and persistence paid off. He knew what to look for, but important signs weren't always easy to see. No doubt other men had stood on this same spot looking for the same thing. If something was there to find, James was determined not to miss it.

James looped his canvas bag over his shoulder. By the end of the day, the bag would be full of samples, and his chart would be marked with notes and calculations. It was a long, meticulous process. James had already spent three weeks exploring Eureka and the surrounding areas. On three occasions, he had gone so far afield, he'd slept on his bedroll under the stars because the ride back would have taken half the night. He didn't mind sleeping on the ground. He'd done it often when he was a cowpuncher on the Butterfly Ranch in Colorado. On a clear night, the stars were so bright, he could almost reach out and touch them. And there was a certain song to the sounds of the night that lulled him to sleep and sent him pleasant dreams.

While James made sketches, Jean-Pierre hiked higher up the rocks, seemingly content to let James take his time. It was a good sign. Impatience usually meant someone was eager to hide something. After James was satisfied with his sketches, he pulled his rock pick and chisel from his bag and started collecting samples of rock, marking them and putting them in his knapsack to take back to Eureka for examination.

"Come look up here," Jean-Pierre said, calling to him from a high crag in the rocks. "Zere are a dozen places zee stone splits."

James climbed up the steep slope, and Jean-Pierre gave him a hand up to a flat shelf where they could both stand. James looked around and took a few samples, marking them in his notebook. Leaving his notebook and knapsack on the flat shelf with Jean-Pierre, he hooked his rock pick around his belt and climbed higher along the jagged rocks where he could get a better view of the landscape below. Clinging to the rough face of one of the rocks, he saw something shiny not five feet below his feet. He squinted against the sun and looked again, then his heart did a somersault. Right there, embedded in the rock, was a fleck of gold, unmistakable in its luster. James sidled along the rock on his tiptoes to get a closer look. A thin vein of yellow metal made a shimmery path down the rock as if a raindrop of gold had splashed on top and trickled down the side.

It was unlikely anyone had ventured up this far, and that was probably why the vein hadn't been discovered. He needed to collect a sample. "Jean-Pierre," he called. "I need a rope. Can you fetch one from my horse?"

Jean-Pierre didn't even blink. He certainly didn't seem to question why James needed a rope. He slid partway down the slope and ran to Jessie the Horse. He returned with a coil of rope and tossed it to James. James anchored himself on the rock, harnessed the rope around his legs and waist, and looped it around one of the rocks in the vicinity. Once secured, he inched along the narrow ledge until he got close enough to the gold vein to take a sample.

Yep, it was gold all right, and a vein like this at the surface promised a bonanza underground.

James was almost giddy. His reward from the London Mining and Ore Company would be handsome, but more importantly, Father would be pleased. James had always been a disappointment to him, but not after James earned thousands from a mine that he had discovered himself. James smiled. Maybe Father would invite him to play a game of chess or ask James to go riding. Or maybe he would break out a bottle of his oldest wine and share it with James in celebration.

James stuffed the samples in his pocket, pulled himself back to solid ground, and untied the rope around his waist. He climbed back to the shelf where Jean-Pierre was standing and handed him the rope. "Deed you find vat you vere looking for?" Jean-Pierre said.

"I think I did," James said. "I'll take a few more samples, and we can head for home."

His heart beat an uneven rhythm. Maybe Jessie would smile at him and tell him what a clever fellow he was. Maybe she'd scold him for bringing a pile of rocks into the boarding house. He looked forward to whatever response she gave him. The thought of seeing Jessie, happy or irritated, was even more exciting than the thrill of finding gold.

Jessie pulled a clothespin from her apron pocket and hung the dishtowel on the line. Laundry was so much more pleasant in the warmer weather. In the wintertime, her fingers grew stiff from the cold, and the clothes froze on the line. Sometimes, icicles hung from the trousers and dresses, and Jessie would have to bring all the clothes into the house to let them finish drying by the stove. In the late spring, a gentle breeze dried the clothes and made them smell like blossoms and fresh air. The sun warmed everything it touched and made the laundry chore almost enjoyable.

James had been gone all day, out on some gold-hunting expedition, which wasn't unusual. Sometimes he was gone for two days straight, sleeping on the trail when he traveled too far to make it back for the night. Hopefully he'd be home for dinner. He livened up any room he was in.

Some nights after the evening meal, the boarders would linger in the dining room, and James would sing for everyone. Some nights, James and Campbell Tomlinson, who was surveying land for the railroad, would swap stories of ranching in Colorado, or all of them, including Alice and Papa, would play games until it was time to retire. Jessie's favorite evenings were when James invited her to walk outside to gaze at the stars. James must have known the name of every star in the sky. He'd point out constellations and tell stories about them, like how Orion fought with a scorpion or that Cassiopeia angered the gods by boasting of her beauty. Jessie sighed. She could listen to that deep, bass voice for hours without ever growing tired of it.

Jessie hung another towel on the line and frowned to herself. She thought about that man way too much. Who cared if he knew Greek mythology or sang like an angel? He was nothing more than a prospector, and she wanted nothing to do with him. For sure and certain, she didn't need a man complicating her life and making a pest of himself on her farm. She could take care of herself.

Then again, it probably didn't hurt to let him help with the chores. He'd be gone soon enough and then she'd be back to keeping up the farm and orchard all by herself. A small break was more than welcome.

The thought of James leaving carried a twinge of pain right to her heart, as if someone had sent it through the laundry wringer. That would never do. She picked up a wet towel and snapped it smooth. That was what Mr. Kelsey could do with his Greek mythology. She was never going to let a man cause her pain again, plain and simple. If she didn't guard her heart, she'd be right back where she had been six years ago.

She finished hanging laundry and fetched the milk bucket. James usually milked the cow in the mornings, but he'd left so early this morning, he hadn't had a chance. It was very kind of him to do it when he had the time. Could she guard her heart *and* let James keep doing some of her chores?

Lily Bell was in the far corner of the orchard, eating the grass that grew under the trees. As soon as that cow heard the handle clank against the milk bucket, she perked up her ears. "Lily Bell," Jessie called. "Hup, hup, hup. Lily Bell, come." Lily Bell lumbered slowly toward the milking post. "Come on, girl. I've got chickens to feed." Lily Bell was a beautiful fawn-colored Jersey. Jessie loved the soft feel of her hide and the pleasant way she ambled to the post for milking.

Suddenly, James was right beside her, startling her a bit with the way he seemed to move so quietly over the ground. Had he been a spy as well as a cowpuncher? His smile could have charmed the quills off a porcupine, but she tried not to stare. In ten short hours, she had forgotten how handsome he was. "I see I've come just in time," he said.

"Dinner's not for another hour," she replied, trying valiantly not to let that smile soften her up.

He chuckled. "In time to milk the cow. Lily Bell and I have become good friends."

Jessie curled one side of her mouth. "Lily Bell is a princess."

"As long as I sing to her, the princess and I get along."

"You're right about that. She can be ill-tempered, but she loves music. It's lucky you can sing because she kicks something awful."

James hooked the rope that was hanging around Lily Bell's neck to the milking post and took Jessie's bucket, giving her an unexpectedly tender smile. "I'm sorry I couldn't milk for you this morning."

"You don't have to apologize. It's not your responsibility." She couldn't leave it at that, not when he'd taken such a burden from her shoulders. "Though, I'm very grateful when you do milk."

He pulled the three-legged stool from beside the back door and sat down. "I wish I could milk for you every day."

"I do too," she teased, in an attempt to get him to stop looking at her like she was somebody important. Jessie smoothed her hand down the fine hair of Lily Bell's nose and listened to the soft ping of milk as it met the bucket. James was a faster milker because he had bigger and stronger hands. She didn't even avert her eyes as his shoulder muscles tensed beneath his shirt and his well-defined forearms tightened. Jessie had seen statues in Salt Lake City. James was a work of art.

But it wasn't polite to stare.

Better to do something productive with her time. Jessie grabbed the pan of kitchen scraps that Alice had left out for the chickens and sprinkled carrot peels and potato skins around the coop. Chickens weren't the smartest of animals, but Jessie loved how happy they seemed to be when she gave them something to eat. Once the chickens were fed, Jessie gravitated back toward Lily Bell and James, but only to make sure he was milking Lily Bell correctly. Easterners didn't always know the right way to do things.

"We're making cheese tomorrow," Jessie said, because she didn't want him to think she had come over there to look at all those muscles.

"Your cheese is some of the best I've ever tasted."

Jessie and James

Jessie grinned. "It's not really my cheese. Alice does all the important things like add salt and mind the curds. I just stir the pot."

"I'm sure you're a fine stirrer." How did he manage to look teasing and sincere at the same time? He nudged his head against Lily Bell's side to get her to hold still. "I have some wonderful news."

"You do?"

"The Frenchman took me to his claim today." He grinned like a schoolboy. "I found gold."

Jessie should have been ecstatic, but her heart sank. Oh, how she hated the very thought of gold and mining. Both had brought her and her family nothing but heartache. "Where did you find it?" she said softly, mustering every bit of enthusiasm she could. James had been searching for weeks. The least she could do was act happy for him.

"The Frenchman has a claim just above Mammoth. I had to climb, but I found a vein of gold, right out in the open. It was so high, I'm sure nobody has ever laid eyes on it before. I came down the mountain and went straight to the telegraph office and wired my company. If they like the idea, they could have money here within a few weeks."

"That soon?"

He glanced at her, his eyes alight with excitement. "Isn't it amazing that a signal can travel to New York so fast? As soon as the money gets here, I can hire an engineer and some miners, and we can start digging."

Hurt and indignation pressed on her chest until she could barely draw a breath. "Then every drifter and opportunist will flock to your new mine in hopes of getting rich, when in truth, they'll be sweating and laboring and dying to make other men wealthy."

His gaze never left her face as he stood up and laid a hand on Lily Bell's back. "I don't understand. You know what I came here to do. Why are you so mad all of a sudden?"

"All of a sudden? I've been mad ever since you tried to steal my shotgun."

He sighed. "Fair enough."

"Lily Bell is going to upset the milk if you leave it there," Jessie said.

He bent over and slowly picked up the pail then gave Lily Bell another pat and unhooked her rope from the post. "What's the matter, Jessie?"

She growled at the gentleness in his tone. She didn't want to be placated, pacified, or sidetracked. "You know what's the matter. I hate the mining business."

"That must be especially hard when you live in a mining town."

She scowled at him, though he didn't deserve it. "Don't tell me I should move. My mother is buried here. I'd never leave her."

"I don't think you should leave. This is your home."

Jessie huffed out a breath. "My home is

overrun with thieves and hypocrites. Mining attracts low men with low morals. They drift into town and make us all the worse because of it. But Papa won't do anything about it. A weekly sermon on repentance would do this place a world of good." Jessie folded her arms. "But those men aren't the worst of it. Mining companies come in with one goal: get the ore and get out of town. They don't care about the miners except about how much work they can get out of them. The wages are shameful, and men with gold fever live in tents because they have a false hope that someday they'll be rich. Mammoth is even worse than Eureka. It's as dry as a bone, and miners pay ten cents a gallon for water hauled up from town."

"Ten cents a gallon?"

"It's highway robbery. Unscrupulous men taking advantage of poor ones."

A hint of a smile played at James' lips. "So you despise the miners and pity them at the same time."

She cuffed him on the shoulder even though he wasn't really meaning to tease her. "I suppose I do. Maybe their poverty makes them ill-behaved."

He drew his brows together. "Maybe it does."

"Mining companies only care about profit," Jessie said, sensing he truly wanted to understand her. "Once the mine goes dry, you'll ride out of town so fast, we'll forget what you look like."

"Who could forget this face?"

She pretended not to think he was funny. "If

someone gets hurt, the company pays them a few dollars for their trouble and sends them packing." Her voice cracked. "There is always another man standing in line to replace him."

"Is that what happened to your father?"

A lump lodged at the base of her throat. "They gave him ten dollars, James. Five dollars for each leg. That didn't even pay for the doctor who amputated."

James put his arm around Jessie's shoulder and led her to the back door. He set the milk to the side and pulled her to sit next to him on the step. "How long ago was the accident?" He wrapped his long fingers around her hand.

Jessie wanted to resist his warmth, but his touch felt too good and she was too downhearted to fight. "Two years before my mother died. He was one of the supervisors, and a beam collapsed. He was trying to get men to safety. A cave-in crushed his legs but not before another man knocked him to the ground trying to get out. That man's selfishness cost Papa his legs."

"Fear can motivate a man to horrible deeds."

"So can greed." A painful memory grabbed her around the throat. She pushed it away. They weren't talking about her past mistakes.

James let go of her hand and propped his elbows on his knees. "Maybe you don't want to hear this, but…"

"That's not unusual. I rarely want to hear anything you have to say."

Jessie and James 79

He gave her a wry smile. "I've noticed. But regardless, another mine will make these men's lives better. With more demand for workers, wages will go up."

"So will prices."

He nodded. "You're right. But if the London Mining and Ore Company doesn't dig a mine, someone else will. If they let me have a hand in establishing the mine, I'll do my best to help the men who work there."

Even though they hadn't known each other long, Jessie had observed James closely enough to know he was a man of his word. He entertained Titus Whitlock every night at dinner so Ann could eat in peace. He helped Alice with the dishes almost every night and Jessie with the cow almost every morning. He had never tried to pull the pins out of her hair, never leered at her during church, and he had run Frank Roberts off with a shotgun. If he said he would try to make the miners' lives better, she believed him.

"Now that you've seen the spot, do you think your superiors are going to be pleased?" she said.

James stared at his hands. "I hope so. My father said it was folly to study geology," he said, in a voice tinged with loss. "He thinks I'm nothing but a gold digger. I hope he'll feel differently when I actually strike gold."

Jessie suddenly felt extremely selfish. She wasn't the only one who had experienced heartache, and she'd do well to remember it. "I'm sure he will."

His mood seemed to shift. He grinned at her and folded his arms across his chest. "Maybe even you will be happy for me when I'm the most famous prospector in the country."

She scrunched her lips together. "You'll be lucky if you're even the most famous prospector in Eureka."

"In a few months, I might be."

"Well, don't expect me to fawn all over you when you make your fortune. I saw the hat you wore into town. You can't put on airs with me."

James laughed. "Even when I'm as rich as Cornelius Vanderbilt, I'm sure you'll tell me exactly what you think."

"You can depend on it."

Lily Bell had been hovering under the nearest cherry tree as if eavesdropping on their conversation. Either she was interested in talk of Cornelius Vanderbilt or she smelled something sweet on James' hair, because she walked right up to James and nudged his hand with her black nose.

"Lily Bell, nice cow," James said, patting the side of Lily Bell's face then pushing her away so she wouldn't tip over the milk or step on someone's foot. James stood and led Lily Bell away from the house. "When I get rich and move into my mansion, I'll have to take Lily Bell with me. She's quite attached."

Jessie giggled. "I won't part with her for less than fifty dollars. You can afford it."

James looked up as if he was thinking about it really hard. "Maybe I'll build my mansion in town. Then I can come visit her here without making that big of an investment."

"So you're not planning on riding out of here as fast as you can?" Jessie said, puzzled by her sudden heart palpitations.

He grinned and fingered the whiskers on his jaw. "I don't want you to forget my face."

Jessie's pulse surged like a racehorse. "I could never forget your face."

He looked at her as if he was trying to read her thoughts. "Really?"

She willed her heart to slow down. It didn't work, but it was a valiant effort. "Well, I mean, you've got half a dozen scars, and your eyes are just a little too close together, and your nose looks like it's been broken about three times."

He smoothed his finger down the bridge of his nose. "Four."

"I like it."

Again with the intense look. "You do?"

She needed to quit talking or she'd soon be revealing all her secrets, like how much she adored his brilliant white smile and how shockingly blue his eyes were, like wildflowers against the desert sand. Or how much she liked that slightly crooked nose, because it meant that even a Greek god had flaws. "Where did you get that scar?" she said, running her finger along the two-inch mark across his jawline.

She felt him tense and withdrew her hand. What was she thinking?

He cleared his throat, but then seeming to relax, he gave her an easy smile. "Let me take you through the history of my face."

"Sounds interesting," she replied dryly.

"You won't understand this scar," he pointed to his jaw, "until you understand scars two and three." He pointed to the line just above his right eyebrow. "I got this when I was five. My brother and I were sledding, and the back of his head met my eyebrow. Hard. There was so much blood, I was certain I was going to die." He pointed to a small scar that cut across his left eyebrow then to the even smaller one that cut across his upper lip. "I got these from boxing."

Jessie gasped. "Boxing? Isn't that illegal?"

He shrugged. "In some states." She must have looked horrified, because his lips curled in amusement. "One thing you need to know about me, Miss Jessie, is that I was an incorrigible young man. I ran away from home at fourteen to be a cowpuncher. After I crawled home with my tail between my legs, I boxed because I had the size for it and I knew my father didn't like it."

"But it's so dangerous."

"All the better if you want to make your father unhappy." Lines of regret appeared around his eyes. "You will be glad to know that by age twenty, I saw the error of my ways and agreed to go to college. My father paid for my schooling in hopes

I'd join his shipping company. But I've always been more interested in rocks."

Jessie didn't know if she dared ask, but she did anyway. "Is your mother...?"

He gave her a sad smile. "I'll never be able to make up for the hurt I caused her when I ran away from home. That's the main reason I went back. She didn't deserve what I put her through. I was angry at my father and God when I left, but when I went back, I realized that all I'd ever really wanted was to make my father proud."

Jessie grunted. "You sure went about it the wrong way."

James laughed. "That's one thing I love about you, Miss Jessie. You'll always tell me exactly what you think."

One thing he loved about her? What kind of talk was that? She wrapped her arms around her knees. "Why were you so mad in the first place? Most fourteen-year-old boys don't run off to Colorado."

James slid his hand along his jaw. "My oldest brother, Marcus, was Father's favorite. There was no getting around it." He paused and grimaced, and Jessie held perfectly still. "There was a boat accident. Marcus and I were rowing on the lake when a storm came up. The canoe capsized, and Marcus decided to swim for shore to get help. I begged him not to, but he wouldn't listen. Marcus always wanted to be the hero. I stayed with the canoe, and Marcus drowned trying to swim to shore." James took in a deep, shuddering breath. "I used to wish I'd been the one who'd died. My father wished it too."

Jessie took James' hand, not even caring how forward it was. "I can't imagine your pain, but I can't believe your father would wish such a terrible thing."

He looked at her as if he needed to apologize for something. "I overheard him talking to Mother the day of the funeral. He blamed me, and he said it should have been me to die instead of Marcus. Marcus was the smart one. My father had hung all his hopes on Marcus."

"Oh," Jessie said, and it came out more as a sob. How could a father treat his son so cruelly, even in his grief?

"I truly believed my family would be better off without me, so I left. I thought if I wasn't home, Father wouldn't have to be reminded what a failure I was, of what he had lost when we went out on the canoe that day. Father started grooming my younger brother Simon for the business."

"You have another brother?"

"I have two younger brothers and two little sisters. My youngest sister Abigail is fifteen." He smiled at the thought of her. "She loves me very much."

"I would suspect they all do."

"All but Father." He shook his head. "I don't mean to paint my father in a bad light. He tries very hard, but money and prestige have always been very important to him, more important than his family."

"I'm sorry, James. To lose a brother so young. How did you bear it?"

"I didn't for many years, not until I had a professor who helped me forgive God."

Jessie widened her eyes. "God doesn't need forgiveness."

James chuckled. "I was mad at Him. Maybe I needed to understand Him better, to understand why He took my brother and why my father blamed me. But God said He would wipe away all tears, and that's what He's done for me."

"I'm glad you didn't leave your family permanently. They would have missed you something terrible."

He looked at her hand as if he'd just noticed it. "I'm glad too. I hate to think I caused anyone more pain than I already have. And now I have a chance to make my father proud. If the mine does well, the company will reward me financially, and maybe Father will stop wishing it was me who had died."

She squeezed his hand. "I hope the mine is the most profitable mine in the whole world. And I'll give you Lily Bell as a gift, as long as you let me visit her."

"You can visit, as long as you leave your shotgun home so you don't scare my servants."

"I don't go anywhere without my shotgun. Visits are cancelled." She laughed at the funny look on his face. "Wait. You never told me about that last scar."

"I got a little distracted." He ran his finger along his jaw. "I got this from a fellow who tried to kill me with a broken bottle after a boxing match."

Jessie widened her eyes. "He tried to kill you?"

James nodded. "He didn't take kindly to being beaten. I didn't duck fast enough."

Jessie winced. "If you had carried a shotgun, that wouldn't have happened."

She loved his laugh. It came from deep within his throat like he really meant it. "I don't think it would have mattered. They jumped me in an alley."

"They?"

"I'm fairly sure I cracked the first man's ribs. I broke the other one's nose and knocked out two of his teeth. They got worse than they gave. After that night, I didn't box again. I wanted to irritate my father, but I didn't want to die. My mother would have been heartbroken."

Jessie was impressed and also relieved James' throat hadn't been slit. "You must have been a good fighter."

"I was young and stupid, so I won most of my bouts, but in the end, I didn't have the disposition for it. As you've seen, I don't like to shoot or otherwise hurt people." He grinned sideways at her. "You would make a good boxer."

"I don't know whether you mean that as a

compliment or an insult."

His eyes sparkled with mirth. "A compliment. I've never seen a woman so confident or so resolute with a shotgun."

She smiled then gave him the evil eye. "Let's hope you never have to find out how resolute I really am."

"I'll do my best to stay on your good side."

"What do you mean *stay*? You've never been on my good side. I don't have one."

Seven

James handed Scully the reins to Jessie The Horse plus a bag of nails he'd purchased in town. "I have the whole day to myself tomorrow," he said. "I'll be down to fix that roof."

Scully spit out a stream of chewing tobacco. "I'd be much obliged."

James smiled to himself. Scully was dirt poor, but he always seemed to have money for tobacco and whiskey. James couldn't fault any man for finding comfort where he could. Scully was old. His days as a cowpuncher had taken their toll. Every joint in his body probably screamed in pain. Whiskey made life easier for men who had lived hard.

James bounded up the slope to the boarding house. It had been a good day, and he couldn't wait to share his good news with Jessie. The London Mining and Ore Company was sending the money to buy Jean-Pierre's claim. It would be here in three weeks. Not only that, but they wanted James to map out the claim, hire an engineer, and supervise the entire project. He wouldn't have to leave Eureka for months. He could spend more time with Jessie. Maybe she would want to spend more time with him.

An unpleasant encounter with Frank Roberts was the only thing that had marred James' perfect day. Frank had been skulking around the telegraph office when James had gotten the message from the mining company. Come to think of it, Frank had been skulking around James' vicinity for a couple of weeks.

James had done his best to keep his gold discovery quiet. Claim jumpers had no scruples about trespassing on another man's claim, and James certainly didn't want one of the other operations in town offering Jean-Pierre more money for a sure thing.

Unfortunately, Jean-Pierre hadn't been able to keep his mouth shut. He had noised it all over town that the London Mining and Ore Company was buying his claim, and Frank Roberts had pounced. As soon as he heard that James was interested, Frank had offered Jean-Pierre more money. Jean-Pierre had no loyalty or obligation to James, and he would have sold the claim to Frank if Frank had actually produced the money.

It was James' good fortune that Frank talked a good story, but couldn't back up his words.

Frank didn't have enough money to buy the claim, and it would take months to round up investors. Jean-Pierre didn't want to wait that long, so the claim still belonged to James as long as the money got there in three weeks.

That didn't stop Frank from pestering James every chance he got. Frank seemed to be just within earshot every time James went to the telegraph office, and he'd been hanging around the land office whenever James went to look at maps. Didn't Frank have anything better to do? James didn't know what else to do but give Frank a dirty look every time he got close, but it was a free country. James couldn't kick Frank out of the telegraph office or shoot him in the foot to keep Frank from following him.

Today at the telegraph office, Frank had actually threatened James, calling him a thief and telling him he'd be sorry for jumping a claim that rightfully belonged to Frank. Being the boxer he was, James had been tempted to sock Frank in the face for slandering his character. But James believed in a fair fight, even against a weasel like Frank, and hitting Frank wouldn't have been very sporting. Frank was a good six inches shorter, with arms and legs like matchsticks. James could have brought him to his knees with a flick of his wrist.

Besides, James had learned long ago that if you picked a fight with every man who spoke badly of you, you'd never be done fighting and your face wouldn't be fit for polite company.

So James had walked away from Frank and treated himself to a new hat. Jessie noticed when he bought a new hat, and he liked it when Jessie noticed. Maybe it was a blessing in disguise that Frank had taken a sudden interest in James' business. While Frank pestered James, he didn't have as much time to trespass on Jessie's farm, which made it less likely that Jessie would go to jail for murder. Better that Frank bothered James and stayed away from Jessie. All in all, it was a good situation.

At the boarding house, the last of the blossoms had fallen from the cherry tree in the front yard, and young leaves grew on the spindly branches. The leaves were a sign of new beginnings for the tree and for James. He was going to supervise the mine from beginning to end, a golden chance to prove himself. Father would be impressed, especially when the mine became profitable. Jessie would be pleased when she heard about his ideas for higher wages and safer working conditions.

She'd be so happy, she'd probably want to plant a kiss right on his lips.

That thought made his heart gallop clear to the edge of the territory.

Even though she hated the very idea of mining, Jessie was softening toward him. Sometimes she smiled at him for no reason at all. She let him carry heavy things and open doors for her. Sometimes she even let him hold her shotgun.

Maybe she was starting to like him just a little bit.

Or not.

Just as he reached the boarding house, Jessie opened the door, her shotgun propped in the crook of her elbow, with a scowl that could have frightened a wolverine. "You missed dinner," she said, as if he'd just kicked her horse.

"I deeply regret that."

"Mr. Kelsey, there is a field of rocks in your room and an inch of dust on the floor. I can't sweep."

"Well, Miss Jessie, I've taken a lot of samples, and I've been cataloguing them in my notebook. I had to spread them out."

She closed one eye and squinted with the other one. "You've done more than cataloguing. You've been hammering and smashing rocks in your bedroom, a clear violation of boarding house rules."

James felt a smile tug at his lips. Jessie was extra pretty when she got irritated. "I don't remember that being one of the rules."

"Mr. Tomlinson's bed is covered with dust. The crushed rock fell between the floorboards."

Campbell Tomlinson appeared at Miss Jessie's shoulder. "I'm not complaining. I found a fleck of gold on my blanket this morning."

James tipped his hat and smiled. "Happy to help."

A growl bubbled up from deep in Jessie's

throat. "Your room is untidy, and I don't dare sweep for fear I'll mess up your rock collection or throw a small fortune out with the dirt."

James couldn't keep himself from laughing. She was just so appealing. "Miss Jessie, you're entitled to keep any gold you find while sweeping up my room."

"Ha," she blurted out. "I'm not setting foot in there until you clean up your rocks. The dust makes me sneeze, and it is very likely I will trip and kill myself." James slid the gun from her arms because it was heavy. She raised an eyebrow in his direction. "You afraid I'm going to shoot you for a messy room?"

"I'm afraid you're going to strain your arms hefting that heavy gun. It's quite a burden to bear."

She stepped back and let him enter the great room. "That shotgun is my best friend. Not a burden."

"You'll have to leave it here," he said.

She tilted her head to one side. "Am I going somewhere?"

He set the shotgun on the floor and leaned it against the wall. "Hatfield House Hotel. I've hired a rig. It will be here in ten minutes."

Jessie propped her hands on her hips. "What are your intentions, sir?"

James laughed, mostly because he had been expecting her surprised, yet appalled, expression. "There's a meeting of owners, operators, and superintendents there tonight. I want you to come with me."

She narrowed her eyes. "Why?"

"I want to present them with a proposal. I thought you could help."

Her eyes were mere slits on her face. "What makes you think I'll cooperate with you?"

"If I promise to clean up my rocks, will you come?"

"James Kelsey, stop being obtuse. Explain yourself this minute."

James smiled, pulled a chair out from under the nearest table, and motioned for her to sit. Jessie sat down, though somewhat reluctantly, and he sat next to her. "When you talked about miners paying ten cents a gallon for water, it got me thinking. What if the owners and superintendents got together and constructed a pipeline to get water from Eureka to Mammoth? The miners in Mammoth wouldn't have to pay for water anymore."

Jessie looked as if she was chewing on his words and trying not to smile at the same time. It was an attractive combination on her face. "You think the owners would fork out their own money to do that?"

"They might, if you came with me to persuade them."

Jessie grunted. "I don't know about that. I'm not well liked."

He pulled a telegram out of his pocket. "I heard from the London Mining and Ore Company today. They're sending the money for the mine."

Half a smile formed on Jessie's lips. "You've been busy."

"I've had a lot of time on my hands."

She nodded. "I know. You spend hours in your room breaking rocks."

"Will you come with me? You've lived here all your life. You've seen the hardships these men have to endure. And you're pretty and feisty and smart. What owner could say no to you?"

Her smile faded. "You want me to talk to a room full of rich men and convince them to donate money?"

He nodded.

Jessie folded her arms. "You'll do fine without me."

He frowned. "But I thought you wanted to make life better for the miners."

"Those men are ruthless, greedy money-grubbers. I wouldn't be in the same room with any of them if you did my chores for a week. Roy Cahill will be there, won't he?"

"Yes, he was one they mentioned."

"Mr. Cahill paid my mother ten dollars for Papa's legs and told her there was nothing else he could do. I'd rather kiss a rattler than lay eyes on Roy Cahill again. They all think they're smarter and better than the rest of us. I'm not having anything to do with that lot."

That wasn't exactly the reaction he'd expected from her, but he could understand her resentment.

Would it make her feel better if he told her she could bring her shotgun? No. The way she felt about it, she'd probably end up shooting somebody. No shotgun.

He tried not to show his disappointment. Jessie wasn't one who could be talked into something once she'd made up her mind.

James pulled the buggy up to the front of the hotel. There were already three other buggies parked there as well as four horses. Hubert Johns had loaned James the buggy because James had planned on bringing Jessie and he had wanted to arrive in something that showed he could afford the luxuries of life. Men with money respected other men with money, and they could spot an upstart from a mile away. Luckily, James had a sophisticated Eastern accent that immediately made him seem more important than he was. He was young and unknown, but he had the education and the background. He'd do just fine. It would have been easier to talk these men into a pipeline with a pretty woman by his side, but he could be persuasive when he wanted to.

Just as James ducked into the hotel, it started raining. The rain came down in plump drops and pelted the ground, stirring up dust before turning everything into mud. A rainstorm in these parts usually lasted long enough to get the ground good and wet, send a creek gushing down the middle of Main Street, and make enough noise to worry the cattle. Any sign of moisture would be gone by morning.

The Hatfield House Hotel was more of a boarding house than a hotel, though many of the mine owners and investors stayed there when they came to Eureka. A dining room much larger than the Madsens' sat off to James' right through a curved stone archway. An official-looking podium stood in the entryway with a guest registry open on top of it, a sure sign that this was a high-brow establishment.

James entered the dining room where eight or nine men gathered for the meeting. Three were smoking foul-smelling cigars. Two had their fingers pinched around cigarettes. A cloud of smoke hung over the room. James took a few shallow breaths to keep from coughing. Father smoked cigars because it was what wealthy men did, but James had never seen the appeal.

James recognized two of the men, but most were strangers to him. John Beck sat in the corner examining an unlit cigar. His salt-and-pepper gray hair was neatly trimmed above his ears, and his bushy white moustache curled at the ends. Beck was from Germany and had been labeled "The Crazy Dutchman" when he'd first come to town because of where he placed his mine. But his risk had paid off. His Bullion Beck mine had made Beck a fortune twenty times over. Beck wore a black velvet smoking jacket and a thick striped tie anchored with a sparkly stud that was surely a diamond.

Arthur Horne sat at a table with two other men James didn't know. Arthur was the supervisor of the Gemini mine, and James had met him his first week in town. Arthur was a hard fellow, not inclined to smile, but with a reputation of being fair and honest with the men. He wasn't well loved, but he was well respected, and in a place like this, respect had a higher value than just about anything else.

James didn't know the other men, but he knew they were the ones he'd have to convince if he had any chance of getting that pipeline.

One man jumped from his seat and rushed to shake James' hand. "You must be James Kelsey," he said, shaking as if he was thrilled for James' company. "Horne told me you were coming with a proposal. I'm Ward Howell, part owner of the Uncle Sam. We're meeting to talk about whether to build a mill or pay to expand the railroad. What do you think?"

James wasn't entirely ready for that question, but he'd done enough research into making a mine here successful that he did have an opinion. "I don't think there's enough water to make another mill practical. Better look to the railroad."

Ward pumped James' hand more vigorously. "Here's one vote for the railroad," he said, loudly

Jessie and James

enough to get the attention of everyone in the room.

Since he had it, he might as well take advantage of it. James turned to the men sitting at the tables. "I'm James Kelsey. Thank you for letting me push my way into your gathering tonight."

The man next to Arthur waved his hand in James' direction. "Frank Roberts tries to push his way in all the time. You're lucky Arthur knows you, or you'd be out in the rain with that pitiful hat."

They didn't like his new hat? James obviously had no sense of fashion. "I'm with the London Mining and Ore Company, and I'm buying and supervising a claim for them above Mammoth." A thrill of pleasure traveled down James' spine. He was going to be supervising a mine. He was going to be somebody important. "I came to talk about water."

"You already told us you don't think there's enough water for another mill. What else have you got to say?"

James took off his hat, because it was only polite and because they hated it. "Since coming to town—"

The door behind him crashed into the wall as if it had been blown open. Jessie slogged into the entryway with her shotgun strapped on her back and her dress and hair soaking wet. The pins had fallen out of her hair, and her long tresses were plastered against her cheeks as if they'd been glued there.

Waterlogged or not, Jessie was a beautiful sight. Her cheeks were flushed with color, and her eyes seemed especially bright by lamplight. Water dripped from her sleeves, and the drops made a pleasant ping as they hit the floor. James stepped into the entryway, shrugged off his jacket, and put it around Jessie's shoulders.

"Not a word," she said, between gritted teeth.

James kept a straight face and whispered back. "I wouldn't dare."

"I changed my mind," she said, lifting her chin and wrapping her fingers around the front flaps of the jacket.

"I can see that," he replied.

She pushed back the hair flattened to her face. "How bad is it?"

"You look magnificent."

Jessie cocked an eyebrow. "That's a mighty fancy word for a girl whose hairpins fell out half a mile back."

The men had gone silent. No doubt everyone wondered at the spectacle in the entryway. Jessie jerked her head toward the dining room. "Are these the ones you want me to talk to?"

James swiped a trickle of water from her cheek. "Do you need some time to collect yourself?"

"I'm scattered from here to the boarding house. There isn't enough time in the world."

That was about what he'd expected she'd say.

Jessie wasn't fussy, and she wasn't one to let a little rain stop her. She'd brought her shotgun, so unfortunately, she was ready for a fight. Would she try to badger them into submission or threaten them with their lives? James had a feeling it was going to be an exhilarating and unpleasant meeting.

A little reluctantly, he led her into the dining room, dripping hair, shotgun, and all. The men jumped to their feet, the chairs scraping behind them. Gentlemen always stood for a lady, but James could see the moment some of them recognized what a beauty Jessie was. Ward Howell snapped to attention. Someone else tightened his brocade vest over his ample stomach. Another man offered Jessie his chair.

Some of the men watched hungrily as Jessie tugged her fingers through her wet hair and fashioned it into a single twist resting on her shoulder. James tried not to tense up as his protective instincts rushed to the surface.

Jessie took the chair offered her, but only after shrugging off James' jacket, removing her shotgun, and shaking out her skirts. She handed her shotgun to James, who was more than happy to take it off her hands. If he was holding it, she was less likely to shoot someone. Her skirts must have weighed ten pounds, but she couldn't stay on her feet without the entire room standing with her.

She nodded a thank you to the man, looked around the room, and gave a small cough. Jessie was as smart as a whip, and she knew when to use her feminine powers. John Beck stabbed his newly lit cigar into the ashtray at his table. The other men quickly extinguished their smoking sticks and sat down. All eyes turned to Jessie. It was the same with James. He couldn't look away, but whether it was out of dread or fascination, he couldn't tell.

Everyone but James sat down. He stood at the front of the room as if he was in charge of this meeting, but it was fairly obvious who had all the attention. He rested the stock of the shotgun on the floor and wrapped his fingers around the barrel as if he was holding a cane.

Jessie folded her hands in her lap and batted her eyelashes. It was obvious she hadn't much practice being coy and ladylike because she looked a little stiff, but it didn't matter. With that wavy long hair and those big, round eyes, she had all of them mesmerized.

James froze as a drop of water trickled down Jessie's neck to the base of her throat. For an eternal moment, all he could think about was wiping off that drop with his thumb. He tightened his fingers around the gun and turned his gaze to the floorboards two feet in front of him. What was happening to him?

It didn't seem to matter what mood Jessie was in. When she was angry, his pulse raced. When she smiled, he couldn't pull his gaze from her face. When she laughed, he found it hard to catch his breath. Whether Jessie was trying to shoot him or

Jessie and James

charm him, she was the most desirable woman he'd ever met.

"Gentlemen," Jessie said, in a voice so not like her own that James had to look to make sure it was coming out of her mouth. "James and I need your help. Mammoth is as dry as a bone. Miners pay ten cents a gallon for water. Ten cents. Life is hard enough for the miners. Having to pay for water is too much."

John Beck nodded. "I used to work underground."

Jessie smiled. "I know you did. I've heard it said that you never forget your own poverty when others are in need."

James didn't know the man sitting next to Beck, but his burgundy velvet vest and pocket watch were signs of his wealth. "What do you want us to do about it? The men are already agitating for higher wages. They'd bleed us dry if we let them."

Jessie's eye twitched, but she answered as calmly as if she were talking about the weather. "We want the owners and operators to build a wooden pipeline from Eureka to Mammoth so the men don't have to buy their drinking water."

Arthur Horne reared back in his seat as if Jessie had said something slightly rude. "You're saying you want us to pay for it?"

James pointed to his saddlebag on the table. "I've got the maps right here—"

"I won't spend another penny on Mammoth," said another man with a shiny black moustache and black pinstriped trousers. "It's expensive enough getting the ore around the mountain as it is."

Ward Howell smiled widely. "No need for water. Most of the miners only drink alcohol."

Just about everyone in the room laughed except for Jessie, James, and John Beck.

"Miss Jessie," Horne said, "Plain and simple, we are not going to spend the money on something that won't do a thing to pull more ore out of the ground. It's bad business."

The room seemed to rumble in agreement. "If the men don't like working Mammoth, they can find work elsewhere," said one.

"We pay them fair wages," another chimed in.

"It's not my business how they want to spend their money."

"Mr. Kelsey," said the man in the brocade vest, "this is a fool's errand. We've mined this area for years. There's no need to change the way we've been doing things."

James tried to be conciliatory. "I'm new here, and I would never want to spend the London Mining and Ore Company's money foolishly—"

Before James knew what was happening, Jessie shot to her feet, grabbed the gun from his grip, and pounded the stock on the floor as if it were a royal staff. The loud clap silenced the room, and every gaze locked on Jessie's face. With her wet hair sagging around her shoulders and her eyes ablaze with indignation, she was a

Jessie and James 105

magnificent, terrifying sight. The gun made her seem all the more frightening.

"I've tried to be nice, but I can only suffer fools for so long."

James winced. It was never a good idea to call a man a fool if you wanted to get money from him. Oh, well. There was nothing he could do now. When Jessie got going, she was like a freight train—mighty hard to stop.

"Here you are, fighting over a few dollars, when men in Mammoth have to buy water just to survive. You should be ashamed of yourselves." She picked up the shotgun and shook it in James' direction. "You should all be ashamed of yourselves."

What was she mad at him for? He was on her side. He pulled the note from his pocket. "Gentlemen, I received a telegraph from the London Mining and Ore Company today. Since their new mine is above Mammoth, they are willing to fund thirty percent of the pipeline project."

Jessie turned so fast, droplets of water flew from her hair. "You didn't tell me that."

"You didn't ask."

She glared at him. "You just got done saying they didn't want to spend their money foolishly." She pointed at Ward Howell. "I thought you were agreeing with him. I thought you were backing down."

"I don't back down, Miss Jessie," he snapped,

a little bit annoyed with her.

She was just as annoyed. "I got all righteous and indignant, and I didn't even have to."

The man with the shiny moustache tapped his finger on the table. "Can you fight about this another time and quit wasting ours?"

Jessie folded her arms around her gun. "The London Mining and Ore Company will pay thirty percent of the cost of the pipeline. What will you contribute, Mr. Nesbitt?"

John Beck nodded thoughtfully. "I will pay an additional thirty percent."

Ward Howell gasped. Arthur Horne pressed his lips into a hard line.

Jessie seemed to soften around the edges. "That's sixty percent of the project already paid for. Who else will help build the pipeline?"

The man in the red velvet vest fingered the cold cigarette in his hand. "If I contribute to this project, I want to know how the miners will help. They should have some stake in it."

Jessie studied his face for a moment. "They stake their lives every day, Mr. Cahill."

Mr. Cahill, the one Jessie especially didn't want to see. Her tone was icy, but polite. James was proud of her. She could control her temper when she wanted to.

Nesbitt smoothed his moustache and nodded. "What are you going to do to help raise the funds?"

James held up the telegram. "As I said, my

Jessie and James 107

company will contribute thirty percent."

Nesbitt gave James a sour look. "Not you, Mr. Kelsey. Miss Madsen."

Jessie lifted her chin even as her cheeks grew pinker. "We...I'm...we haven't the money."

She didn't lower her eyes or cower in the face of opposition or the nine intimidating men staring at her. Maybe the shotgun gave her confidence. Maybe she knew it was no shame to be poor.

Nesbitt folded his arms and leaned back in his chair as if he'd won the argument. "It's easy to spend another man's money. It's mighty hypocritical to tell me I'm greedy when you aren't willing to put in any of your own."

Ward Howell's mouth fell open, probably surprised Nesbitt had dared call a lady a hypocrite.

James was a bit surprised too. This Nesbitt fellow seemed to know Miss Jessie, but he obviously didn't know her well. Wasn't he aware that Jessie might start shooting at such an insult? And if she did, could James wrestle the gun away from her before she killed somebody?

Jessie didn't change her expression, but the muscles of her jaw worked back and forth as she clenched and unclenched her teeth. "You can't justify yourself by calling me names, Mr. Nesbitt. But as a show of good faith, our family will sponsor a fundraising dance at the boarding house Friday after next." She swallowed hard. "Men can pay ten cents apiece to dance with me."

A slow smile grew on Nesbitt's face. "I just

might take you up on that, Miss Jessie."

Jessie straightened her spine. "As long as you can pay."

James could muster only one thought at that precise moment. Mr. Nesbitt was not getting one dance with Jessie Madsen. James would make sure of that if it was the last thing he did.

Eight

Jessie growled as an errant lock of hair fell out of her bun. She was entirely too distracted to do her hair well, and tonight of all nights, her bun needed to be as impenetrable as Fort Douglas. She stabbed four extra pins into her hair and looked in the mirror. It would have to do. If a man tried to mess with her hair, maybe he'd get skewered with a hairpin.

She growled even louder when she heard voices in the other room. James and Papa talking over last-minute plans for the dance.

The dance. Jessie hated the very thought of it.

Not only were men going to put their grubby, unwashed hands on her waist, but she was going to get her feet stepped on and probably come away with a sprained ankle before the night was over.

"Ouch," Jessie hissed, as she stabbed herself with the pin attached to Mamma's broach. She wasn't one for wearing adornments or decorations, but tonight the memory of her mother would give her comfort when one more miner asked her to dance, and if that miner got fresh, she could stab him with the broach pin. The broach would be her secret weapon, since she couldn't very well dance with a shotgun strapped to her back. Papa had strictly forbidden it.

She clenched her teeth. James Kelsey had gotten her into this, and somehow, some way, she was going to pay him back. That man was the very devil himself sent to torment her for her sins.

Jessie expelled a heavy sigh. Maybe the dance wasn't completely James' fault. Seeing Roy Cahill at that meeting of fancy-pants mining executives had made her blood boil. Then Watson Nesbitt had called her a hypocrite, and she hadn't been able to think of another way to shut him up. The measly two or three dollars she would raise tonight by dancing with anyone willing to pay wouldn't buy much pipe or labor, but at least people would see Jessie and her family making an effort for the miners in Mammoth.

She smoothed her hand down her skirts. The dress had been her mother's, and it was so fancy Jessie had only worn it four other times. The bodice was purplish blue with darker blue and maroon stripes. The skirt was the same purplish blue as the bodice. It didn't quite go to the floor because Mamma had been shorter than Jessie. Alice had offered to take the hem down, but Jessie didn't want to risk ruining Mamma's dress. Besides, it would be easier to dance if she wasn't worried about having her skirt stepped on all night.

Alice had decided the dining room wasn't large enough for a dance, so they were dancing in the front yard under the cherry tree. Alice had spent two days making cookies and pies and cakes, James had spent at least that much time filling in the uneven spots in their front yard with dirt, and Jessie had spent a week and a half dreading it. She fully anticipated having to stab a few hands with her broach and slap a few faces. It wasn't a dance. It was a battle, and she wasn't going to give an inch of ground.

Jessie stood up straight, glanced at her hair one last time in the mirror, and marched out of her room like a good soldier. Every man who dared dance with her would know she was ready for a fight.

James and Papa stood next to the stove conversing in hushed tones. When Jessie came out of her room, they moved apart and pretended they hadn't been talking about anything. Jessie wasn't fooled, but she wasn't going to ask them to explain themselves when she wasn't likely to get an answer.

James bloomed into a dazzling smile. "Miss Jessie, don't get mad at me for saying this, but you're prettier than a sunrise."

His appreciative gaze made her feel giddy,

which in turn made her irritated that she was giddy. "If you think your flattery will get you a free dance, you can just think again. You pay like everybody else." Jessie's heart pounded in her ears. Would James want to dance with her?

Did she want to dance with him?

She refused to answer such a dangerous question. It didn't matter one way or the other, because tonight she would be dancing with men who were willing to pay. What did she care if James would rather not spend his money? Jessie caught her bottom lip between her teeth. Unfortunately, she might care too much.

James laughed. "I knew you'd get mad, but I had to try anyway."

She tried to size up James without staring. He wore a crisp blue shirt that stretched across his wide shoulders and strained around his hard upper arms. His light hair was still damp from being washed, and the stubble that often covered his face after a long day on the trail was shaved clean. He had a strong jaw, four fascinating scars on his face, and blue eyes that put the sky to shame. She had never before seen any man quite so magnificent. She cleared her throat. She'd do well to remember that James was a prospector at heart who only cared about one thing. It was all that kind of man ever cared about.

Papa smiled, transferred both canes to one hand, and took Jessie's wrist. "You look very much like your mother, my dear. You'll break at least a

Jessie and James

dozen hearts tonight, no doubt."

James pressed his hand to his chest. "You've already broken mine."

Jessie arched an eyebrow in his direction. "You'll pay for your dances just like everybody else."

James merely laughed.

Papa pointed to the ledger sitting on the nearest table. "I've written the numbers one to ten on the back page." He glanced at James as if there was some secret between them. "Any man who wants to dance with you will sign his name, pay me the money, and wait his turn."

Jessie pursed her lips. She couldn't bear the thought of dancing more than ten dances, but ten cents a dance wouldn't bring in much money. "That's only one dollar in profits."

Papa cupped her chin in his hand. "It will be enough. I don't want you to suffer any more than you have to."

"Thank you, Papa."

"Besides, we are charging two bits for admission. Any money you bring in is extra. That should satisfy even Mr. Watson Nesbitt."

Jessie nodded as some of the tension of anticipation fell from her shoulders. Only ten dances. The torment would last less than an hour. She could bear it.

"Are you ready?" Papa said. "They'll be arriving."

Jessie forced a smile onto her face. A scowl

would drive men away, and despite her reluctance to dance, she truly did want to help raise money for the pipeline. "I'm ready."

James offered his arm. Jessie hesitated. The arm she really wanted to take was Papa's, but with two canes, he couldn't give her any assistance. She reluctantly hooked her arm around James' elbow. His muscles were rock hard, and warmth radiated from his skin. "Don't worry, Miss Jessie," he said, with a smile that stole her breath. "I won't let any harm come to you."

Immediately comforted by his strength, Jessie tightened her hold on him. He was like an anchor in her own private storm, a warm fire for her chilly heart. He was a boulder that would not be moved.

When she found her voice, she tried to be flippant so James wouldn't know how his touch unnerved her. "I'd rather have my shotgun."

"It won't be as bad as all that," Papa said. "These are a good sort of men, hard workers who have a hard life."

Papa always saw the best in everyone. Jessie couldn't be so charitable. She certainly wasn't going to let down her guard tonight. These men needed discipline, and she would insist they mind their manners.

James opened the front door, and they walked outside. Alice had strung five lengths of rope from the cherry tree to the eaves of the house. Each piece of rope was tied with fabric scraps that looked quite festive in the gathering dusk. Jessie and

James had carried out two tables from the dining room that Alice had loaded with desserts. It definitely looked like a party. If not for the dancing, Jessie might even have anticipated a good time.

Even though the dance had been Jessie's very bad idea, Alice had done most of the work preparing for it. Jessie had kept the farm and boarding house running while Alice baked and made fabric streamers. Papa was going to collect money, and Alice was going to play her concertina while Handy Milsap sawed his fiddle. Handy was one of the miners on the Uncle Sam, but Jessie suspected he made more money playing his fiddle than mining.

Alice was arranging the last of the plates on the table when she saw Jessie. She abandoned her cookies and took both of Jessie's hands. "You look like a princess."

"Prettier," James said.

"Save your breath," Jessie said, tempering her scolding with a small smile. If he didn't stop with the flattery, she'd start to believe he actually meant it.

Alice nodded. "You're right, Mr. Kelsey. I once saw a real princess in Denver at one of those traveling shows. Jessie is much prettier than that." She spread her arms, motioning to the tables. "What do you think?"

James smiled. "I think no one has eaten this well since Thanksgiving."

Alice seemed pleased. "I want everyone to get their money's worth."

"They'll get more than their money's worth, Miss Alice. I don't know anyone who can cook like you, even the fancy chefs in Boston."

Alice giggled. "I'd like to see that. I surely would."

Papa sat down at a small table facing the road in the direction most of the miners would come from. Some arrived on horses. Some families came in buggies. Most came on foot. Only the most prosperous among them could afford the luxury of a horse. Jessie gazed past Papa to the stable where her own horses were kept. Her family owned two strong horses, a flock of chickens, and a milk cow. She tended to focus on her misfortunes more than her blessings. Maybe they had more blessings than she realized.

Alice and Handy started to play music as more people arrived. Most were miners, but there were some families that lived in Eureka, and even a couple of older girls who were willing to dance with the miners. Lou Johns from the mercantile came with his wife. Emmaline Johns was a strait-laced, severe sort of woman, but she was also willing to dance when she was needed. And she was always needed.

The barber, Orson Parker, brought his wife and family of six girls and three boys. Mabel Tyson also came with her three children in tow. Mabel was a single woman who owned a bar in

Mammoth. She wasn't especially respectable, but everyone was welcome to a dance like this. Jessie hardly knew Mabel at all, except to know that she needed to sorely repent for serving the demon liquor, but Jessie wasn't going to be the one to tell her.

Jessie drew her brows together as she watched Mabel shepherd her young ones up the hill. Mabel needed to repent, but it was also said that she had a heart of gold. Three different people had left their babies on Mabel's doorstep on three separate occasions, and Mabel was raising those children as her own. Maybe she wasn't such a lost soul after all. Maybe a water pipeline to Mammoth would make Mabel's life a little bit easier.

Papa was taking money and feverishly writing in his ledger. Jessie's dread surfaced all over again. She didn't know what she dreaded more, that someone would want to dance with her or that no one would.

"You okay, Miss Jessie?" James said, coming up behind her and planting himself like an immovable cottonwood tree at her back.

She borrowed some of his strength and squared her shoulders. "Yes. Let's get this over with. The sooner it's finished, the sooner I can find it in my heart to forgive you."

He laughed. "Forgive me? I hate to remind you, Miss Jessie, but you got yourself into this. Mr. Nesbitt provoked you."

She wasn't about to let him be right. "You're

the one who invited me to that fool meeting."

"I hope with all my heart you can forgive me for everything I've ever done to offend you, Miss Jessie."

There was so much affection in his voice, she turned and studied his expression. He was grinning with his whole face, and that grin was completely irresistible. "You are a charmer, Mr. Kelsey. A smooth-tongued charmer," she said, unable to suppress a genuine smile.

"I'd walk three whole weeks in the desert just to see that smile, ma'am."

She rolled her eyes. "Any more of your flattery, Mr. Kelsey, and I'll have to throw you out on your ear."

"You can't throw me out. I've paid my two bits just like everybody else."

Alice and Handy climbed onto the wagon they were using as a stage. "Welcome," Alice said. "We hope you enjoy yourselves tonight. Two treats per person so we don't run out."

Alice wasn't much for speeches, and Handy had a stutter, so that was all the greeting the dancers were likely to get. Alice said something to Handy that Jessie couldn't hear, and they started playing a lively, toe-tapping song Jessie didn't recognize. That was all the invitation most of the people needed. Every woman had a partner within seconds, and some of the miners danced with each other.

A miner with dirt-caked fingernails

Jessie and James

approached. At least his face was scrubbed clean, and it looked like he'd made an attempt with his shirt. He tipped his hat. "Good evening, Miss Jessie."

"Are you my partner?" she asked.

"Nah," he said, glancing at James. "I ain't getting that pleasure tonight." He headed for the dessert table.

Three more miners headed in her direction. They all tipped their hats and moved on, none of them claiming her hand for the dance. Their destination was the food. Jessie's heart couldn't take the suspense. One thing was for sure. She needed to get out of the way of the cookies.

Jessie stepped aside and scanned the crowd. Any second now, the miner who had paid for the first dance was going to find her, and she'd have to leave the safety of James' strong presence. The wretched waiting was the most uncomfortable feeling in the world.

James gave her a tentative smile. "May I have the pleasure of this dance?"

That accent of his floated into her brain like a beautiful melody, and she found him nearly irresistible. But she would have to resist tonight. And tomorrow. And every night for the rest of her life. She shook her head. "I have to find my first partner."

James seemed unsure of himself for the first time today. "Well, Miss Jessie, I hope you don't mind, but I am your first partner."

Her mouth fell open, and her heart was like to leap out of her chest. "You want to dance with me?"

"Oh, yes."

She gathered her wits and tried to talk herself out of whatever conclusion her heart had jumped to. What possible reason could he have for wanting a dance? She cocked an eyebrow. "You want to rub it in, don't you?"

"Rub what in?"

"The fact that I have to dance with anyone who pays. Even you."

"Because you wouldn't dance with me otherwise?" He attempted a teasing smile and failed miserably, his expression hijacked by uncertainty.

Realization struck her and made her dizzy. It wasn't possible that Mr. Kelsey actually wanted to dance with her just to dance with her, was it? And even more astounding was that he seemed to want her to *want* to dance with him.

Jessie's mouth went dry, and she couldn't swallow past the lump in her throat. Every flippant or scornful response she might have given him flew out of her head like a flock of pheasants from a coyote. Mr. Kelsey wanted to dance with her. And maybe she wanted to dance with him. It didn't mean she had to like him or trust him or give him her heart. It was just a dance. And James had paid for it.

She laid a hand on his arm, hoping to make

that pained look on his face disappear. She couldn't be so cruel as to put him through any sort of discomfort. "Mr. Kelsey, you milked the cow this morning. I would be very happy to dance with you."

His smile could have lit up the entire evening sky. "I'm glad Lily Bell and I are such good friends."

Her heart had never beat so fast as when he took her hand and pulled her close. The wonderful scent of leather and sharp, strong soap attacked her senses and made her wobblier than she already was. Of course she wanted to dance with him, just for the pleasure of that smell. He placed his hand lightly on her waist and took her other hand in his. She rested her hand on his firm shoulder.

Most people in the territories didn't know any proper dance steps. Jessie certainly didn't, but James did. He tightened his hand around her back and led her around the yard as if they were floating. It was the most heady feeling Jessie had ever experienced.

It took her eight measures to catch her breath. "You know how to dance."

"Every son of the upper class knows how to dance, but it's also a good skill to have if you want to be a boxer. Proper footwork wins many a match."

"You must have been a very good boxer."

He laughed. "Good enough. My little sisters love to dance, so they made me help them practice.

I spent more time dancing than I did boxing. It's much safer."

"I'm sorry I'm not a better partner."

James slowed his steps and pulled her to the edge of the group of dancers. He bent his head so his mouth was close to her ear. She shivered as his warm breath tickled her cheek. "Miss Jessie, you are the best partner I've ever danced with."

That couldn't be true, but she wasn't going to argue with him, not when she couldn't even speak.

They stood like that for a few seconds, swaying back and forth but not really dancing, until James seemed to remember he'd paid for a dance. He pulled her closer and whirled her around the yard. She laughed at the feeling of flying in a circle. She liked dancing better than she would have thought.

"Who is that girl over there?" James said. "In the green dress."

Jessie turned to look. "That's Clara Parker." She tried not to frown. Was James interested in dancing with Clara next?

"Are you and Clara friends?"

She pressed her lips together. "Do you want me to introduce you?"

He studied her face, his eyes shining with something deep and unreadable. "Miss Jessie, there isn't another girl here tonight I want to dance with."

"Oh," she said, because his look rendered her unable to form a clear thought in her brain.

Jessie and James

"I'm just curious. Who are your friends in town?"

"Clara is only seventeen. We don't really know each other. I'm too busy with the farm and house, and Clara goes to the church on Main Street. We don't cross paths often."

James furrowed his brow. "But do you have any other woman friends?"

Jessie shrugged. "The married women don't pay any heed to a woman who doesn't have a husband. The girls are too young and silly. I have too much work to do to develop the patience for them."

Concern saturated his features. "You don't have any friends?"

Jessie took a deep breath to squeeze out the sudden ache in her chest. "In case you haven't noticed, I'm not that easy to get along with. Nobody wants to be my friend."

"I don't believe it." James suddenly shrugged off whatever somber mood he'd fallen into and smiled. "Clara looks like a girl who would be eager to learn how to shoot a shotgun."

Jessie cracked a smile. "Every girl should know how to shoot."

He pointed to Edith Lund, the daughter of one of the mining supervisors. "I'll bet that girl would like to know how to prune cherry trees."

Jessie giggled. "That's Edith. She'd only thirteen. I don't know if she'd care to be my friend. I'm ten years older."

"Oh. She looks older."

"She's tall for her age."

The song ended, and James squeezed Jessie's hand. "That was even better than I dreamed it would be. Thank you."

She rolled her eyes. "You're a charmer, Mr. Kelsey. I'm inclined to disbelieve every word you say."

With tight hold of her hand, he pulled her dangerously close. "I would never lie to you, Miss Jessie. I hope you know that."

She couldn't look away from those blue eyes. "I...I suppose I do."

He lost the intensity of his gaze and smiled. "Let's go ask Clara if she wants to learn how to shoot your gun."

She cuffed him on the shoulder and tried to pull her hand away. "There's no time for making friends. I have to find my second partner."

He tugged her back and gave her a sheepish grin. "Well, Miss Jessie, as it turns out, I'm your next partner."

"You...you're my next partner?" A thrill of pleasure pulsed through her veins. Even at her peril, she didn't try to ignore it. "You paid for two dances?"

"Miss Jessie, I paid for them all."

Jessie was struck mute. James had bought all her dances?

He watched her doubtfully. "I knew you were uncomfortable, and I didn't want you to have to suffer through all those dances. If you want, I can cross my name off your father's ledger, and you can dance with whoever you want."

James was a very thoughtful man. He helped with the farm chores. He pitched in after dinner. He bought all her dances so she wouldn't have to suffer tonight. So why was she so miserable all of a sudden? "Oh. Well." Her smile withered no matter how hard she tried to keep it alive. "Thank you. You're so kind. I appreciate your consideration."

He must have seen something he didn't like in her face. No wonder, because her smile probably looked as fake as a soiled dove's colored hair. He took her by the shoulders and stared into her eyes. "I thought you'd be happy."

"Of course I'm happy." She sounded so pathetic, she didn't even convince herself. "You're so kind, James, but I won't hold you to it. I'm glad I don't have to dance with anyone else, but you shouldn't be forced to dance with me all night. I can go in the house and read the Bible, which is what I'd rather do anyhow."

Exasperation tugged at his mouth. "Yes, I'm sure you would."

"I'm very grateful."

His hands tightened around her shoulders. "Miss Jessie, seventeen men came to your father this week asking to be put on your dancing list. Seventeen!"

"They did?"

"And I wouldn't stand for it." He ran his fingers through his hair and messed up its perfect shape. "I paid your father a dollar a dance, and he wrote me in on every slot."

A dollar a dance? It was an indecent amount of money. "You're very kind to all of us, Mr. Kelsey."

"Miss Jessie, if you call me kind one more time, I'm going to tear the legs off Alice's dessert table."

Jessie frowned. Didn't he like being kind? Now he was just talking crazy. "Alice would have your hide."

He glanced at the dessert table as if he might just do it. "I wasn't being kind. I was being selfish, because I couldn't stand the thought of your dancing with anybody but me."

Jessie's heart raced so fast, she thought she might pass out. Was it possible to faint from pure happiness? Maybe she'd just faint with shock. "Oh."

"Yes, *oh*," he said, more irritated than adoring. "If you don't want to dance with me, don't dance, but I'd just as soon dance with you clear into next Sunday if you let me."

Jessie's wits were scattered to the north wind. It was as if she was wandering through a very pleasant dream where she couldn't understand what anyone was saying. "Would we take time out to eat?"

He paused. A smile grew slowly on his lips,

and he held out his hand. "Will you dance with me, Miss Jessie?"

"I...think I'd like that very much."

Nine

Holding Miss Jessie in his arms felt like he'd finally found his missing puzzle piece. And James wasn't about to let go. Unfortunately, he had to let go when they did the Virginia Reel, but every time she came back around to him, he held on that much tighter. The best part about dancing was that he had leave to keep Jessie close to him, and nobody, not even Jessie, thought it was improper or forward. God bless the person who had invented dancing.

By dance number six, he could tell Jessie was getting tired. He truly could have danced until Sunday, but he didn't want to wear her out or wear out his welcome. Keeping tight hold of her hand in plain sight of everyone, he led her to a spot under the tree where they could sit.

She gave him a drowsy smile when he brought her a drink of water. "The next dance has started. You're not going to get your money's worth."

"I got my money's worth before the music even began."

She laughed. It was a deep, throaty laugh he liked very much. "You're a charmer, Mr. Kelsey, no doubt about it."

It was getting dark, but George had lit some lanterns on the porch and the dessert table. Two lanterns sat on the wagon bed on either side of Alice and Handy. There was plenty of light to see by, but still James couldn't quite make out the features of the man strolling in their direction with his hands in his pockets.

"Miss Jessie," he said. "Mr. Kelsey has stolen all your dances for himself."

James vaulted to his feet as Frank Roberts stepped into the light of a lantern hanging from the cherry tree. Jessie stood up with him. "I don't think you were invited to this party, Mr. Roberts," James said.

Frank smirked. "Oh, everybody was invited. I paid my two bits. I was hoping to dance with Miss Jessie here, but George said you was all sold out."

Jessie folded her arms. "It's just as well, Frank, because I'd just as soon shoot you as dance with you."

Frank laughed, trying to sound amused but only managing to sound nervous. "I only wanted a friendly dance. You won't let me get within ten feet, and I'm itching to tell you what I've found on your claim. We could both be rich."

"You'd be wise to stay off my claim. Don't make me come after you again." Jessie seemed more irritated than angry, as if Frank was a fly bothering her milk cow.

James didn't know what to do. He wasn't afraid of Frank, and neither, it seemed, was Jessie. Frank was a gnat, a nuisance and hard to get rid of, but he couldn't do much to hurt anybody. James couldn't very well throw Frank off the property. He didn't want to make a scene, and he didn't want to ruin Miss Alice's dance. He still had four more dances coming.

He'd just have to hope that Frank would behave himself. It didn't bode well that Frank had sought him out, as if he was looking for a fight. He cupped his hand around Jessie's arm and nudged her in the direction of the dancing. "Well then, enjoy your evening, Mr. Roberts."

Frank wasn't having any of it. "The Frenchman was going to sell me that claim."

James clenched his teeth. "Are you still gnawing on that bone?"

"He said he'd wait until I came up with the money, then you come to town and suddenly he ain't willing to wait."

Frank drew the attention of some of the miners standing near the cherry tree. James wouldn't argue with him. He already said his piece at the telegraph office, and Frank didn't want to hear it. James stepped very close to Frank so their toes touched. His size gave him an advantage, and he was going to use it. "Mr. Roberts," he said softly, with a hint of violence in his tone. "Don't ruin this nice evening for all these folks."

Frank narrowed his eyes and stood up taller, as if that would make a difference. He was a head shorter than James. He could stand on his tippy toes and James wouldn't bat an eyelash—but he might laugh at the little man trying to play at being tough.

Frank stared at James for a few seconds and then backed down, just as James hoped he would. "I'm just saying. I deserve that claim." He took a step away from James and looked at Jessie. "Don't you see what he's doing? He's trying to soften you up, convince you to sell him your claim."

James eyed Jessie and was relieved that she didn't seem to believe it. "Don't try that with me, Frank," she said. "I ain't selling to nobody."

Frank smiled bitterly. "Just ask Reuben Pierce."

Jessie stiffened. "I ain't selling."

Frank must have sensed Jessie's agitation, a way to get under her skin. "Reuben would have given you the moon if you'd asked him, and all he wanted was to explore your claim."

Jessie stood ramrod straight, her eyes flashing with anger and pain. That pain tore right through James' chest. He balled his hands into fists.

Unwisely, Frank kept talking. "You're a cruel, cold woman, Jessie. Not even Reuben Pierce could touch that hard heart of yours."

James shot out his arm and wrenched it around Frank's neck. He didn't want a fight, but nobody was allowed to hurt Jessie. Frank grunted in pain and shock as James dragged him by the neck around to the side of the house where no one would see. Hopefully nobody but a few miners and Jessie saw him remove Frank from the premises. He wrapped his fingers around Frank's throat and pushed him against the house. Frank gasped, but he couldn't speak. It was better that way, even if Frank didn't realize it. If he'd said another word, James might have slammed his head into the rock wall.

Frank clawed at James' arm, but James wouldn't let go until he'd said what he had to say. "I've tried to be neighborly, Mr. Roberts, but now I'm just angry. Don't talk to Miss Jessie like that again. In fact, don't talk to Miss Jessie at all. You stay ten feet from Miss Jessie at all times, even if you have to stay in your house to avoid passing her on the street. Do you understand?"

Frank gurgled and struggled. James loosened his grip slightly so Frank could speak. "Let me go, you snake."

Jessie appeared around the corner of the house, her eyes filled with alarm. "James, don't."

James didn't relent. "I don't think you heard me, Mr. Roberts. I said, *do you understand*?"

"I understand. I understand. Just let me go." James released Frank's neck, and Frank clutched his throat, fell to his knees, and coughed until he gagged. "You could have killed me."

"Remember that next time you want to upset Miss Jessie."

Without wasting another minute, Frank stumbled to his feet and ran back toward the dance and the safe crowd of people. He caught sight of Jessie and squeaked as he staggered to make a wide berth around her.

"Ten feet," James yelled, but Frank was already long gone.

Jessie folded her arms and leaned against the house. "You didn't want to shoot him the other day."

"I wasn't in the mood."

"Frank is a weasel, but I'm never really serious about killing him," Jessie said.

James brushed off his sleeves. "I wouldn't have killed him, but as long as he thinks I wanted to kill him, that's good enough."

One side of her mouth curled upward. "I've never seen any man drag another man away so fast."

"I didn't want to risk offending Alice or any of the other ladies present. I had to be quick."

She laughed as if she'd been holding it in for a long time. "I owe you another dance for doing me such a great service."

He smiled, even though he was still mad as a hornet. "If that's my reward, I'll start looking for other varmints I can throw off the premises."

His heart beat double time when she came close and smoothed down his collar. "Do you know your accent changed when you threatened Frank? You sounded like a Texan."

He stifled a grin. "Something I learned in Colorado. Out here, the working men don't take you seriously if you sound like you were raised to be a gentleman. I use the western accent when I really mean business."

"Hmm," she purred. "I like it."

He switched into his drawl. "Then I'll talk this way all the time."

She smiled. "No. I like your real accent better. You sound foreign, like an exotic bird."

He cocked an eyebrow. "An exotic bird? Like a parrot?"

"Maybe." Her smile faded, and she turned her face away. "I'm not as coldhearted as everybody says."

"Of course not. I don't believe it for a minute."

"Even though I tried to shoot you once?"

"You didn't mean it."

That coaxed a wisp of a smile from her, but it soon disappeared. "Reuben's mama spread all sorts of rumors about me. She said I drove him away. She said I broke his heart. She called me a liar." Her voice cracked.

"Hush, hush, sweetheart," he said, caressing her cheek with his thumb. "You never have to explain yourself to me. I know your heart."

A soft moan escaped her lips. "No, you don't.

You don't know how foolish I've been."

He ached to take her in his arms and kiss away that wounded look in her eyes. "It doesn't matter. We all regret things in our past."

"I do have regrets, but not the ones Frank accuses me of."

"I wouldn't believe Frank if he swore an oath on the Bible."

Jessie sighed. "Would you feel cheated if we skipped the rest of the dancing and sat on the back porch? The moon is pretty tonight."

He took her hand. "I'd like nothing better."

They strolled to the back of the house. The spindly silhouettes of cherry trees stood out against the darkening sky. A rock wren twittered in the distance. A coyote barked, and it seemed like a million crickets chirped in harmony. The music from the dance floated in their direction, but it felt like they were miles away.

They sat down on the back porch step where they had spent many evenings looking at the stars and talking about constellations. The breeze was chilly. He sidled close to lend her some of his warmth. "I'm sorry about what Frank said."

"I'm sorry too." Jessie wrapped her arms around her knees. "This is my favorite spot on the farm. The hills watch over our little vale, and the trees wait like friends with their arms outstretched. There are no headframes or mining timbers on the hill to ruin the view. The Colorado Chief mine is just over that second hill, but you can't see it from here."

"I've been to the Colorado Chief. It's a monster."

She frowned, studied his face, then pointed above the cherry trees to the north. "Reuben Pierce put up a headframe right there. It looked like Goliath crouching for an attack."

James stared at Jessie in surprise. "You...there was a mine up there?"

She smiled sadly. "I let him talk me into it. He was even more charming than you are."

Considering that the very name of Reuben Pierce seemed to bring Jessie a great deal of pain, James didn't take that as a compliment. "The one Frank was talking about? He built a headframe on your claim?"

Jessie peered out over the hills. "Yes."

"You don't have to say another word, Jessie. I don't care who Reuben Pierce is."

"I want you to know the truth, not Frank Roberts' or Ida Pierce's version of the truth." She leaned back on her hands and expelled a deep breath. "I was seventeen, missing my mother and starved for affection. Papa and Alice had each other, and I had no one. That was why Reuben was able to fool me so easily. He grew up in Eureka but spent three or four years away in the Army. When he came back, he was taller and handsomer, and to a backward girl like me, he seemed very sophisticated, a man of the world."

James drew his brows together. No wonder

she had been so hostile when he'd come to town. She'd definitely seen him as a man of the world.

"I didn't know it," Jessie said, "but he had his eye on our claim from the minute he came back to town, but really, he just had his eye on our money. He started hanging around the boarding house, coming to Papa's Sunday morning sermons, bringing me flowers or candies from the mercantile. He talked so pretty, and I believed every word he said. He said our claim was rich with gold and if we let him mine it, we'd be the richest family in the territory." Her voice faltered. "He asked me to marry him."

"He did?" James' gut felt as if it was full of stones. It was already obvious this story didn't end well for Jessie.

"I was seventeen, so Papa said I had to wait. I was devastated at the time, but now I am nothing but grateful for his caution. I thought I loved Reuben and I wanted to make him happy, so I convinced Papa to let Reuben start mining the claim even though we weren't married. Reuben borrowed money from Watson Nesbitt and built a headframe."

"Watson Nesbitt from the meeting last week?"

Jessie winced, as if the mention of his name was painful. "We have some history." She fingered her broach. "Reuben built the headframe but didn't have enough money to start digging. I thought I loved him, and I wanted to make him happy. He promised we were going to be rich beyond our wildest dreams." She closed her eyes and pressed her hand to her forehead. "So I gave him the money my mother left me when she died. That was what he was after all along."

"How...how much?"

A quiet sob escaped her lips. "Five hundred dollars."

James tried to temper his expression even though his shock was acute. Jessie felt bad enough as it was. Five hundred dollars was an enormous sum, more than the average miner could make in a year.

"I didn't tell Papa about giving him the money, because I thought he might say no. I wanted him to be surprised when we pulled our first gold out of the ground and made him rich." James had never seen Jessie cry before, not when she talked about her mother's death or her father's mining accident, but a tear rolled down her cheek. "Reuben never planned on mining it. Instead, he was gone the next day with every cent. I was so ashamed about the money, I never told anyone the truth about Reuben. They thought he left town because I broke his heart. He left because I'd handed over every penny I had."

James couldn't resist any longer. He wrapped his arm around her shoulder and pulled her close. She seemed to melt into his embrace. "I'm so sorry, Jessie. I'm so sorry he hurt you."

"Oh, yes," she said, her voice cracking in

Jessie and James

about a million places. She lowered her eyes and stared at her hands. "It hurt very bad."

He wanted to reassure her that he wasn't like Reuben Pierce, that he would never hurt her like that, never lie to her or break her heart. But a man didn't prove anything with his words, only his actions. "It's too bad Reuben Pierce wasn't here tonight. I would have enjoyed throwing him out."

She regained a little of her composure. "Oh, he's long gone. Mr. Nesbitt came to us for the money because Reuben used our claim as collateral. I sold the timber from the headframe and some men from the Retribution hauled it away. It still took me another year to pay Watson Nesbitt the balance of what Reuben owed him. I don't think Mr. Nesbitt has trusted me since."

"But you paid him back."

Jessie blinked away her tears. "I also got rid of the headframe. Men like Watson Nesbitt think you're sick in the head if you don't want to mine your claim."

James drew his brows together. "Did you ever try to find Reuben and get your money back?"

She shook her head. "I was too humiliated, and it was no use. I had freely given the money to him. I hear tell he's in California trying his hand in the railroad business."

James gritted his teeth. "He's a snake."

"It's my fault. I trusted him, and I should have known better."

He pulled her closer. "Jessie, you were

seventeen, and you had no reason to doubt him."

"I should have been smarter. He made me believe there was gold on our claim, when I'd never seen any evidence of it. I believed him because I wanted to believe him."

"You have nothing to be ashamed of. Unscrupulous men are very good at preying on unwitting victims."

She nudged herself from his embrace. "That's why I determined never to be a victim again." She lifted her chin. "And never to trust anyone who promises to find gold on my property."

He couldn't blame her. She was protecting herself and her family the only way she knew how, but he was still so angry he could spit. Angry at Frank Roberts for stirring up bad memories, angry at Watson Nesbitt for being so hard-hearted, and angry at Reuben Pierce for giving Jessie a wound that still hadn't healed. Because of Reuben, Jessie didn't trust a soul except maybe her papa and Alice. She saw most men as irredeemable sinners, and she refused to open her heart to the possibility of real love.

James had been in Eureka long enough to discover two things. First, Jessie Madsen was desperately lonely. She was surrounded by miners and townsfolk and boarders, but she had built a sturdy fort around her heart, and she was singlehandedly trying to defend it. She didn't dare let anyone in for fear they might be an enemy.

Second, he never wanted to dance with

anyone but Jessie ever again.

His heart beat a wild rhythm as they sat in silence, gazing at the hill behind the house and the place where Reuben Pierce's headframe used to be. With Jessie by his side sharing the quiet stillness of the evening, James had never been more content and less restless in his entire life. He might feel differently in the harsh light of day, but if his mine never struck gold, if Father never approved of him, this feeling would be enough. Jessie would be enough. "Are you cold?"

She wiped away the last trace of tears from her face. "It's the last dance. Should we go back?"

"How do you know it's the last dance?"

"Alice is playing *Goodnight, Goodnight, Beloved*. It's always the last dance. So slow it will put you to sleep."

He chuckled. Nothing could put him to sleep if he was dancing with Jessie. "I would never pass up a chance to dance with you, Miss Jessie, but we don't have to go back if you don't want to. There are still some stars we haven't looked at."

She gave him a genuine, maybe-you're-not-so-hopeless smile. "There will be plenty more nights to look at the stars, but this may be the last dance of my lifetime."

"Your lifetime?"

"Watson Nesbitt will never trick me again."

He laughed. "Well, then, I'd be a fool not to take the last dance you'll ever give." He stood, took her hands, and pulled her to her feet. "I hope

Goodnight, Goodnight, Beloved is a long song."

"It might be, if you pay Handy a little something."

James pulled a silver dollar from his pocket. "This should get me an extra fifteen minutes. Are you up for it?"

She gave him a teasing grin. "I would be devastated if you didn't get your money's worth."

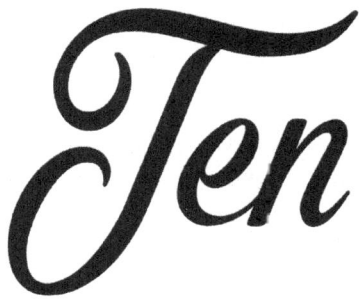

Ten

June in Eureka was quite fickle. One day would be chilly and windy, and George Madsen would build a fire in the stove in the dining room. The next day would be sunny and hot, and James would find it hard to sleep in the heat of the attic. The last of the snow had finally melted off the hilltops, the first day of summer was three days away, and James had finally finished digging the trenches for Jessie's new irrigation system.

James had built one wooden trench from the well to the farthest corner of the cherry orchard. Then he'd dug furrows down the rows of trees and trenches around each tree. All Jessie would have to do was carry the water from the well and pour it into the wooden trench where it would run to each of the furrows.

James looked over his work. It wasn't an ideal irrigation system, but it would save Jessie hours of watering time.

Jessie came out the back door with the milking bucket in one hand and a cup in the other. She gave him a brilliant, breathtaking smile. It was good James was leaning on his shovel, or he might have fallen over. It had been nearly a week since the dance, and he still wanted to take her in his arms and dance with her every time he saw her. He had a suspicion that desire would never go away. "I can't believe how much work you've done out here," she said, setting down her bucket next to the milking post.

He couldn't keep from grinning like an idiot whenever he saw her. "I can't do a thing on The Frenchman's claim until the money comes in. I wanted to make myself useful."

"You certainly have done that. This is going to save me a mountain of time."

"I hope so."

She handed him the cup. "It's lemonade. Alice made it especially for you since you've been out here using those muscles all afternoon."

"I'm much obliged, Miss Jessie." He took a long drink and finished off the whole thing in three swallows. "Delicious. Where did Alice get lemonade?"

"A man up from St. George. He gave her two lemons in exchange for supper."

James raised an eyebrow. "And she saved them for me? That is mighty nice."

Jessie traced the dirt with the toe of her shoe.

"You're Alice's favorite boarder, probably that's ever stayed here. And you got rid of Frank Roberts the other night. Alice doesn't like Frank. He asked her to marry him once."

James coughed in surprise. "He did?"

"Then she turned around and married Papa. It was a real blow to Frank's pride." Jessie took the cup from James and picked up her milking bucket. Lily Bell, who had been lounging under one of the cherry trees, heard the noise and started toward Jessie.

"Miss Jessie, I hope you're not planning on milking the cow. You know that's my job."

She laughed. Oh, how he adored that sound. "I've grown too accustomed to you doing all my chores. I'm going soft."

He took the bucket from her hand and smiled widely. "Good. I'm hoping to soften you up enough for another dance some time."

Her cheeks turned a darker shade of pink. "You'll be waiting a very long time, Mr. Kelsey."

He pretended to think about that. "How many more cows will I need to milk?"

She cuffed him on the shoulder. "Too many."

Lily Bell nudged his hand with her nose, and James welcomed the distraction. He'd been sorely tempted just now to gather Miss Jessie in his arms and kiss that enchanting grin right off her face. He cleared his throat and tore his gaze from her lips. It had been a dangerous thing to dance with Miss Jessie. Now he didn't have to imagine what it felt like to hold her in his arms. He knew exactly how nice it was to bask in a smile meant just for him, to feel her subtle, graceful movements as they moved together in the dance. He knew how good Miss Jessie felt, and the longing to be close to her almost overpowered him.

Lily Bell had come barging in at just the right moment. James' mother had raised him to be a gentleman. He wouldn't do anything to disappoint his mother. Besides, Alice might have something to say about it if he kissed her stepdaughter in broad daylight. She might have something to say about it if he kissed Jessie at all.

Jessie propped her free hand on her hip. "Those trenches would have taken me all summer to dig. Even most miners don't have the arms you do."

He hitched Lily Bell to the milking post. "All the better to milk with."

Jessie smoothed one of Lily Bell's ears. "I still don't understand why the water isn't just going to soak into the dirt before it reaches the end of the row."

He retrieved the milking stool and sat down. "Well, it still could, but I don't think it will. That dirt is as hard as a rock. I don't know that even a week of flooding would soak through, but if you're serious about growing cherries, you should move to Santaquin or Provo where they take water from the rivers and streams for irrigation. It's a thousand times easier."

"I know."

"It's next to useless to farm here. There just isn't enough water."

Jessie drew her brows together. "I know. Drawing from a well is an inefficient and time-consuming way to water the cherry trees, but I love my trees. Without them, Eureka would truly be a wasteland."

James wiped a trickle of sweat from his neck and started milking. "You seem to have a low opinion of your hometown."

"It's just a fact. Nothing grows here but sagebrush and juniper. If we want any beauty, we have to make sacrifices. Emmaline Johns has a rosebush. The Parkers grow tomatoes. They haul their water from their wells."

He looked up at her while he milked. "And you insist on growing cherry trees, which take gallons of water to keep alive."

Her lips twitched upward. "Hubert Johns told me I couldn't do it, so I set out to prove him wrong. I'm stubborn that way."

James smiled. He loved that about Jessie. Stubbornness was one of her best qualities. "Since you're not planning to move out any time soon, I want to make it as easy on you as possible. My next project was to install a pump so you won't even have to carry the buckets to the wooden trench, but that will take more money than I have."

She frowned. "Don't even think about paying for improvements on our farm. That's our responsibility, not yours."

"But you can't afford anything as fancy as another pump."

She stiffened. "We might be poor, Mr. Kelsey, but there's no need to pity us." Stubbornness was also one of her worst qualities.

Could he defend himself without digging a deeper hole? "I didn't mean it like that. You work yourself to the bone, Miss Jessie. I want to help where I can."

She pursed her lips resentfully. "We were doing just fine before you got here, and I dare say we'll do fine after you leave. We didn't need you to come in and fix us. We still don't."

He finished milking, stood up, and handed her the bucket. "Of course you don't need me, but you don't have to hold the world up by yourself either."

"And you don't have to feel sorry for me."

"I don't."

"Good. I don't like a man who's too big for his britches."

Maybe he should mention he didn't especially appreciate a woman who was too proud to admit she needed help. And maybe he should shut his mouth, because that was not at all how he felt. Sure, he wanted to help Jessie, but he also loved that she was determined to make her own way without depending on anyone else. Jessie was strong and independent and certainly didn't need a man to help her make her way through life. Of course, that meant she didn't need James, and that thought poked a hole right in his heart. Jessie didn't need anybody, so she pushed people away, refused to trust, isolated herself so she couldn't be hurt.

Yep. He should definitely shut his mouth.

He watched her march into the house, milk sloshing over the lip of the pail as she went. How quickly her mood had turned. How quickly James had fallen from grace, all because he wanted to help Jessie and her family.

She had no idea how easy James could make her life if she let him. But she wouldn't let him, and he'd never tell his secret.

He'd found gold on Jessie's claim.

James paced the wooden walkway in front of the mercantile, telegram in hand, heart pounding an uneven rhythm. He was usually stone-cold calm in situations like this. It was why he was such a good boxer. But he couldn't help but be agitated, because this delivery meant the beginning of everything for him. If he could successfully supervise the digging of a mine and if that mine proved as rich as his research said it was, he would do more than ensure himself a job. He would earn the respect of the company, the town, and maybe even Jessie Madsen. The London Mining and Ore

Company had put a great deal of trust in his word alone. He could not let them down. He *would* not let them down. Maybe his success would help mend the decade-long rift with his father. Maybe Father would finally approve of his second son, the son who should have died, the son who had been such a disappointment to him.

And maybe Jessie, who hated the very thought of mining, would see he wasn't a gold digger or an opportunist but someone who wanted to make life better for the miners. And for her. Maybe she'd stop fighting and let him behind those walls she'd so carefully built and guarded over the years. Maybe she'd finally let him into her heart.

And suddenly, there she was, like an angel from heaven, if angels wore blue calico and carried shotguns strapped to their backs. Jessie walked toward him, her heels tapping along the walkway, completely oblivious to the attraction of her swaying hips.

He couldn't help but smile at the way she casually strolled down the walkway, as if she hadn't anything better to do on a Tuesday afternoon. "Fancy running into you," he said.

"I came to scold you for leaving another big pile of rocks on your floor," she said, a wry, tempting smile on her lips. She lifted her foot. "I stubbed my toe."

He cocked an eyebrow. "Did it bleed?"

"No, but I think I'm going to lose a nail." She

fluttered her eyelashes.

Oh, how he loved those brown eyes. "You need to be more careful, Miss Jessie. Always watch where you're stepping."

Her mouth fell open in mock indignation. "You aren't even going to apologize?"

He grinned. "Miss Jessie, I'm sorry if I did anything to bring you pain or discomfort. Please forgive me."

She shook her head. "An apology won't bring my toenail back."

"How about two-bits for your trouble?"

She smiled as if she'd been holding it in for a long time. "You are insufferable, Mr. Kelsey."

He made a slight bow. "I'm happy I can be of service, ma'am."

"Oh, I know. You always want to help."

He laughed. After their conversation about cherry trees and irrigation, her irritation with him had only lasted a few days. She'd forgiven him for whatever it was she was mad about. "Are you shopping for Alice today? I didn't see you drive up in the wagon."

She shrugged. "It's a nice day for a walk."

"It's good to see you get out more. All you do is sit inside that musty boardinghouse and knit mittens."

Her lips curled upward. "The world needs more mittens, especially in June." She drew in a deep breath. "Today is a very important day for you. I came because I wanted to give you some company."

James melted like butter on a skillet. Jessie cared about him just a little. "Well, Miss Jessie. Well. That is mighty nice of you."

She patted the strap that sat diagonally across her torso. "And since you left your gun in your room, I will protect both of us and your money."

He chuckled. "I don't think I'll be needing any protection. The land office is two blocks down the street, and my brawny physique will discourage any robbers."

The twitch on her lips grew into a self-conscious smile. "I can't argue with that, but it won't hurt to have my shotgun with us." She adjusted the strap. "I take that back. It will hurt very much if someone comes between my shotgun and your money."

"I hope we won't have to find out."

She shaded her eyes and looked to the east. "When is this delivery wagon supposed to be coming?"

"Any minute now. I'll get the money from them and take it to the land office where The Frenchman will meet me and sign over the land and the claim to me. Then I can hire an engineer and a team and start digging. We're going straight down. I saw a promising vein right at the surface. If my calculations are correct, we could hit gold at less than a hundred feet."

She studied his face. "That would be wonderful. I'm very happy for you, Mr. Kelsey.

Your father will be so proud."

His gut clenched. "I hope so."

"How much money are they sending?"

"A thousand dollars. That should be enough to get the mine up and running. If the reports are good, they'll send another thousand in a few months."

Jessie reached into her apron pocket and pulled out three shotgun shells. She leaned close and whispered. "Just in case we need them. A thousand dollars is nothing to sneeze at."

"Not one sneeze." He loved that Jessie cared enough to bring extra shells, but there wouldn't be any trouble. Eureka was full of hard men, but they weren't criminals, and James wasn't helpless.

A creaking wagon appeared over the crest of the hill, lumbering down the road as if it was nearing the end of its journey. James' heart sped up. This was the delivery wagon. Two armed teamsters sat atop the seat, and the cargo was covered with a gray tarp secured with thick rope. Most of the cargo on the wagon was meant for the mercantile. Both James and the London Mining and Ore Company thought it would draw less suspicion if the money was hidden among the dry goods delivered to the store.

One man jumped from the seat, a six-shooter at the ready by his side. The other man stayed on the wagon, his rifle propped lightly in his elbow. He caught sight of Jessie's gun, and his jaw twitched.

The first man tipped his hat to Jessie. "Ma'am."

"Good afternoon," Jessie said, squinting her eyes at the man as if she suspected he would try to steal the money even though he was the one delivering it.

The man shook James' hand. "I have a delivery. What is your name, sir?"

James handed the teamster his telegram. "My name is James Kelsey, and I am authorized to take delivery of a box in your possession."

The teamster read James' telegram and motioned to his partner. The other man untied the knot that seemed to be holding the entire rope in place. The rope came loose, and the man pulled up a corner of the tarp. "Which one is it, Hobbs?" he said.

"Number seven. That box right there."

The man stood on a spoke of the wheel, pulled a barrel from the wagon, and handed it to Hobbs. Hobbs set the barrel on the ground. Right below the barrel was a rough wooden box with the number seven painted on the top and on the side. The man hefted the box from the wagon bed and gave it to Hobbs. Hobbs held the box in his arms, getting a feel for the weight of it. The box was the heavy part of the shipment because the mining company said they were sending paper money.

"Here is your shipment, Mr. Kelsey," Hobbs said. "I suggest we go into the mercantile so you can make sure everything is in order."

Jessie and James

James nodded. They didn't want to be counting the money out here. Better to be cautious. The mercantile door stood open, and James motioned for Jessie to go first. Hobbs followed, and James entered last.

Lou Johns stood behind the counter measuring some fabric for a woman in a brown dress. He glanced up. "Hello, Mr. Kelsey, Mr. Hobbs. Nice to see you, Miss Jessie. Is my shipment here?"

Hobbs nodded. "Cutler's outside."

Lou smiled at his customer. "As soon as I finish with Mrs. Lange, I'll get Hubert."

Hobbs raised the box so Lou could see it. "Have you got a place we could go?"

Lou motioned toward the backroom. "There's a table in there."

They made their way to the back room. Jessie was still tense, as if it really was her job to guard James' money. Hobbs set the box on the table, took a small key from his pocket, and unlocked it. A money pouch sat inside the box. Hobbs untied the string around the pouch and handed it to James. Jessie's eyes widened as he pulled out five small bundles of ten-dollar bills. James slowly counted the money in each bundle. There were twenty bills in each. He took two tens and handed them to Hobbs. "Here is your payment as agreed."

Hobbs pulled a folded piece of paper from his pocket. "Will you sign this, Mr. Kelsey, saying you received the delivery?"

James took the pen sitting on Lou's table, dipped it in the inkwell, and signed Mr. Hobbs' document. Hobbs blew on the paper until the ink dried, then folded it and returned it to his pocket. He shook James' hand. "Thank you, Mr. Kelsey. If you will leave the box here, I will retrieve it after I unload Mr. Johns' order."

Without another word, Hobbs left the room. Jessie let out a breath, as if she'd been holding it since Hobbs first arrived. "I've never seen that much money in my whole life."

James grinned. "Neither have I." He put the money back in the pouch and slid the pouch into his pocket.

Jessie shook her head. "It looks like you're carrying a prairie dog in your pocket. That will never do."

James gave her a teasing wink. "But who would want to steal a prairie dog?"

She snatched the pouch out of his pocket. "Put it in here." She stuffed the pouch in her apron pocket.

It didn't look any less suspicious. "Now it looks like *you're* carrying a prairie dog."

She giggled. "Everyone expects a woman to carry all sorts of supplies in her pocket. No one will even look at me twice."

"Oh, Miss Jessie, how little you know. Everyone looks at you at least twice, sometimes five or six times, and mostly they never stop looking."

Jessie and James

A very attractive blush overspread her cheeks. "That is the biggest load of hogwash I've ever heard."

He laughed. "What exactly does hogwash sound like?"

They walked out of the mercantile, James tipping his hat to Lou Johns as they left. Hobbs, along with Cutler, Hubert Johns, and two other adolescent boys unloaded goods from the wagon as fast as they could go. No doubt the teamsters wanted to get back on the road before too long.

Jessie gave James a mischievous smile and sashayed across the walkway, making a special point to show off that bulge in her apron pocket and making James laugh out loud. She was teasing him, and he'd never been so enchanted in his life. What would he give to see that playful curve of her lips every day?

Jessie stepped off the walkway and strolled up the north side of Main Street, glancing back occasionally to make sure he was looking. Of course he was looking, even when Hubert Johns called to him. "We got some new hats, Mr. Kelsey, if you want to come and look."

James flicked his gaze in Hubert's direction. "I might take you up on that. Maybe tomorrow."

Hubert waved at him. "Come in anytime. We'll have new shirts too."

Jessie was a block and a half ahead of him, still walking as if she had the world at her feet, still looking back to make sure he was following. James jogged to catch up with her. Miss Jessie wasn't going anywhere by herself with that money. It wasn't safe.

She made it to the next corner when suddenly she jerked to her left and disappeared around the side of the hotel. What in the world? James' heart leaped into his throat, and he started running. Miss Jessie hadn't been that far ahead, and it took him less than five seconds to race to the corner.

He pulled up short and took in his breath sharply when he went around the side of the building and came face to face with a six-shooter, or rather, two six-shooters. Dizzy with shock, he instinctively raised his hands and took a step backward. Two men, their faces hidden under bandanas, stood in the narrow alleyway. The taller, darker one pointed two guns at James' head. The shorter one had one hand wrapped around Jessie's waist and the other pressed against Jessie's mouth. Her shotgun lay on the ground at her feet.

James gasped. It felt as if someone had taken a knife and ripped his chest open. "Don't hurt her," he said.

The bigger man stepped closer and pressed the barrel of the gun to James' forehead. "Shut yer mouth and don't move, or the lady gets hurt," he whispered.

It was plain to see why he whispered. The teamsters and Hubert Johns were just two blocks away. All James had to do was take three steps back out from the cover of the building and get their attention. Neither would it be hard to whip out his hands and slap those guns away. If he had only himself to think of, he'd take the risk in a heartbeat, but he couldn't risk what they might do to Jessie. He felt sick with the possibilities.

James' pulse pounded in his own ears. The sound was deafening. Jessie struggled mightily against her captor, but though he was on the small side, she couldn't match his wiry strength. Jessie's eyes flashed with raw anger as she tried stomping on her captor's foot, but she didn't make contact. She squeaked as he tightened his grip around her to maintain control.

Don't fight, Jessie. It will only make them more desperate. "Please," James said. "Please, let her go."

Jessie didn't seem to be afraid. His heart swelled as he gazed at her. She wasn't afraid. She was mad. Fear could be paralyzing. Anger gave her some power. Jessie was fierce when she was angry.

The fear James saw belonged to the man who held Jessie fast. His face was covered, but he couldn't have been more than sixteen or seventeen years old, and the terror in his eyes was unmistakable.

The man with the guns took three steps back. "Give us the money."

James nodded. "Okay, okay. Let her go, and I'll give you the money."

"Money first."

Jessie squeaked, and her eyes told him no, but

what could he do? He couldn't bear the thought of Jessie in danger.

"The money is in her apron pocket," James said, earning a glare from Jessie. It didn't matter what he did, she was always irritated with him.

The man kept one gun trained on James and reached into Jessie's pocket with the other hand. He pulled out the pouch and shoved it into his own pocket. A miner's pocket on a miner's pair of trousers. Did these men work one of the mines in the area?

The man with the guns nodded to his partner. "Let's go. And bring her along."

Rage and desperation boiled in James' chest. "You've got your money. Leave her and get out."

The younger man's eyes widened like saucers. "We can't take her, Pete."

"We can if we don't want to get kilt." He grabbed the younger man by the shirtsleeve and pulled him backward, with Jessie still in tow. He aimed his gun at James' chest. "Don't follow us, or we put a bullet through her head. Do you understand?"

James felt so helpless, he could barely see straight. "You don't have to do this. Anson, is it? You've got your money. Just let her go."

"Keep your voice down, mister. We'll let her go as soon as we're safe."

"That's not good enough," James said, his desperation rising to fever pitch.

Anson slipped one of his guns into his pocket,

and without letting his gaze or his aim move from James' face, he stooped over and picked up Jessie's shotgun. Anson didn't have a holster for his gun. A professional criminal, a killer, would have a holster. Anson was definitely a miner, or at worst, a drifter who had seen an opportunity and taken it. The thought gave James a little hope even as fear for Jessie tormented him.

Anson slung the shotgun over his shoulder. "Now, mister, we're going to ride out of here, and if I see one trace of you, this lady will be dead, and I don't think you want that on your conscience."

James held perfectly still as they backed away from him to the other end of the alley, Jessie fighting them all the way. James flinched as Anson grabbed hold of Jessie's apron and tore one of the straps off. "Be still and be quiet," Anson hissed, "Or I shoot that one in the chest."

For the first time since they been in the alley, James saw fear in Jessie's eyes. She seemed to lose all her fight and let the little one drag her away. As soon as they were out of sight, James ran to the end of the alley and peeked around the corner of the hotel. Two horses stood at the hitching post. With his hand still over her mouth, the younger man dragged Jessie to the bay horse. Anson jumped on and lifted Jessie on in front of him. He said something to her, and they both turned to the spot where James was hiding, obviously not that well hidden. Anson pointed his gun in James' direction, and Jessie clamped her lips together and shook her head.

The younger one got on the other horse, and they rode east as if the devil was at their heels. He was, because when James caught them, he was going to send them to Hell.

Eleven

Jessie's heart pounded with a fury she'd never felt before. How dare they threaten James like that? How dare they take his money? How dare they think they could kidnap her and nobody would come for a reckoning?

How dare they take her shotgun?

They rode so fast that every bounce knocked the wind out of her. As soon as they were out of sight of James, Jessie started struggling against the arm that held her fast. "Let me go," she demanded. "Give me back my money, and let me go."

When she nearly fell off the horse, Anson the outlaw turned into a sheltered ravine and stopped. He snatched her down from the horse, pressed her against a boulder, and tied her hands with his bandana. This meant he had to take it off his face, and when he did, Jessie gasped. Anson was tall and muscular, but he was just a boy, no older than

Jessie, and likely much younger.

The other one got off his horse and started pacing. "Anson, we can't do this. We gotta let her go. Please. We gotta let her go and run away."

"Shut up, Denny," Anson said. "We can't let her go. That fancy fellow will come after us."

Denny pulled the bandana off his face and moaned. "We're gonna get kilt, Anson. I told you we shoulda said no."

"We take her to the mine and then decide what to do with her."

Jessie momentarily stopped struggling and stared at the other one. Denny was younger than Anson, maybe fifteen or sixteen. They were just boys. What had brought them to this kind of trouble? She held out her bound hands. "You should be ashamed of yourself, pointing a gun at an upstanding citizen and kidnapping a woman. And you ripped my apron. What kind of monsters are you?"

Denny only moaned louder. Two tears escaped his eyes and made trails in the dirt on his face. "What are we gonna do, Anson? What's to become of us?"

"Shut up," Anson said. "We go to the mine and think. That's what."

"Shame on you," Jessie said. "Repent of your evil ways or the Lord will smite you as sure as I'm standing here."

Anson snatched the bandana out of Denny's hand and tied it around Jessie's mouth. Tight.

"You shut up too, ma'am, or come nightfall, you won't be able to talk."

Jessie didn't want to cower, but Anson was young and desperate, and desperation made men do reckless things. She closed her lips around the bandana. It certainly wouldn't have prevented a scream, but there was something raw and wild in Anson's eyes, and she'd rather not tempt fate.

When they got to the mine, wherever that was, she could make a plan for escape. For now, she'd let them take her farther from home. Farther from Papa and Alice. Farther from James.

Jessie clamped her eyes shut and said a silent prayer of gratitude. She was in the hands of evil men, but at least James was safe.

They rode east for over an hour, keeping off the main trail and tucking close to the thick junipers that grew alongside the canyons. As the sun hovered over the western hills, they turned to the south and followed a steep trail to a tiny brook bubbling out of the rocks beneath a grove of aspens. Patches of snow still survived under the trees, and Jessie shivered as a breeze teased a strand of hair from her bun.

Denny and Anson dismounted, and Anson pulled Jessie off the horse. They tied their horses to two trees near the brook so they could drink. Anson still had Jessie's shotgun slung over his shoulder and a six-shooter in each pocket. It made Jessie's blood boil to see her beloved shotgun in the hands of a scoundrel.

Anson slipped the saddlebag off his horse, pulled out five canteens, and handed them to Denny. Denny filled each canteen and handed them to Anson. Anson stuffed them back in his saddlebag and draped the bag over his shoulder. He nodded to Denny. "Let's go."

Denny pointed to Jessie, drawing his brows together as if he was concerned about her. "She'll need more air."

Anson growled and untied the bandana from her mouth, then loosed her hands as well. "Don't try to run off or you'll fall off a cliff. Stay on the trail or I can't be responsible for what happens to you."

Jessie rubbed her sore wrists. "Where are we going?"

"Some place your fancy friend won't find us." He pulled one of the canteens out of the saddlebag. "Carry this."

Denny started up a scarcely visible trail. "It's steep. You'll need your whole mouth to breathe, and you'll need both your hands or you'll fall."

"What about the horses."

Denny shrugged. "They can't make the climb. He'll come and get them in the morning."

"Denny," Anson said, "Why don't you shut up about it."

Denny frowned. "What did I say?"

"I want my gun back," Jessie said, in a last-ditch effort to make them see reason.

Anson gave her a scornful smile. "Maybe you should shut your mouth. And maybe you'll be glad

I'm carrying it when the trail gets rough."

Denny led the way with Jessie in between Denny and Anson. Back when they had stopped the horses the first time, she'd noticed Denny had a slight limp. Now climbing up the hill, his limp seemed more pronounced. When she had been trying to get away back there in town, she'd stomped on his foot. Had she stomped hard enough to injure him? Not likely. His boots were thick, and she hadn't stomped that hard.

It was getting dark, and Jessie found it hard to see more than five steps ahead of her. After ten minutes of walking, the climb got steeper, the rocks got bigger, and the trail narrowed. There were places where the mountain dropped sharply on one side or the other, and the height literally stole Jessie's breath.

How would she ever find her way out of this canyon? The maze of trails and the treacherous climb would make escape difficult and rescue nearly impossible. This thought stoked her anger. She didn't care if Anson had told her to shut up. They were going to hear her indignation. "The wicked shall fall by his own wickedness," she said, directing her wrath at Anson behind her. That was one of her favorite scriptures.

Anson didn't reply. Either he was ignoring her or contemplating his sins.

"God's justice will smite you if you don't let me go. Repent before it's too late."

Still, Anson didn't say anything. She glanced

back at him, but it was too dark to make out his features. Jessie thought of all the sermons she composed inside her head whenever Papa preached about love and mercy. She would have given Anson and Denny a sermon, but the trail was unbelievably taxing, and she needed to save her breath for the climb. Sermons could wait until they got to their destination. She got so weary that she was tempted to sit down and tell them to go on without her. But if they left her there, she'd surely be eaten by wolves or attacked by a bear or fall off a cliff or into an abandoned mine shaft trying to find her way down.

One thing Jessie knew for sure. She didn't want to die. Papa and Alice would be destitute. And she wanted to see James again, if only to tell him *I told you so* for doubting her when she'd brought her shotgun.

A little warm spot grew at the center of her chest. She loved telling James *I told you so*. She loved the grin on his face when he pretended to agree with her but really didn't.

Jessie pressed her lips together and tamped down the melancholy that threatened to bring her to tears. She needed to save her tears for her sins and her energy for the trail ahead. Who knew how long it would be?

Denny's gait became more labored the farther they went. They walked for another half hour until it was so dark Jessie was sure they would all unintentionally walk off a cliff. The trail suddenly

Jessie and James

veered downward to a few square feet of flat area and the entrance to a cave. Well, it didn't look so much like a cave as a horizontal mine shaft with a front door. Jessie wanted to cry. It was one thing to walk two hours up an insanely steep mountain. It was quite another to find a mineshaft waiting for you at the end of it.

Instead of going into the mineshaft, Denny went past it and climbed up a set of rocks that looked as if they'd been placed for stairs. At the top of the steps was a shack made of wood and stones. It was almost too dark to see, but the shack couldn't have been more than ten feet wide and ten feet long, but compared to the prospect of sleeping in a mineshaft, it looked like a mansion.

Denny opened the door and gestured for Jessie to enter. Hmm, someone had taught him some manners. She stopped just inside the shack for fear of cracking her shin on a piece of furniture or bumping her nose on something hanging overhead. She might as well have been completely blind. A rancid smell all but knocked her over, and she wrinkled her nose, wondering if she might not prefer the mineshaft after all.

Denny reached over her, and she heard the metallic creak of a lantern as he took it from a hook on the ceiling. He moved past her, set the lantern on a table, and struck a match. Lifting the glass chimney, he held the match to the wick. The wick caught fire, and the light bathed the shack in an eerie yellow light. Jessie shivered as she looked around the room. She would have preferred the mineshaft.

The lantern rested on a small, dusty table that looked as if it might collapse if anything heavier than a lantern was placed on it. Two milking stools sat on either side of the table, and Jessie couldn't imagine them holding up under anybody's weight. Two bedrolls were laid out on the floor, which seemed to have been chiseled and smoothed right out of the foundation rock at her feet.

Strands of cobwebs hung from the roof beams, floating in the air like forlorn ghosts. A railroad potbelly stove stood in the far corner next to a small pile of coal. A collection of boxes, rusty tins, and filthy sacks sat on a dusty shelf next to the table. Jessie's stomach growled, but the thought of eating anything from one of those sacks made her ill.

A pile of rocks similar to what James often kept in his room sat against one wall. Anson and Denny were miners, with no morals and absolutely no sense of cleanliness. She shuddered slightly and took a step backward, but Anson was so close behind her, she met with his rock-solid chest. She turned and glared at him, mustering her righteous indignation despite her weariness. "This place is a filthy, disgusting pigsty. I won't stay here," she said. "Take me back this instant."

Anson scowled. "Shut your mouth, lady. We ain't shamed by your uppity ways." He pointed to one of the milking stools. "Sit down."

Jessie and James

Jessie was loath to follow any orders from a robber, but her legs were about to give out on her and the room tilted slightly to the left. It would do no good to faint. She lifted her chin, harrumphed in Anson's face, and lowered herself to the milking stool. One thing was for sure. They needed proper chairs. Her shoulders were at the same level as the top of the table. The height would make it very difficult to eat supper. She screwed the lid off her canteen and drank the last of the water.

Anson took her precious shotgun off his shoulder. "Watch her, Denny. I'll be right back." He narrowed his eyes at Jessie. "If you run off and die, I won't be held responsible."

Jessie glared at him but didn't give him the satisfaction of a reply. Anson's threat was meaningless. She couldn't run. She didn't even have the energy to stand up. She'd never been so weary.

Denny kept his distance, but gazed at her as if he felt sorry. She must look a sight. What was left of her bun sagged at the nape of her neck, and the rest of her hair fell in spindly strands around her face. Her apron was torn in about seven places, having snagged on sagebrush and junipers along the path. Her hands were smudged with dirt and there was an inch-long line of blood where she'd scratched her hand against a cedar.

"We're real sorry, ma'am," Denny said. "We wasn't expecting he'd have a woman with him. We was just going to jump him and tie him up so's we could get away."

They wouldn't have been able to overpower him if they'd jumped him. James was too strong. She's witnessed with her own eyes what he could do with those powerful arms. The only reason Denny and Anson had gotten away with the robbery was because Jessie had been there. James' concern for her safety kept him from beating Denny and James to a pulp.

Oh.

Maybe she wouldn't be able to say *I told you so* after all.

"Shame on you," she said. "Thou shalt not steal. Or kidnap."

Denny frowned. "Kidnapping isn't one of the Ten Commandments."

He was right, but how a filthy, delinquent miner knew that was a mystery. "You still shouldn't do it. God will smite all sinners."

Denny's eyes flashed with pain. "We wasn't stealing. We was just borrowing. That's what Anson said."

She turned her face away so she wouldn't see the youth and vulnerability in his eyes. She had to harden herself against these men if she had any chance of escape. "That's just the excuse someone like you would make."

Denny pressed his lips together and pulled something brown and lumpy out of his pocket. "Are you hungry? It's my last piece of jerky, if you want it."

Jessie and James

Jessie shook her head. She was starving, but she didn't know where those hands had been and she didn't know where that jerky had been. She could live off water until she escaped.

Denny hesitated then took a bite for himself. "What's your name?"

"I'm not telling," Jessie said. She had a suspicion that telling him her name would soften her up, and it would give him some sort of power over her.

Her resistance seemed to upset him. Good. He *should* be upset. His sins should nettle his conscience, torment him until he was compelled to let her go. "My name is Denny Waller. That's my brother Anson. We've been up here by ourselves almost five years."

Five years? She wanted to ask how old Denny was, but she didn't want him to think she wanted to be friends, so she kept her mouth shut. But that kind of isolation at so young an age wasn't healthy. Loneliness could drive a man mad.

Anson came back in the shack and slammed the door behind him. Dust rained from the ceiling. "Don't talk to the prisoner, Denny. We got enough trouble without her knowing anything about us."

"Where is she going to sleep, Anson?" Denny asked, giving voice to what Jessie had been dreading since she got here. The floor would be hard and cold, and those blankets were surely infested with fleas. But the biggest obstacles were staring at her. She would not lie down on the floor next to these two men. It wasn't proper, it wasn't decent, and it wasn't safe. It would be too easy for Anson to do her harm in the middle of the night.

She studied Anson's face. Despite his youth, the hard lines around his eyes spoke of a difficult life. His scowl was a permanent fixture on his face. He'd threatened James with his life and told Jessie to shut up more than once. Despicable as he was, he didn't seem the type to take advantage of a woman, but Jessie's instincts could be wrong and she wasn't about to find out the hard way.

"The two of you will be sleeping outside," Jessie said, with more confidence than she felt. If she made it sound like a matter of fact, they were less likely to disagree with her.

Anson rubbed the dark whiskers on his chin. "Okay then. But we get the blankets."

Jessie scowled even though she wasn't especially angry about the blankets. They were filthy. She'd be cold, but she'd be less likely to catch a disease and she could use her apron as a pillow. "Would you build a fire?"

Anson narrowed his eyes. "If you burn down our house, you'll burn with it. It's a horrible way to die."

Jessie didn't want to argue about whether their tiny shack could be considered a house. "I'm not a fool," she said.

Denny took another bite of jerky. "You don't need to fret about us. We're used to sleeping outside."

Jessie and James

Why would she fret about two kidnappers? "It's what you deserve," she said, spitting the words from her lips like venom.

Denny looked as if she'd slapped him. She looked away.

"Don't bother trying to escape," Anson said. "I'll sleep right outside the door. If you open it, I'll catch you."

Jessie glanced at the two windows in the shack. Instead of being glass, they were covered with waxed parchment paper. She couldn't climb out of one of those. They were no wider than a foot. "I'm not going to try to escape, but you should let me go. The longer you hold me, the greater your sin."

Anson smirked. "Ma'am, my list of sins is too long to count. I don't reckon a couple more will make much of a difference." He glanced at Denny. "Start a fire. I'll get the blankets."

Denny wouldn't look at her as he took a match from the shelf and limped over to the potbelly stove. Jessie folded her arms around her waist and tried to push the guilt away. She couldn't possibly have upset him. Criminals didn't have feelings.

There was one more thing, and she'd have to mention it sometime or end up very uncomfortable very soon. She felt her face get warm. "I must...relieve myself," she said. Another humiliating necessity.

To her surprise, Anson didn't scowl. "We got

an outhouse. I'll take you. But don't try anything dumb or you'll fall over the edge, and you'll never see your fancy friend again."

Jessie swallowed hard. Would she ever see James again?

She squared her shoulders and stood up, bracing herself against the wall to keep from falling over. She had to stay strong. Her determination was the only thing that would get her off this mountain and back to James. Until then, the memory of his tight embrace would keep her warm.

Jessie sat cross-legged and warmed her hands at the potbelly stove. What could she do? How was she going to escape?

She had awoken this morning with a stiff neck and a sore back from sleeping on the floor of the shack. Denny had built a fire last night, but she'd spent half the night shivering because the stone floor was ice cold, as if it had frozen with the ice in the winter and hadn't thawed yet. She almost envied the Waller boys and their threadbare blankets.

Denny had knocked on the door before sunrise, let himself in without being invited, and stoked Jessie's fire, even though she was perfectly able to do it herself. She'd gotten up and did what

Jessie and James

she could to refashion a bun on her head. It couldn't have been acceptable, but under the circumstances, it had been adequate.

Breakfast had consisted of jerky, dusty hardtack, and a cup of water, and Jessie had been too hungry to refuse it.

Then they had waited. Anson and Denny seemed to have no other plan but to sit in the shack. That is what they did all day. Just wait. Sometimes Anson would go outside as if he was expecting a visitor. Sometimes Denny would join him, leaving Jessie sitting on the milking stool by herself just staring at the walls or watching the cobwebs float in the air and trying to stay warm.

Whenever the Waller brothers were inside the shack, Jessie took the opportunity to remind them of their wickedness and admonish them to repent. Her lectures annoyed Anson, but with every word out of her mouth, Denny grew sadder and more troubled. She had to keep it up. She was getting to him. Maybe he would realize the error of his ways and agree to take her home.

As the day had gone by, the brothers had spent more time outside. Their consciences were obviously tormenting them, and they couldn't bear to hear Jessie speak the words of truth.

Supper and dinner were also hardtack and jerky. It was obviously what they lived on up here. When night fell, Denny built Jessie another fire, and he and Anson had gone outside to sleep.

Jessie sat by the stove and pictured the farm

and her cherry trees. Who would milk the cow and feed the chickens while she was away? By the Lord's good grace, she'd be home before it was time to water the cherry trees again, or maybe James would do it for her. James cared about her trees. He'd water them, and he'd make sure Frank Roberts stayed off her property. She didn't need to worry about Lily Bell or the chickens, and James would look after Alice and Papa until she returned. Since James had come to town, he had been as much help to Alice as Jessie was. With James at the house, everything would be okay until she got back.

Even though the hardtack sat like a stone in her gut, Jessie was hungry. She stood, picked up the lantern, and batted a cobweb from her face. Surely there was other food in this shack. She went to the column of shelves where they kept the tin of hardtack. She opened the flour sack on the bottom shelf. It was full, and it didn't look to have any weevil. There was a tin of baking powder, a small bag of white sugar, and a large tin of coffee. Why hadn't Anson made coffee? A steaming cup would have been nice when she'd gotten up this morning.

Behind the coffee was a yellow apple, shriveled and soft, but still good to eat. It had obviously been there since last fall. She cradled it in her hand then took a bite. To Jessie's empty stomach, it tasted better than one of Alice's pudding cakes.

Jessie sighed. Wouldn't she love a thick piece

Jessie and James

of apple pie right now?

She finished the paltry apple and scanned the shelves for more treasures. There was something like a box on the very top shelf, but she couldn't tell what it was. The ceiling wasn't high, so she could reach the box without even standing on her tiptoes. She pulled it from the shelf and a puff of dust came with it. Jessie caught her breath as she saw what it was. The Waller boys had a Bible!

It obviously hadn't been used in a long time. Heedless of the dirty cover, Jessie clutched the book to her chest. Now she could read the Wallers all the passages about sin. With the Word beside her, she could convince them of their wicked ways and talk them into letting her go.

She opened the Bible and thumbed through the pages before turning to the front. Facing the title page was a handwritten page of names and dates. Jessie placed the Bible on the table and set the lantern beside it.

June Swigert born October 16, 1846 Berlin, Ohio
Married Thomas Anson Waller born circa 1840 Clay Co, Missouri
Anson Isaac Waller born October 1, 1865
Dennis George Waller born March 23, 1870

Jessie smoothed her thumb over the page. Denny and Anson's family history. She quickly did the math in her head. Anson was only nineteen years old, Denny barely fifteen, the same age as

James' sister Abigail. Jessie's heart clenched. Jessie was sixteen when Mother had died. She had been so young, just like Denny. Denny was only a boy. Anson was barely a man. Where were their parents?

Jessie's heart sank. Thomas and June Waller were surely dead, and Anson and Denny had been left to fend for themselves. Jessie gazed around the small shack. They weren't fending very well.

Jessie ran her finger down the block of closed pages. A piece of paper protruded between two of the pages. Jessie pulled it out. It was a letter in almost illegible print addressed to Anson. Jessie hesitated. She shouldn't read something that wasn't meant for her, but she was too curious to stop.

The person who wrote the letter obviously hadn't gone to school. Most of the words were misspelled and the handwriting was crude, but Jessie could make it out well enough. She leaned closer to the lamplight to read.

My dearest Anson,
By the time you see this letter, I will be dead. I am so sorry to have to leave you. The doctor said I am too far gone with the consumption. I hope you can find someone to read this to you so you will know how much I loved you. I know how sad you were when I took you and Dennis and ran from your father. You were too young to understand, but I could not go on letting him hurt us. When you have your own children, I hope you will

understand a mother's love. Take care of your brother, say your prayers, and glorify God in all things. I wish I could have given you a better life, but all my hope for you is now in Jesus and the life to come. God bless you, my son, and know that with my last dying breath, I thought of you and Denny.
　　Mama

The words blurred as Jessie blinked back tears. What would she have done if she hadn't had Papa when Mama died? Would she be living in a shack trying to eke out a living from the hard stone ground? Jessie marveled at the sacrifice June Waller had made for her children. How many mothers would have been so brave in the face of a violent husband? How many women would have had the courage to save her sons at the expense of everything else?

What would June have had to say about the way Jessie had treated her sons?

Oh, of course, they had kidnapped her and threatened James and stolen a thousand dollars, and June, no doubt, would have scolded them and demanded they make things right. But then Jessie imagined June would have held them in her embrace and showered them with a mother's love, fortifying their resolve to do better next time.

What would Jesus have done? Would He have railed at Denny and Anson about their sins, or would He have taken them in his embrace and loved them back to the fold of God? Jesus was confronted with all kinds of sinful people, but to the woman taken in adultery, He said, "Neither do I condemn thee. Go and sin no more."

In spite of the fact that Denny had grabbed her in Eureka, he had treated her with respect. Anson had told her to shut up about a thousand times, but he hadn't been cruel. That didn't excuse what they'd done, but maybe it meant they deserved a second chance.

In a sudden rush of insight, she heard her papa's voice in her head. "For God sent not His Son into the world to condemn the world, but that the world through Him might be saved."

Jessie was a little ashamed of herself. What damage had she done with all her righteous indignation? How many hearts had been changed because of her criticism? Maybe love spoke louder than outrage. Maybe it was time to stop preaching repentance and start showing some kindness.

Jessie thumbed through the New Testament to a scripture Papa quoted often, one that Jessie liked to forget. *Though I have all faith so that I could remove mountains, and have not charity, I am nothing.*

Love came naturally to Papa, like judging did to Jessie, but according to Paul, Jessie was nothing if she didn't have love. June's sons were misguided, but Jesus died for the Waller boys. How could Jessie ask more than that of Him?

Twelve

Jessie flipped the griddlecake and smiled. Sometimes she impressed herself with her own ingenuity. Well, maybe she wasn't too impressed, because the Waller boys had lived up here for many years without her help. But what had some philosopher said about necessity being the mother of invention? Jessie badly needed a proper breakfast, so she'd turned a tin plate into a griddle and made three giant griddlecakes. One for her, one for Anson, and one for Denny.

Luckily, the Waller boys had a coffee pot, and Jessie had brewed up some strong coffee, using the last of the beans in the tin. She felt bad about using the last of it, but what better time to drink it than at this new beginning for all of them.

She had found a small chunk of lard in one of the tins, and it proved to be more precious than gold. The lard kept the griddlecakes from sticking to the tin, and it gave them a richer flavor. Jessie was no cook, but after hardtack and beef jerky for two days straight, she hoped her griddlecakes would taste like heaven.

Like yesterday morning, Denny knocked softly on the door then limped into the shack to light the fire. He didn't know she'd lit it half an hour ago. His eyes went wide when he saw the two steaming griddlecakes on the table. "Anson," he called. "You better get in here."

Anson must have been hovering right outside. He shot in the door as if there were a fire, a menacing scowl pasted on his lips. Jessie couldn't blame him for being alarmed. She had been threatening all sorts of hellfire and damnation since she got here. "What's going on?" Anson asked, before he even got a good look at what Jessie was doing.

"You better eat before it gets cold," she said. Smiling, she motioned to the table where she'd set two tin plates, two tin cups, one fork, and a spoon. She hadn't been able to find another fork. "I made coffee."

Denny's lips curled into a tentative smile. "For us?"

"Something to warm you up after a cold night on the ground."

Anson eyed her suspiciously. "Did you poison it?"

After being so hostile, Jessie couldn't blame Anson for not immediately warming to her. But good food and hot coffee always softened men up. She wouldn't underestimate the power of a warm griddlecake. "Of course I didn't poison it. You think I carry cyanide with me when I go to town?"

She meant it as a joke, but Anson didn't crack a smile. "You might have. They's pulled arsenic from a mine in Tintic."

Jessie cocked an eyebrow. "Sit. Those griddle cakes aren't getting any warmer."

Denny cheerfully sat on one of the milking stools, but Anson didn't budge. "You hate us."

Jessie blew a puff of air from between her lips. "Maybe I've changed my mind. And maybe I can't bear another day of biscuits and jerky. It's indecent the way you boys eat. You're half starved, and I won't stand for it."

Anson didn't smile, but his lips twitched as if he might be considering what she said. "You take the first bite."

Jessie sighed as if she might just have to throttle him, picked up the fork, and pulled a small chunk out of the top griddlecake. She popped it in her mouth. It wasn't bad, a little bland, but when all you had to work with was flour, baking powder, and salt, you got what you got. "Delicious," she said. "And I didn't die."

Anson narrowed his eyes. "The poison might take a few minutes."

"Then we all might as well enjoy ourselves before we kick the bucket."

Anson relaxed slightly. With his foot, he

scooted the milking stool toward Jessie. "You sit. I'll stand."

Well, she couldn't fault him for being a gentleman, but she wanted him to shrug off the stiff tension he'd been carrying since they'd met in Eureka. "I still have one griddlecake to tend to. You sit, and I'll pour the coffee."

"You take the first drink," Anson said.

She laughed. "If you insist."

She hesitantly held out both her hands to the brothers. She'd been planning this all morning. "Shall we say grace?"

Denny burst into a surprised smile. Anson rolled his eyes. "Are you trying to trick us?"

"What's the trick?" Jessie said. "You boys need a little religion."

Anson groaned. "You gave us enough religion yesterday."

"You're right," she said, her hands still outstretched. "Too much of the wrong kind. Can we start over?" Denny took her left hand. Anson reluctantly took her right and reached across the table to join hands with Denny. She grinned. "That wasn't so hard, was it?"

"I'm only holding your hand so's I know right where's you are when my eyes are closed."

"That's good enough for me." Jessie bowed her head and closed her eyes. There was no way to know if the boys followed suit. "Dear Heavenly Father, we thank Thee for this bounteous meal. Please forgive us our trespasses. Amen."

"Amen," Denny said. Without hesitation, he dug into his griddlecake as if it were a king's feast.

Jessie used her apron to pull the coffee off the stove and pour Denny and Anson each a cup. Anson gave her one suspicious glance, picked up his cup, and held it under his nose to savor the aroma.

Denny took a drink. "Hmm. Try it, Anson. Best thing you ever tasted."

Anson sipped as if he was afraid he would choke on it. He didn't comment on the taste, but he closed his eyes as he swallowed.

"I hope you enjoy it," Jessie said. "Because that's the last of the coffee. I wanted to make it nice and strong."

"Best I ever tasted," Denny said again, holding up his cup for a refill. Jessie poured more for him. "We got more."

"You do?"

"Yup. We keep all our foodstuffs in the mine cuz it's cool in there. It's depleted since the winter, but we've still got a few potatoes and a bag of apples. And some lard and bacon."

Jessie's heart skipped a beat. "Bacon? You've got bacon?"

Denny seemed overjoyed that this news made Jessie happy. "Almost three pounds."

She turned to Anson. "And yet all we've eaten is hardtack and jerky."

Anson shrugged. "It's easier."

"Easier?" Jessie said in mock outrage.

"Hardtack and jerky isn't easier. It's a travesty."

Denny laughed. "I don't know what that means, but it sounds mighty bad, don't it, Anson?"

Anson took another slow sip of coffee. "Can you both shut up about it? I'm trying to enjoy some quiet with my coffee."

Jessie smiled to herself. Nothing softened a man's heart like a good cup of coffee. And a little kindness.

Denny finished his griddlecake in about four bites, and Jessie couldn't bear the thought of him still being hungry. She carried her makeshift frying pan to the table and flipped the last griddlecake onto Denny's plate. Denny's eyes lit up before he drew his brows together and shook his head. "I couldn't, ma'am. You haven't eaten yet."

Just more evidence that someone had taught Denny manners. Jessie pushed the tin plate closer to Denny. "If you could see it in your heart to fetch me a bit more lard, I'll make a whole other batch of griddlecakes, and you can have all you want."

Denny looked at Anson, the anticipation shining on his face. "Can I, Anson?"

Still sipping his coffee, Anson motioned with his head. "Go. And don't get killed."

Denny sprang to his feet. "You always say that."

He ran out the door as if he was shot from a cannon. Jessie laughed. Anson looked at her sideways but kept silent. "Why did you say, 'don't get killed'?"

Anson set down his empty cup. Jessie quickly refilled it. "Our mine goes horizontal twenty feet then drops forty feet straight down. We work it almost every day, but I don't like the thought of Denny falling. He ain't cautious with his bum foot."

Jessie nodded. "Who is cautious at fifteen?"

Anson studied her face. "How did you know Denny is fifteen?"

Jessie didn't want to lie, but she didn't want to mention the Bible she'd found unused and tucked on the top shelf. Anson would think she'd been prying, which she had. "Isn't he about fifteen?"

Anson nodded. "He's just a boy. It's my job to take care of him."

Jessie wanted to ask who was taking care of Anson. In most ways, he was just a boy too. "You're doing a fine job."

"I'm not," Anson said. "I just got both of us into a heap of trouble."

"Maybe you have, but Denny trusts you. You're doing your best."

Anson stared at Jessie until she had to turn away. She set the coffee pot back on the stove and threw another piece of coal into the fire just to look busy. Anson set down his cup and folded his arms. "Why are you being nice to us all of a sudden? Because if you think we're going to let you go if you're nice, you can forget it. I was more inclined to cut you loose yesterday when your sermonizing gave me a headache."

She curled one side of her mouth. "I'm sure it did." She shrugged. "I realized I should behave as Jesus would."

"You think He would make us griddlecakes?"

"Maybe not. Maybe He'd spread out some loaves and fishes. But I know He would try to make things better for you."

Anson shook his head. "Jesus wouldn't even pay us any heed. He forsook our family a long time ago."

Jessie wanted to argue with him, but what did she know about it? Sometimes she blamed the good Lord for taking her mother. She didn't have the words to convince Anson otherwise. She swallowed past the lump in her throat. "I'm sorry for whatever bad things have befallen you and Denny."

"Tain't yours to apologize for."

Jessie was a breath away from telling Anson that she knew about his mother, but he didn't trust her, and her sympathy would only anger him. But he had brought up another topic she needed answers to. She sat on Denny's milking stool and tried to make her voice as gentle as possible. "I'm not just being nice so you'll let me go, but I do wonder. How long are you planning to keep me here?" His gaze shot to her face, and his eyes flashed with anger. "Although, you didn't plan on taking me in the first place, so maybe there is no plan."

"You got in the way. I didn't have no choice."

She had resolved to be kind and agreeable this morning, but she felt the irritation bubble up inside her. "Neither of us had a choice, Anson, but I'll warrant I had less of a choice than you did."

"I done what I done, and you can just shut up about it."

Jessie expelled a deep sigh and mustered some patience. "I don't mean to make you mad, but it would be nice to know how long I'm going to be here." She stole his coffee cup and took a sip. "I'm fair certain you're not planning to murder me."

He snatched back his coffee cup and grunted as if she was the most irritating woman in the world. "I haven't decided yet."

"That's a comforting thought," she said wryly. "You might not be in a hurry, but I can't imagine you'll enjoy sleeping outdoors much longer."

"We almost always sleep under the stars in the summer. It's too hot in the cabin."

Well, then. She wasn't going to convince him with that argument. "You might not mind it, but I don't want to sleep on the floor. And I want my shotgun back. I get a little testy without it."

He stared into his coffee and smiled. "I never seen a lady carry a shotgun like that. Right into town on your back."

"Then you can see why I'm anxious without it."

Anson grunted. "Your shotgun is safe. Safer with me than it is with you cuz I don't wanna get shot."

"You're right to be cautious. I would have shot you in town if I'd had the chance."

Anson acted as if this news didn't surprise him. "You fought hard. I knew you didn't just carry that gun for show."

Denny burst into the room with a sack and what had to be a whole pound of lard wrapped in crunchy white paper. "Miss..." He stopped and his face fell. He didn't know her name. "Ma'am, I brought lard and all the apples, just in case you need them for something."

Jessie laid a hand on Denny's shoulder. "My name is Jessie Madsen, and I'm sorry I didn't tell you sooner."

Denny's smile returned with full force. "Jessie. I like that name. Nice to meet you."

Jessie took the lard and apples from Denny and gave him a sisterly smile. "Okay, Denny, how many griddlecakes do you want?"

His eyes lit up. "Can I have three?"

"You can have seven, if you like."

He laughed as if he'd never heard of something so wonderful. "Then I'll have seven."

Anson finished his griddlecake in spite of thinking it might be poisoned, then stood up and gave Jessie the evil eye. "I have to go out, and I'll be gone all day."

"Where are you going?" Jessie said.

Jessie and James

"Nothing you need to know. I'm leaving Denny here to look after you. Don't try to run away, or you'll get lost and fall into a mine shaft or get eaten by a bear."

"He's got to meet a man," Denny said.

Anson turned his displeasure on Denny. "You just shut up about it." He pressed his lips into a hard line and studied Jessie's face. He reached up, took the Bible from the shelf, and held it out to Jessie. "I want you to swear you won't try to run away. Swear it on the Bible."

Jessie was trying to be accommodating, but she wasn't going to swear to any such thing. The possibility of escape was slim, but it was still a possibility and she wasn't going to back herself into a corner. "I won't do that."

"You can swear, or I'll leave you tied up all day. That could get mighty uncomfortable."

Jessie bit her tongue on an insolent reply. She was trying to be nice and treat Anson as Jesus would have treated him. He was certainly making it very hard. Wasn't he the least bit grateful she'd made him breakfast? She grabbed the Bible from Anson's hand and pressed it to her heart. "I swear I won't try to run away today. I can't promise I won't try to run away tomorrow, but I will stay put today."

Anson nodded in satisfaction and tried to take the Bible.

She pulled back. "And I want to encourage Anson to make a plan so that I don't have to sleep on the floor indefinitely."

"What does *indefinitely* mean?" Denny said.

"It means I want to go home."

Denny drew his brows together. "I'm sorry, Miss Jessie. We didn't mean to snatch ya. That fancy man was supposed to be by himself."

Anson pulled the Bible from her arms and set it back on the shelf. "I'll be back after dark."

Jessie pinned Anson with a stern look. "I don't know where you're going, but if you find some butter and eggs, bring them back. And I can make bread with some yeast."

Anson didn't say anything. He walked out the door and closed it not so softly.

Denny looked at Jessie with utter pity in his eyes. "I'm sorry, Miss Jessie. You just wasn't part of the plan."

Jessie huffed a breath and shook her head. "No use crying over spilled milk now. Let's see that your belly gets full for once."

Denny grinned. "Okay. I like that plan."

Jessie made griddlecake after griddlecake for Denny, who ate them like a starving man. Jessie had never gotten so much satisfaction out of cooking for anybody. Denny loved every bite. He complimented her cooking over and over. When he started talking about what a good cook his mother was, Jessie found her opening. "Where is your mother now?" she asked, fully knowing what the answer would be.

Denny squinted as if he was concentrating very hard on the past. "She died not six years ago. The good Lord gave her consumption."

"I don't think the good Lord makes people sick. I think dying is just part of living."

Denny shook his head. "Anson says the good Lord coulda healed Mama if He'd wanted to. He healed lots of folks in the Bible."

Jessie pretended she hadn't read that letter. "Did your daddy take care of you after your mama died?"

"No. My papa had trouble with the bottle. He used to throw things at us and say bad words. Mama would huddle us in a corner and pray, but it didn't stop Papa from coming after us. He hated me the worst cuz of my broken foot." Denny pulled up his sleeve to show Jessie a ragged scar across his forearm. "Papa hit me, and I fell and put my arm through a window. After that Mama said we had to get out." He motioned around the cabin. "This here is my mama's claim, left to her by her daddy. We came here and hid out so my papa wouldn't find us. Then Mama got consumption, and we could only afford to see a doctor once. She wasn't with us much longer then. After that, we found enough silver in our mine to trade for food and mining supplies when we need them. But we didn't find silver until after Mama was gone."

Jessie swallowed past the lump in her throat. "Your mama was a brave woman."

"I sure miss her cherry pie. And when I cried, she'd rub my foot with liniment to make it feel better."

"What is wrong with your foot, Denny?"

Denny looked down at his boot. "Anson says it's a malformation. I don't know what that means, but the doctor says he can fix it with an operation. But we don't have the money. I don't mind cuz I don't never want to go under the knife. You don't come back if you go under the knife."

Jessie frowned. "Is that why you stole the money? So you can pay the doctor?"

Denny looked at her as if she was crazy. "I told you. We didn't steal the money. A man paid us fifty dollars to take it, but we're going to give it back. My mama would be ashamed of us if we stole."

Jessie longed to ask how his mama would feel about kidnapping, but Denny was giving her a lot of good information, and she didn't want to shut him down by preaching to him. "What man?" she asked.

"I don't know. The man in town told us that your fancy friend stole his money. He paid us fifty dollars to steal it back. That's all." Denny studied her face in puzzlement. "You seem like a nice lady. Why was you with that no-account thief?"

Jessie felt her face get warm. "James isn't a thief. That money was from the London Mining

Jessie and James

and Ore Company, meant to buy a claim and start a mine in Mammoth. I don't know who told you that James stole his money, but James didn't steal anything."

"Well, now. I don't know about that. All I know is that Anson's going to give it back today. That's why he done gone down the mountain."

Jessie's heart flipped over. Anson was giving that money to someone it didn't belong to. But even if she could stop Anson, he wouldn't believe her. Was James' money gone forever? Well, she had plenty of other things to worry about. When she got home, maybe she could find a way to get James' money back. She put her hands on her hips. "Is there a way to get water besides going back down to the brook at the bottom of the mountain?"

Denny brushed the crumbs off his trousers. "Sure. From the mine. What do you need water for?"

"I need to wash the dishes."

"We usually just scrub them off with dirt."

Jessie's stomach turned over. "You'll make yourselves sick doing that. Everything needs to be washed properly. Have you got any soap? Or a scrub brush?"

"We got a little soap." He rifled through the tins on the shelf. "See? We got soap right here, but we don't use it but once a month to take a bath."

Jessie couldn't give him more than a weak and queasy smile. "Have you a scrub brush?"

"No scrub brush."

Jessie sighed. "Very well. We'll make do without."

"What are you going to do?"

"We are going to clean this place top to bottom."

Denny made a face. "But why?"

"Because I won't sleep another night in this filth, and cleanliness is next to godliness." She smiled at the horrified look on Denny's face. "I'm going to be your big sister for a few days. You need someone to take care of you. Go get a bucket of water, and let's get started."

Denny seemed to like the thought of Jessie as family. "For a big sister, you sure are bossy."

"Save your breath. I've heard it a thousand times before."

Thirteen

James clenched his jaw so tight, his head felt like it was going to explode. He'd suffered a skull-splitting headache for the past four days, plus a sharp ache in his chest, and a gaping hole in the pit of his stomach.

He couldn't find Jessie, and he thought he might go mad.

He took off his hat and pulled his fingers through his hair, hoping that something would come to him. Was there some clue he'd overlooked? Some trail he and Jessie the Horse hadn't been down yet? Some miner who might know Anson and the younger boy and where they holed up when they weren't committing crimes and kidnapping people?

James shuddered and clamped his eyes shut. He hated to think what could happen to a woman at the hands of an evil man. Hated to think of what might have already happened. The thought that Jessie might be hurt made him ill. The thought that she might be dead drove him to the edge of insanity.

If Jessie died, his entire world would descend into darkness. There would be nothing but desolation and despair left to him.

Scully was waiting for him when he arrived at the stable. "Any news?" he said, taking the reins while James slid off his horse.

James just shook his head, unable to speak while the world disintegrated around him. He pulled his saddlebag off Jessie the Horse and gave her a pat before leaving her to Scully and taking the painfully short trek up the little hill to the boarding house. He didn't think he could feel any worse, but he still hated the thought of delivering the bad news to Alice and George. Four days in the saddle, and he hadn't been able to restore their daughter to her parents' loving arms. They would be heartbroken.

He couldn't think about that terrible day without getting the wind knocked out of him all over again. The second those thieves were out of sight, with Jessie as their captive, James had raced to the mercantile and asked Lou to round up a posse. Precious time had been wasted because he had to run to the boarding house and get his horse and his six-shooter and tell George and Alice what had happened. By the time he'd returned to town, three miners, Hubert Johns, and Watson Nesbitt were waiting for him with horses ready and guns at their sides.

They rode hard in the direction the thieves had left town, but they never found a trail, and there was no way of knowing which way the thieves had actually gone. The two had ridden east with Jessie, but they could have turned north or south or even west once they were out of sight. James and the posse had ridden like the wind until they reached Santaquin, but no one in Santaquin had seen or heard anything, which meant the thieves had likely veered in a different direction, and their trail had gone ice cold. James' fear had been like a raw, open wound.

The posse had spent the next two full days searching the hills to the north and the south of Eureka, but there was too much ground to cover, and they'd found no trace of Jessie. After two days, the miners had to return to work or starve, and Watson Nesbitt had a mine to run. Hubert Johns stayed with James the third day, and Campbell Tomlinson, the surveyor, rode out by himself to look west of town, just in case.

By the second day, James had been frantic, and his panic had come with the realization that he loved Jessie to the very marrow of his bones. If he lost her, he didn't know that he would ever find meaning in life again. He didn't care about the money. He didn't care anymore about the mine or the claim or making his father proud. All he cared about was Jessie.

James draped his saddlebag over his shoulder and opened the boarding house door. Last night, after Hubert had gone home, James had spent the night on the trail and gone farther north in hopes of finding any traces of Jessie or the men who took her. He found an abandoned wagon with a juniper growing up between its slats and the skeletons of three cows but not a sign of Jessie. He didn't know where else to look, and he didn't know what else to pray for.

Alice greeted him at the door, her face pale, her hands clasped so tightly her fingers were white. "James," she said breathlessly, "did you find her?"

"I didn't," James said, his voice cracking in a million places. Suddenly his legs couldn't hold him up. He sank into the nearest chair, buried his face in his hands, and sobbed out his anguish.

Alice was immediately hovering over him, clucking her tongue and cooing as if he were a newborn baby. She placed her hand on his shoulder. "There, there, Mr. Kelsey. It's going to turn round right."

James heard George clomp into the room, his canes tapping on the ground as he made his way to the table where James sat. James looked up. George nodded earnestly. "Where did you go today?"

"Up past the Colorado Chief then back east."

George rubbed his hand along his jaw. "That's some rough country."

James swiped his hand across his eyes. "I don't know where else to look."

"Campbell," Alice said. "Could you please fetch James a cup of coffee?"

James hadn't even noticed Campbell when he'd come in, but Campbell pushed off from his place by the wall and disappeared into the kitchen.

George pulled a chair closer to James and motioned for Alice to sit. Then he pulled another chair for himself and sat next to Alice. "They've got to be hidden somewhere in the mountains," he said.

"If they are, they're hidden very well. I've been in so many canyons and gullies, I think I've got the whole territory memorized."

George nodded. "There's just too many places they could have gone."

Campbell came back with a cup of coffee for James. James took a slow drink and set the cup on the table.

"Do you think they've left the area?" Campbell said, pulling up a chair next to them.

Thinking of that possibility paralyzed James like almost nothing else. "I hope not. We sent a wire from Santaquin that will go all the way to Salt Lake. The locals will be on the lookout."

Alice lifted her chin. "She's still here. If they'd tried to take her anywhere, she would have fought them tooth and nail. Someone would have noticed. I've no doubt she would have escaped."

James took a deep, shuddering breath, but it

did nothing to ease the pain in his chest. "I'm riding out again tomorrow. I promise I won't rest until I find her."

Alice's eyes filled with compassion and resolve. She reached out and took James' hand. "Don't you worry, Mr. Kelsey. Our Jessie is no shrinking violet. She's strong and stubborn and determined. I have no doubt she's alive and well, and she'll find a way to get back to us." She placed her other hand on top of his. He felt the warmth of it down to his bones. "God will bring her back to us."

"I pray for that every minute."

"Pray as if everything depended on God and work as if everything depended on us. That's what I always say." Alice squared her shoulders. "I'll ride out with you tomorrow. Four eyes are better than two."

James gave her a sad smile and squeezed her hand. "Miss Alice, you know I depend on you for so many things, but you'd only slow me down."

Alice's lips twitched with disappointment. "I love your honesty, Mr. Kelsey, but hate the truth of it. What can I do? I want to help."

"You can pack me enough food for two days and pray for my safety. That is the best help I could get."

Campbell placed a hand on James' shoulder. "I'll ride with you tomorrow. My reports can wait another week."

Campbell's kindness rendered James mute.

Jessie and James

All he could do was brace a hand on Campbell's elbow and nod his thanks. Overcome with emotion, George bowed his head and leaned heavily on the canes in his right hand.

Alice seemed to be the only one keeping her composure. "My Jessie will be just fine. She's probably giving those thieves a piece of her mind and calling them to repentance as we speak. If she's ornery enough, they'll let her go."

James nearly smiled. Jessie had stared down a whole room of mining executives. She'd have those thieves cowering before her in a matter of hours.

"I'll go see about borrowing a horse," Campbell said. He went outside, presumably to find Scully at the stables.

James flinched as he remembered something he needed to give the Madsens. "I almost forgot. Can you wait here for a minute?"

Finding enough strength to stand, he tromped up the stairs, climbed the ladder to his room, and retrieved the jar he'd been keeping in the chest beneath his clothes. He went back downstairs where Alice and George were waiting, hands clasped together as if they were each holding to a lifeline. James handed George the jar. "Since the money was stolen, I haven't had enough to pay for my board. This isn't my gold, but I hope this will tide you over until they send me more money."

George gasped as he gazed at the jar half full of shiny gold flecks. He turned it over in his hand, and the gold caught the light and glowed like sunshine on a brilliant summer day. No wonder men built tunnels beneath the earth and risked their lives to find this treasure. There was almost nothing more exquisite than the rich, beautiful color of gold. "Where did you get this?" George asked breathlessly.

"Like I told you, this isn't my gold. It's yours. I found it in the water when I dug trenches to Jessie's cherry trees. It came up from the well and ran down the trenches. All I had to do was pull it out of the dirt."

George handed the jar to Alice, who took it as if she wasn't quite sure what to make of it. "You mean there really is gold on our land?" George said.

"Oh, yes. I estimate this is the richest vein of gold in Eureka, probably the whole territory. More than is on the Frenchman's claim. More than even the Colorado Chief can boast."

A line gathered between George's eyes. "You've been collecting this for many days. Why didn't you tell us this sooner?"

Alice handed the jar back to George. "Isn't it obvious?"

George glanced at James. "Jessie can't abide talk of mining our claim."

"Jessie can't abide talk of mining at all," Alice said. She studied James' face. "A claim like this would make you and your mining company very rich."

"Yes."

Jessie and James

"But that doesn't matter to you, does it?"

James pressed his hand to his forehead. "Nothing matters but Jessie."

Alice seemed to be clinging to her calm self-assurance with all her might. "You love her."

"With all my heart." Saying it out loud made it seem all the more real, all the more painful if he lost her. He closed his mouth and tried not to disintegrate.

"Oh, my dear," Alice said, releasing her tears and letting them flow freely down her face. She surprised him when she burst into a smile. "Isn't love the most wonderful thing?"

James didn't know if he agreed with her, because right now, love was making him crazy. He'd bask in the wonder of love after he found Jessie. For now, he was just surviving.

The door opened, and Jean-Pierre Bonheur walked into the boarding house, hat in hand, looking as if the world had come to an end. "I am zorry, but may I speak vith Mr. Kelzey?"

In all the upset about Jessie, James had almost forgotten about the money and the claim Jean-Pierre had agreed to sell him. He stood and shook Jean-Pierre's hand. "I'm sorry about the delay, Jean-Pierre. I've wired the London Mining and Ore Company. They're making a decision about sending more money. As soon as I know, I'll contact you."

Jean-Pierre strangled his hat in his hands. "Zat is zee zing, Mr. Kelzey. I cannot wait for your money. I have sold zee claim to Frank Roberts for a hundred dollars less."

A vice squeezed the air out of James' lungs. "You sold the claim?"

"I am sorry, but I must get to California. Frank offered me zee money zis morning. I had to take it. I must get to California." Jean-Pierre smoothed down his hair, but the gesture didn't matter. His hair was plastered to his head with pomade. "Maybe Mr. Roberts vill sell the claim to you ven you get zee money."

Not likely. Frank had wanted that claim for himself ever since James had found it. James could barely speak past his anger. "You should have come to me. I would have worked something out."

"Zere is no time. I leave for California tonight." He reached out to shake James' hand, but James kept his arms securely at his sides. "I am zorry about your lady friend. I hope you find her safe. But now I must go."

James stood frozen to the floor as the Frenchman closed the door behind him. Jessie was missing, and now James had no claim. He couldn't feel worse than he already did, but it was a hard blow all the same. Would he have a job by the end of the week? Would it even matter?

The best he could do was take one day at a time, not worry about what he would do without the claim, not worry what he would do if he never found Jessie. Only think about the next place to look, the next direction to ride, the next mountain in his way.

He would find Jessie, because nothing else would be enough.

Fourteen

"*Miss Jessie, what did you carve* on the top of that pie?" Denny sat on the milking stool, holding his little cup of cinnamon and sugar at the ready while Jessie set the top crust onto the apple pie and sealed the edges.

"It's an A and a D."

"Why?"

Jessie pinched the edges of the pie with her thumb and fingers to give it a pretty, decorative look the way Alice always did with her pies. "The cuts let the air vent while the pie is baking."

"But why A and D?"

"A is for Anson. D is for Denny."

Denny's face fell. "Oh. I shoulda known that. Mama taught me all my letters, but I long since forgot them."

"Do you want to learn to read, Denny?" Jessie said.

"Anson says it ain't no use reading when you're a miner."

Jessie smiled. "But you might want to read the Bible some time. Or write letters to people."

Denny snorted. "I ain't got nobody to write to."

Jessie sprinkled the top of the crust with water. "Okay. I'm ready for the sugar and cinnamon."

Denny took their one and only spoon, scooped some sugar and cinnamon from the cup, and sprinkled it carefully over the top of the apple pie. "How long will it take to bake?" he said. "I ain't had apple pie since I was a young'un."

"It should take about an hour, then another hour to cool. It will be ready after dinner."

Denny clapped his hands and his eyes flashed with excitement. "I'm sorry we kidnapped you, Miss Jessie, but I'm also not sorry. We ain't never ate so good."

Jessie had no trouble believing that. The Waller boys lived like vagabonds, eating jerky and hardtack, seldom bathing, and pulling silver from their mine when they needed more food.

Jessie slid the pie into the potbelly stove. It barely fit, and she had spent an hour trying to make the temperature just right so she wouldn't burn the pie to a crisp. This was the first pie Denny had eaten in ages, and she was not going to ruin it.

"There it goes," Denny said, looking at the stove as if it held all his hopes and dreams.

"If you want a real thrill, go outside for about half an hour then come back in, and your whole cabin will have the most heavenly aroma you've ever smelled."

Denny didn't need to be told twice. He grinned like an idiot, limped outside, and slammed the door behind him. Jessie sighed. She'd have to train Denny how to close the door properly.

Or maybe she wouldn't be here long enough for that.

Jessie's heart sank to her toes. She wanted to help the Waller boys. She really did, but she couldn't stay here any longer. She was either going to have to attempt an escape or convince them to let her go. At this point, she didn't know which would be harder.

Four days ago when Anson had made her swear to not escape, Jessie and Denny had scrubbed the cabin so clean there wasn't a speck of dust anywhere. Jessie had fried bacon and potatoes for dinner, and if she hadn't won Denny over after breakfast, he was definitely on her side after dinner. Anson had come back well after dark, bringing yeast, sugar, butter, eggs and cinnamon with him. Jessie had been astounded at the bounty and even more astounded that Anson had brought it.

She'd been able to bake bread and make better meals for the boys, even though their pantry was still sorely lacking. Yesterday, Anson had brought home a rabbit he'd shot with Jessie's shotgun, and rabbit stew was bubbling on the stove—rabbit stew with potatoes from the mine and wild onions that grew on the hill above the cabin. With the apple pie for dessert, it was going to be a feast.

The last three days, Anson had left Denny to look after Jessie and spent most of his days working the mine. Anson was young, fiercely loyal to his brother, and unsure or unable to show his love. It was clear that Denny was Anson's only concern and that he was doing everything he could to pay for the operation to fix Denny's foot.

Jessie couldn't approve of Anson's methods, but his love for his brother was obvious enough. Even though Anson loved Denny fiercely, it was a private kind of love. Denny was starved for affection and company, and sometimes Jessie wanted to gather him in her arms and tell him that she would take care of him. But she couldn't make such a promise. Someday, Anson and Denny were going to have to pay for their mistakes, and Jessie feared the day of reckoning would be swift and harsh.

An hour later, Jessie hiked down to the entrance to the mine, opened the door, and called the brothers to dinner. The mine wasn't very deep, and they could hear her from the top. Jessie looked over the edge of the vertical shaft. There was a natural underground stream at the bottom and the water filled a shallow depression in the rock before spilling down to disappear between the stone walls. With that plentiful water supply, the boys could live up here for a long time without needing to go down the mountain. No wonder nobody knew them in town. They rarely went.

She went back to the cabin and pulled the pie from the oven. It was the perfect golden brown, and steam rose from the top. The sweet smell of apples and cinnamon did indeed fill the space. Jessie closed her eyes and breathed it in. It was a far cry from the stink that had met her nose when she'd first set foot in the cabin. Thanks to Denny, some strong soap, and lots of water, that smell was only a distant bad memory.

She set the pie tin atop four stones that acted as a trivet on the table then set the stew pot on another set of stones. The table would burn like kindling if it met that much heat unprotected. Anson had found her a bucket that served as a third chair at the table so they could all sit down and eat together. It was really quite a nice arrangement, all things considered.

She could hear Anson and Denny outside the door washing their hands in the basin she'd set out there. If they wanted to eat, they had to wash their hands, and since Jessie's cooking was far superior to what they'd been eating, they washed their hands eagerly.

Denny and Anson walked into the cabin together and stopped as if they'd run into a wall. "Hurry, Anson. Close the door," Denny said. "You'll let out all the smell."

For once, Anson obeyed his brother without even a nasty look. Both boys stood like stone pillars with their noses in the air and smiles on their faces. Denny closed his eyes and sighed. "Miss Jessie, I ain't never smelled anything so delicious in my life."

Jessie smiled. "I hope it tastes as good as it smells." She motioned to the table. "Sit. I don't want the stew to get cold."

The boys sat down on the milking stools, and Jessie sat on her overturned bucket. They held hands while Denny said grace. After the third day of her saying grace, Jessie had insisted that the boys take their turns. Anson had resisted mightily, but hunger had driven him to surrender. Considering his past, Anson gave very eloquent prayers. Denny's were more childlike, but just as sincere. Their mama had taught them, and for that, Jessie was grateful.

After grace, Jessie dished up the rabbit stew, which smelled so good her mouth watered. Denny got the spoon, and Jessie and Anson ate their stew with their forks. She'd made some hearty bread that they all could use to sop up the stew at the bottom of the bowls. Anson tore a piece of bread from the loaf and ate eagerly. It always amazed Jessie how much a man could eat when he set his mind to it. Anson and Denny ate as if they didn't know where their next meal was coming from, and Jessie took it as high praise. She wasn't the one who got complimented on the cooking at home, and it was nice to be appreciated.

It couldn't last forever, and she decided to broach the subject while Anson was enjoying the best meal he'd probably had in years. She set her fork down and clasped her hands in her lap. "Thank you for the rabbit, Anson. I was growing tired of plain potato soup every night."

Anson dipped his bread into his bowl. "That's a real nice shotgun. I could get a pheasant or maybe even a wild turkey for you every day with a shotgun like that."

She cocked an eyebrow in his direction. "I'd like a turkey, but you can think again about using my shotgun. That shotgun is my prized possession, and I'm not keen on you putting your grubby hands all over it."

Anson spread his palms and looked at his hands. "They're clean enough."

Jessie cleared her throat. "But how many wild turkeys can we eat before it's time for me to go home?"

Denny paused eating long enough to give Jessie a doubtful look. "Why don't you stay the summer? You could cook us a turkey and an apple pie every night. Wouldn't that be nice, Anson?"

Anson's brows had been inching closer to each other ever since she said the word *home*. Now they were touching, and his frown looked as if it was etched into his face. "I can shoot a lot of wild turkeys."

"That's not really the question, Anson, and

you know it."

Anson set his bread on the table and wiped his mouth with his sleeve. "I don't have the answer, Miss Jessie."

Jessie reached out and dared to wrap her fingers around Anson's wrist. "I've been here seven days, Anson. We've all tried really hard to get along, but nothing can change the fact that I'm your prisoner."

Anson scrubbed his hand down the side of his face. "I know." He had lost his anger about three days ago, and he seemed to feel sorry for her, but that wasn't enough.

"You have to see it in your heart to let me go," Jessie said. "Come what may."

Anson expelled a deep, frustrated breath. "Come what may is the hard part."

"I know this is hard. There might be consequences, but I can't stay here."

Denny screwed up his face as if he was going to cry. "Why can't you stay here, Miss Jessie? I'll help with the cleaning every day, and Anson will bring you cinnamon and butter and all the wild turkeys you want."

Jessie smoothed her hand down Denny's arm. "Think about how much you loved your mama. I have a papa and a mama who love me. They're waiting at home, and they don't know what has become of me. I imagine they're sick with worry, thinking maybe I'm dead, not knowing if the men who took me were kind or scoundrels."

"What is a scoundrel?" Denny said.

Anson folded his arms across his chest. "Someone who takes advantage of a woman. It's bad, and our mama taught us never to do such a thing."

Jessie nodded. "I know, and I'm glad I fell in with your lot instead of the other kind. You aren't scoundrels, but my parents don't know that. My friend James, who you stole the money from…"

"Borrowed it," Denny said. "And the man who paid us told us your friend is a bad man."

"My friend James is not a bad man. He is one of the best men I've ever known. He works for a mining company and that money was supposed to help him start a mine. He is surely looking for me."

Anson pressed his lips into an unyielding line. "He's looking, all right. There was a poster at the store."

Jessie's heart jumped like a flea on a griddle. "A poster?"

"I can't read, but some of the customers was looking and talking about it."

Anson couldn't know how this news sent the emotions spinning inside her head. James was looking for her! The thought took her breath away and knocked the wind out of her at the same time. It was good news and bad news, because someone was going to get hurt. "No matter how well hidden you think we are, it is only a matter of time before James or someone else finds this shack. Then what do you think will happen? Someone will start shooting, and someone is bound to get hurt, if not killed. It could be me or Denny, but there is no way a fight ends well. You've got to see that, don't you, Anson?"

Anson turned his face away from her as if he didn't want to listen anymore.

Jessie sighed. "James is a fighter, and he knows how to use a gun. I've seen him shoot, and he doesn't miss." She took Denny's hand and squeezed it. "I don't want to see either of you dead on my account."

Anson gazed at her with raw intensity in his eyes. "But if we let you go, what then? You'll send a posse up here to kill us. We're dead either way." He tried to act angry, but Jessie saw nothing but fear. Anson was just a boy. His circumstances were out of his control, and he was terrified.

Jessie looked from Anson to Denny and back to Anson again. A week ago, she would have liked nothing better than to see the Waller boys locked away for what they'd done to her. Now, she found to her surprise, that there wasn't an ounce of indignation or retribution in her heart, only pity for two boys who'd lost their mother and were trying to survive in a world that had treated them harshly. "I understand why you want the money," she said, glancing at Denny so Anson knew she really did understand. "And I have no ill will in my heart. If you let me go, I promise never to tell where you are. James will not come looking for you, and neither will the sheriff or a posse. But if you continue with your life of crime, I won't stop the law from coming after you for something else."

Anson's expression softened around the edges. "We ain't never committed a crime before, and we don't aim to commit one again. You was enough trouble for three lifetimes."

Jessie laughed. "Good. I have two conditions for my silence."

"Conditions?"

"I won't reveal your identity or tell anybody where you are if you tell me the name of the man who hired you to steal the money."

Anson grunted. "I reckon we got more than we bargained for. I don't mind telling you, except I don't know his name."

Jessie's disappointment was profound. She was hoping to go home with a little gift for James. "What does he look like?"

Anson turned his body and leaned against the wall. "He's a puny fellow with a fancy moustache and a scar on his right hand, like maybe he laid it on a stove or something."

Anson might as well have conked her over the head with the stew pot. She should have known. How had she not guessed it already? "I think I have a pretty good idea who that might be."

"What's your second condition?" Anson said.

"I want my shotgun back."

James was so weary, he thought he might crumble into a pile of dust and blow away with the wind. He walked out of the telegraph office and found he could go no farther. Desperation and despair had crippled him to the point of exhaustion. He sat down on the step just outside the door, not caring if he was in anyone's way. If they wanted to go inside, they'd just have to step over him. The only thing that had kept him going for the last seven days was the hope that he would find Jessie just around the next bend or over the next hill. But as the days wore on, his hope was waning, and he could no longer see the road ahead.

James pulled the telegram out of his pocket and read it again, just to make himself feel worse. The company wasn't sending more money. They weren't going to wait for him to scout out another claim. As of this minute, he was no longer an employee of the London Mining and Ore Company. As bad as this was, James felt almost numb to the pain. He couldn't think straight, let alone decide what to do next. He might buy a tent with the little money he had left, camp along the side of the road like a miner, and spend the rest of his life searching for Jessie. It was as good a plan as any.

James hung his head and said another desperate prayer, one of about a thousand he'd said since he'd lost Jessie. Was God listening anymore? Did He even care? Had He already answered James' prayer and the answer was no?

James couldn't bear that thought. The answer had to be yes.

A cloud of dust rose in the distance as a horse and rider came over the crest of the hill and into town. James looked closely. It wasn't Jessie, so he didn't care who it might be. He didn't even tip his hat as the rider passed by the telegraph office. If he wanted a warm welcome, he'd need to find someone besides James to give it to him.

He pulled another letter from his pocket, the one he'd received yesterday from his father. *Your mother and I are pleased with your progress in the mining business and hope the claim you found produces a wealth of gold for your employer. A pursuit in geology seems to have been a fine idea after all.*

Even though it wasn't especially effusive, a letter like that would have sent him to the moon a week ago. Father and Mother were *pleased*, which was quite close to being proud. James would take any bone they threw his way. But now the letter meant nothing. Father would find out soon enough that James had lost the company's money and lost his job. He was loath to go crawling home with his tail between his legs, but he might have no other choice. He options were shrinking.

Another puff of dust appeared down the street to the east, but this time whoever it was didn't ride a horse into town. He was walking. James squinted into the waves of heat that rose from the street. *She* was walking. And it looked as if she had a tree branch sticking out diagonally from her neck.

It was either a branch or a...shotgun.

James jumped up so fast, he tripped on the step and nearly fell on his face. Only his boxer's balance kept him upright. And then he ran. Ran like a madman toward the woman tromping down the street with a shotgun slung over her shoulder.

Jessie Madsen, with her hair half up and half down and her face layered with dust, was the most beautiful sight James had seen in all his twenty-seven years. He reached out, wrapped his arms all the way around her, gun and all, and pulled her into an embrace as if she were his missing piece. He lowered his lips to hers and kissed her hungrily. She might have been surprised, but she slid her hands around his neck, rose on her tiptoes, and pulled herself closer to his heart.

James had never, never been so deliriously happy in his entire life. He wanted to stay like this forever, with his arms around the woman he loved, kissing her until he lost the use of his wits.

But he also needed to breathe before he passed out from the sheer joy of it.

He pulled away from her, and she gave him a wry, I'm-about-to-scold-you look. "Don't you even want to know if I'm okay first?"

He pulled her to his chest and laughed in utter relief. "No, ma'am. Kissing first, talking second."

Her smile was like the sunrise after a fearfully dark night. "You gave my shotgun a hug too. Admit it, you missed her more than you missed me."

"Miss Jessie, if we weren't in the middle of the street, I'd show you the hole in my chest where I missed you something fierce. I didn't care a whit about your shotgun, except for hoping it might keep you safe." He shuddered at the notion of Jessie being in danger. It was the thought that had dominated his life for seven long days.

"It kept me from starving, anyway," she said, reaching out and cupping his face in her hand. Her eyes went as soft as melted chocolate. "You look like you've been through the wringer washer, Mr. Kelsey."

He wrapped his fingers around her wrist and kissed her knuckles. "I'm better now. Never better."

She closed her eyes and sighed. "Hmm. Me too."

He brushed away some strands of hair that dangled in front of her face. "Did they hurt you? Is there anything I can do?"

Jessie lifted her skirts almost to her knee. James tried not to stare at the enticing view of lovely white leg. "I scratched my leg on a branch, and I'm in sore need of a bath, but other than that, I am no worse for the wear."

She dropped her skirts, and a shard of glass seemed to pierce through his heart when he noticed a fading red welt around her wrist. He took her forearm and pushed up her sleeve. "What's this?"

"They tied me up, and I tried like the dickens to get loose."

James' relief turned to rage in an instant. "I swear, Jessie, I'll make them pay for this." She grunted her disapproval and folded her arms stubbornly. It wasn't the reaction he expected. "You'll do no such thing." She traced her finger around the welt on her wrist. "This is nothing. You know how much worse it could have been."

He did, and he didn't want to think about it. "It doesn't matter. They kidnapped you, Jessie. That's more than enough for me. I won't show them any mercy. They didn't show you any."

"But they did. And you shouldn't get all worked up when you don't know the whole story."

James swiped his hand across his mouth. Jessie wasn't making any sense. She had a stronger sense of justice than he did. "Don't tell me not to get worked up," he snapped. "I thought I'd lost you. Do you know what torture that was?"

Jessie slid her hand around his back and tucked herself under his arm. She fit there perfectly even though her gun stuck up between them. She pressed her palm to his chest as if to calm his pounding heart. "I am sorry. I didn't mean to hurt you. I didn't want any of this to happen."

"Of course you didn't."

She lifted her head and kissed his cheek. He turned and caught her lips with his mouth in a feather-soft, fleeting motion. "All is well," she said softly. "You found me."

James let out a slow breath. This was what he had been praying for all week. "I didn't do anything. I was sitting on the telegraph office steps, and you just happened to walk by."

She grinned. "Well, at least you didn't pass up a golden opportunity. You caught me in a moment of weakness. You'll never steal a kiss so easily again."

James let his mouth fall open in mock indignation. "You think that was easy? I slept four nights on the trail, ate next to nothing because I didn't have the stomach for it, and lost my hat. I spent a whole week working up to that kiss."

"Well, never forget that I carry a shotgun at all times to ward off men who try to take liberties with unsuspecting young women."

James might have laughed, but the pain of almost losing Jessie was still raw. "I don't mean to cut this nice conversation short, but I would like to know where you have been for the last seven days and how you got away."

"I will tell you everything, but..." She touched her hand to her forehead. "I think I need to sit down."

James didn't waste a second. He scooped Jessie into his arms, and despite her weak protests, carried her to the nearest door, which happened to be the mercantile. He went inside and set her on one of the barrels by the front counter.

Jessie and James

Lou Johns came out from the back room, and his face lit up like a stick of dynamite. "Miss Jessie, you're back!" He turned his head and called behind him. "Hubert, Miss Jessie is back."

Hubert rushed into the room, wiping his hands and grinning widely. "Well, my stars. Miss Jessie. How are you? We thought you was dead." He glanced at James. "Not that we wanted you to be dead, but most of us gave up after a few days. James never gave up. I thought he would go to his grave looking for you."

Jessie laid a hand on James' arm. The touch sent a ribbon of warmth through his entire body. "Thank you," she whispered.

"I had to find you." He motioned to Hubert. "Can you get her a drink?"

"Water or hard liquor?"

Jessie's lips curled upward. "Water will be most appreciated."

Hubert hurried away. James knelt next to Jessie's barrel. He wasn't going to let her out of his sight again. "Can I get you something to eat?"

She tucked some errant hair behind her ear. "I just want to get home. How are Alice and Papa?"

"Worried. But Alice never doubted for a minute. She kept saying you would escape. She thinks the world of you."

"I don't know why."

"I do," James said. Jessie's worth was obvious to everyone but her.

Hubert brought Jessie some water. She drank

it then stood up. James put his arm around her waist. She didn't seem very sure on her feet. "I need to get home. I don't want Alice and Papa to fret one more minute."

James bent over to pick her up. She raised her hand. "You are not carrying me all the way home."

"I won't let you walk."

She pinned him with the stink eye. "You've had a harder time of it than I have. Try to carry me, and you'll fall into a ditch."

James would have done anything for Jessie, but he felt the truth of her words to his bones. "Lou, can I borrow your horse? I need to get Jessie home."

"You're welcome to her. I'll have one of the young ones fetch her back later."

"Thank you."

Lou nodded. "I'll spread the word that Jessie's home. There's a lot of folks who'll be mighty glad to hear it."

James tried to pick Jessie up again. She cuffed him on the shoulder. "Don't even try it, Mr. Kelsey."

"But, Jessie, I just want to help you to the horse."

"I've got two strong legs, and I know how to walk. You're just as likely to fall over as I am. I'll walk by my own power, thank you very much."

James gave her an exasperated smile. His Jessie was back, and he'd never been so happy about being scolded.

Jessie and James

James rode right up to the door of the boarding house. He slid off the horse to help Jessie down, but she dismounted almost as quickly as he did. After tying the horse to the cherry tree, he opened the door for Jessie. The great room was empty, but they could hear two people talking in the kitchen.

"Hello?" James called.

George hobbled out of the kitchen first and stopped in his tracks when he laid eyes on Jessie. Alice bumped into him as he stood like a statue just outside the kitchen.

Alice gasped. "Jessie? My dear Jessie, you're home." She pushed her way past George, almost knocking him over, reached out, and placed her hands on either side of Jessie's face. "Oh, my darling. Oh, my darling. We were worried sick." She pulled Jessie in for a hug, and George joined them, putting his arms around the two of them, a cane in each hand.

Tears streamed down Alice's face, and George was no less affected. Watching such a profound family reunion, James could scarcely contain his emotions. The Madsens loved each other fiercely, and despite all their problems, they had each other to depend on every day of their lives. James was jealous of the bond among them. He'd never had that with his parents, and he never would. But he couldn't feel sorry for himself. Jessie and her parents were reunited. There was no cause for anything but joy.

Alice broke away from Jessie and George and took both of James' hands. "Mr. Kelsey, we will never be able to thank you adequately for bringing our Jessie back to us, but I want you to know you will always have a place with us."

James hung his head. "I wish I'd been the one to find her, Miss Alice, but she just walked into town not half an hour ago."

Alice patted his cheek and nudged him to look at her. "You found her all right. Your hope kept every last one of us going, and don't you ever forget it." Alice turned back to Jessie, cupped her hand around Jessie's elbow, and led her to a chair. "Sit, my darling. You must be worn to the bone. I've got rabbit stew on the stove. I'll dish you up a bowl."

An indefinable emotion traveled across Jessie's face. "Rabbit stew." James helped Jessie off with her shotgun and leaned it against the table.

George and James pulled up chairs on either side of Jessie. George sat down and took Jessie's hand across the table. "What happened? How did you get away?"

Jessie propped her elbow on the table and rested her chin in her hand. "They let me go, Papa."

James' mouth fell open. "Let you go?"

She playfully raised an eyebrow. "I was ornery, and they got tired of me."

Jessie and James

"I don't believe it for one minute," James said, though he knew Jessie could take care of herself.

Alice came from the kitchen with two bowls and two spoons. She set one of the bowls in front of James. "Eat. You haven't hardly touched a thing for a week, and I'm starting to worry you don't like my cooking."

Suddenly realizing he had an appetite, James picked up the spoon. "Miss Alice, I've never tasted better cooking than yours."

Jessie took a bite of stew. "So much better than what I made," she said.

Alice sat down next to George. "I don't remember that you've ever made rabbit stew."

George patted Jessie's hand. "Tell us what happened."

Jessie paused between bites. "I can't tell you everything, because I promised I wouldn't, but…"

James' temper bubbled to the surface. "You promised?"

Her eyes flashed with a rebuke, as if he was the one who was being unreasonable. "Just remember it could have been much worse."

"It was bad enough."

She pretended not to hear him. "The two boys—I can't tell you their names…"

"You can't tell us their names?"

She arched an eyebrow, and he shut his mouth. One kidnapper was Anson. He remembered that from that horrible day. He'd find out who both of them were, and then there'd be the devil to pay.

"They are only fifteen and nineteen, young and motherless," Jessie said.

Alice frowned. "Oh, those poor boys."

James clenched his teeth. Alice shouldn't encourage Jessie like that. Boys or not, they were going to feel the full force of James' fists.

Jessie nodded. "The younger boy needs an operation. They got paid fifty dollars to steal James' money. I wasn't supposed to be with James that day." She smiled at him and took his breath away, even though he was irritated with her. "They're just boys. That's why it was a good thing I was there, or James would have given them a good beating."

"Yes, I would have."

"But instead, he was worried about me getting hurt, so the brothers had to kidnap me for their own safety. They're just boys. They got scared and didn't know what else to do."

James clenched his teeth. The kidnappers might have been young, but they were old enough to know better. They'd hurt Jessie and stuck a gun in James' face. He wasn't likely to forget that anytime soon.

"They took me to their…well…hideout, and I tried to convince them to repent, but they wouldn't listen to me. The older one said he wanted to throw me off a cliff just to make me shut up."

James balled his hands into fists, but he didn't say anything. That boy, probably named Anson, would pay for threatening Jessie.

"Oh, dear," Alice said, pressing her hand to her throat.

Jessie reached out and squeezed Alice's hand. "I knew they weren't going to hurt me. They're just boys."

James choked on his own spit and coughed loudly. But he'd keep his opinions to himself. He didn't want Jessie to scold him again, even if he was the one who seemed to have any sense left.

"That's when I found the letter."

"Letter?" Alice prodded.

"I found a letter their mother had written them right before she died. Den—the younger brother was nine years old and the older was thirteen when the good Lord took their mother. They were left to care for each other."

"Oh, my, so young." Alice could be as sympathetic as she wanted. James wasn't going to budge.

"The poor boys were practically starving up there, so I cleaned their cabin as best I could and made hearty meals out of whatever they had on hand. Last night, I made them an apple pie and told them my family was missing me terribly. I promised if they let me go, I wouldn't tell who they were or where to find them. They're just boys, and they deserve a second chance."

James folded his arms and tried to keep the bitterness out of his voice. "Now they can afford to hire a cook."

Jessie grew intensely serious and clutched James' arm. "I told you. They were hired to steal that money. They didn't keep it for themselves." She patted her stomach. "Will you excuse me?" She stood and hobbled into the kitchen. Before James decided to go in after her, she returned holding a dark brown pouch that looked suspiciously like...

If James hadn't been sitting down, he would have fallen over. "My money!"

"Anson didn't have a chance to give it to Frank, because everybody in town was suspicious of strangers." Jessie clapped her mouth shut, and her eyes flashed with irritation.

No wonder. She'd just revealed two important names, though James already knew about Anson. "Are you talking about Frank Roberts? What does he have to do with this?"

Jessie handed him the pouch. "Count it. It's all there except fifty dollars. The boys felt entitled to keep it. I gave them permission."

The outrage bubbled to the surface again. "You gave them fifty dollars of my money?"

"That's what they'd been promised."

James' heart and his temper raced out of control. "Jessie, you're not making any sense."

"You keep interrupting me," she snapped.

Alice patted James' hand. "Now, now, let's not get cross with each other."

James took a deep breath and remembered that despite how aggravating she could be, he loved Jessie with his whole soul. "I apologize, Miss Alice." He turned to Jessie. "If you will explain yourself, I will do my best not to interrupt."

She gave him an arch look. "It will be a Herculean effort, I'm sure."

James didn't know whether to glare at her or laugh. She was so endearingly headstrong. "I'm listening," he prodded.

Jessie studied his face. For what, he wasn't sure. "The boys didn't know his name, but they told me a short man with a moustache and a burn on his hand hired them to steal your money."

"Frank," James muttered, his anger rising like heat from the desert floor. He should have shot Frank when he had the chance.

Jessie nodded. "It can't be anyone but Frank. He wanted the Frenchman's claim bad enough to steal for it. The older boy—"

"Anson?" James said. When Jessie's eyes flashed at him, he shrugged. "Might as well use his name so we don't get confused."

Jessie sighed as if she was utterly fed up with James. "Okay, his name is Anson. Anson came to town on Monday to give the money to Frank, but he got spooked by all the people keeping an eye out for anything suspicious. He bought some supplies at the mercantile and left town without meeting with Frank." She wrapped her fingers around his wrist. "Anson said you made posters. That was very sweet."

James gave her a half smile. "Alice made the

posters. She and Emmaline Johns hung them all over town."

Alice grinned. "Emmaline is very good with a hammer. I held the posters, and she nailed them to things."

Jessie's face lit up like a starry night. "Thank you. The posters sort of scared Anson off. They made him realize that people were looking for me and that he wasn't going to get away with kidnapping. When they let me go, I convinced them to let me bring the money back. Frank is going to be very angry when he realizes the boys don't have the money anymore. Now you can buy the claim as planned and move ahead with the mine. It's only a week's delay."

James grimaced. "I can't. Frank bought the claim right out from under me not three days ago."

Jessie's frown took over her whole face. "What? I don't understand. He didn't have the money."

"Do you remember that Frank said he was working on securing investors for the claim? The price of the claim was only a small portion of what the company sent me. Frank was working on getting the money to buy the claim. The brothers bought Frank more time. Jean-Pierre was in a hurry to get to California, and he thought my money was gone for good. He got impatient and took less for the claim just to get something out of it. Once Frank secured the claim, he would have used the other money to do what I was going to do:

get a mine started."

"That snake," Jessie said.

"Oh, yes," James said. "He's going to feel my wrath with his entire body."

Jessie shook her head. "I know you want to punish him, but—"

"You can't talk me out of it, Miss Jessie."

"Talk you out of it? I want to be the one to do it. With my shotgun."

James wouldn't allow that. "They'd send you to prison, or Frank would end up shooting you. I'll take care of this one."

"I'm the one who got kidnapped."

"And I'm the one who's been living in torment, in dread of how they were hurting you, not knowing if you were dead or alive."

Jessie seemed to soften around the edges. "You...you were really that upset?"

"Of course I was. I love you, Jessie." He glanced at each one of them in turn. "And I don't care who knows it."

Jessie burst into a smile. Alice sighed and clasped her hands together. George seemed mildly amused.

Jessie sat back and folded her arms. "We can argue about who gets to hurt Frank Roberts later. What are we going to do about the claim?"

James pressed his lips together. "It's legally Frank's now. I don't know how we can get it back unless Frank goes to jail. Even then, since he didn't buy it with stolen money, we might not be able to do anything about it."

"He can't go to jail without the brothers testifying, and if they testify, they'll be in trouble for kidnapping me." She slumped her shoulders. "So Frank goes free."

James longed to point out that the brothers *should* get in trouble for kidnapping Jessie, but they could have that argument another time. "I won't let Frank off easy. Maybe he'll end up walking with a permanent limp."

Jessie frowned. "You've got to find another claim for the company."

"It doesn't matter," James said, his heart as heavy as an anvil, despite the return of Jessie and the money. "The London Mining and Ore Company has dismissed me from their employment."

Jessie stared at him with wide eyes. "They...they fired you?"

"For not being more careful with their money."

"But, James, that's not fair."

He shrugged. "I lost their money. They can't very well overlook that."

"Oh, dear," Alice said. "I'm terribly sorry."

Jessie drew her brows together. "But if you contact them and tell them you found the money, won't they give you your job back? Then you can just find another claim and carry on as before."

"I will contact them immediately about the money, but they don't trust me and they're not interested in mining in Eureka anymore. They've already dispatched a new geologist to Idaho." James massaged a spot just above his eyebrow. "I'm truly a failure."

Jessie squeaked in protest. "None of this was your fault."

James wished that was true. He wished he didn't have to write home and admit that Father had been right all along. It really should have been James who had died in that boat. Marcus would have been the perfect son. Marcus would have made Father proud. "I shouldn't have been so confident. If I'd been smart, I would have hired three or four men to walk me and the money to the land office. Then Anson and his brother wouldn't have been able to rob me. They wouldn't have taken you either." He took Jessie's hand. If she couldn't forgive him, he didn't know what he would do. "I'm sorry. I lost the money and couldn't keep you safe. It's no one's fault but my own."

Jessie glared at him, pulled her hand away, and smacked his arm. "Don't be ridiculous. If it's anyone's fault, it's mine. If I hadn't been there, you wouldn't have had any trouble taking care of Anson and his gun. You were more concerned about me than you were about the money. Another man might have let them kill me."

"No one would have let them kill you."

Her glare narrowed. "You think too highly of manhood in general. Frank Roberts would have let them kill me. But it doesn't matter because Anson and Denny wouldn't have hurt me. They aren't killers. They're just boys."

James slapped his hand on the table, his irritation swallowing his misery. "If you say they're *just boys* one more time, Miss Jessie, I'm going to go out front and tear all the branches off that cherry tree."

Jessie harrumphed her displeasure. "You are not. You're going to suck in all that anger and show those boys a little compassion. Their father beat them, and they lost their mother. They've promised me they won't commit any more crimes. That's good enough for me."

"It's not good enough for me."

"I don't care."

"Well, then," Alice said, smiling with all her might, "Who would like a piece of strawberry shortcake? The strawberries are just ripe, and they're delicious."

"I'd love a piece of shortcake," Jessie snapped, directing all her irritation at James.

"Not as much as I'd love one," James shot back.

He was going to make Jessie see reason, but after shortcake. Shortcake would put everybody in a better mood.

Fifteen

Jessie woke with a start, her heart racing like a freight train. She sat up in bed and looked around her dark room. She couldn't see much, but with her eyes open, she reminded herself of what was real and what was just a dream. Seeing the familiar surroundings of her room gave her an anchor in her sleep-confused head and made it easier to push the nightmare back into the shadows of her mind. She'd suffered through the same nightmare every night since she'd been home—three nights in a row. Trying to calm herself, Jessie took several deep breaths. She'd been through a harrowing experience. Bad dreams were only to be expected. When Mama had died, she hadn't slept well for months.

This recurring nightmare wasn't about being snatched in the street or being tied up and taken to a shack, or even about eating hardtack and jerky for two days straight. In this dream, she saw James walking backward, not taking his eyes from her face, then tripping into a mineshaft and falling to his death. Jessie always reached out her hand to catch him, but her effort was too late and James still fell.

Jessie didn't know what it meant, but it was the worst nightmare she could have imagined. She wouldn't lose James, couldn't lose James, and yet he was slipping away from her as sure as the sun rose in the morning. And she felt helpless to stop it.

Jessie sat up straighter as she heard the door open and close softly in the great room. Was someone coming in or going out? With her heart doing all sorts of somersaults, she quickly lit her lantern, slipped on her robe, and grabbed her gun. Holding her gun at the ready, she hooked the lantern handle over the barrel of the shotgun. She had to be ready to shoot, but she also had to be able to see what she was shooting at. She tiptoed so she wouldn't wake Papa and Alice in the next room, but she didn't need to be quiet for the thief or intruder or whatever he was. If he was in the boarding house, he'd see her light first thing.

Jessie held her breath as she gazed around the great room. Nothing to see. No robbers waiting to seize her, no one hiding under one of the tables or behind the stove. She pressed her lips together. Okay then. Most likely it had been one of the boarders. Sometimes one of them would go out in the middle of the night to the outhouse, but they always went out the back door.

Jessie slid the lantern off the barrel of her gun and peered out the window. Someone was out there, lingering near the cherry tree, looking up at the stars. Probably seeing how many constellations he could count.

Not caring about the propriety of going outside in her nightgown, she propped her shotgun by the door and slipped outside with her lantern. James immediately turned around when he heard the door open. When Jessie got closer, the light of the lantern illuminated his features. He smiled at her, but the smile didn't quite reach his eyes. "Did I wake you, Miss Jessie? I'm sorry."

"I had a bad dream. Then I heard something. I got spooked."

He nodded. "Understandable."

He'd been ecstatic when she'd walked into town three days ago, but his happiness hadn't lasted long. So many things were troubling him, she couldn't begin to know how to comfort him. "Couldn't sleep?"

One side of his mouth curled upward. "I'm not complaining, but the attic is the hottest place on earth tonight."

Jessie smiled playfully. "That's why you had to pay extra for it."

His grin faded. "Not for much longer. I'm out of money."

Jessie didn't want to talk about money or the

London Mining and Ore Company or James' future. "I hope you're not out here plotting revenge on Frank Roberts without including me."

"Oh, no, Miss Jessie. I have already plotted my revenge, and it most assuredly does not include you." Frank Roberts probably didn't know it yet, but he was in big trouble. Both Jessie and James were planning different kinds of retribution. "I went to his house the night you came home. He wasn't there."

"I know," Jessie said. "I followed you. And I followed you the next night and tonight as well."

James rolled his eyes. "I know. You're not a good spy, Miss Jessie."

Jessie let her mouth drop open in mock outrage. "How did you know I followed you?"

"You don't sneak very well."

Jessie huffed out a breath. "It doesn't matter. Nobody has seen hide nor hair of Frank for three days. Do you think he ran off for good?"

"Not likely. Not now when he's got the Frenchman's claim."

"Well," said Jessie, "as soon as he returns, I'm paying him a visit. Don't try to beat me to it."

"Miss Jessie, I can't allow you to have anything to do with Frank Roberts."

Jessie gave James the stink eye. "It's not your decision to make. I'm the one who got kidnapped. He's going to get *what for* from me."

Suddenly James was so close, she could smell the soap he used to wash his hair. He wrapped his

Jessie and James

arms around her possessively and pulled her to him. Jessie held her breath as her lantern dangled from her fingers. The move was bold of him, but not unwelcome. His embrace was even warmer than the night air. "Jessie," he whispered. "Please don't try anything. If you got hurt, I don't know what I'd do. I think I'd go insane."

Without warning, he bent his head and brought his lips down on hers. She shivered with pleasure at the sensation of his touch. Was there anything better in the world than being kissed by James Kelsey under the canopy of a million stars? He kissed her until she was sure she wouldn't be able to walk a straight line ever again.

He pulled back slightly, so that his lips were barely an inch from hers. "Will you let me deal with Frank Roberts?"

She sighed with her whole body. "But if you got hurt, I'd never recover either. You should think of my feelings. I can't bear to lose you."

He smiled slowly, as if it took him some time to grasp what she was saying. "Really? Do you…do you like me?"

"If I didn't, I wouldn't have let you kiss me the other day. Men know that's the quickest way to get shot around here."

James laughed softly. "I'm glad you didn't shoot me. I want to be this happy for a hundred more years."

She smoothed some hair behind his ear. "But you're not."

"Not what?"

"Happy."

He tried to cover up his sadness with a smile, but he wasn't a very good pretender. "How could I not be happy? You're back and unharmed, and you let me kiss you."

"Yet you're not happy. You're not one to haunt the halls of the boarding house at night."

"I suppose not."

"The London Mining and Ore Company made a foolish, hasty decision. They'll come to regret it. It's too bad I can't march into their office tomorrow and show them my shotgun. That would knock some sense into them."

"I doubt it." He sighed and pulled away from her. "I got this today." He slid his hand into his pocket and pulled out a piece of paper. A telegram. "It's from my father. I wired him about the stolen money and the lost claim. I thought he should know." He cleared his throat. "I...I asked him about taking a position in his company."

Jessie stared at the folded telegram in stunned silence. James had asked his father for a job? How humiliating that must have been for him, not to mention the fact that James would be utterly miserable working in any office, his father's or otherwise. "What did he say?"

He handed her the paper. "Perhaps what I expected."

Jessie took the telegram and read it silently by the light of the lantern. *Don't come home. You are accountable for your own mistakes.* "Oh, James," she said, her voice disintegrating at the very thought of such an unyielding father.

He took her into his arms, and she could tell he was trying to borrow what comfort he could from her. "He's right, but I had hoped for a kind word."

"How could he cast off his own son like that?"

"He wants me to learn something, and he's got his heart set on my brother Simon now. As far as Father is concerned, I'm just as dead as Marcus is."

Jessie wanted to throw her arms around him and tell him it wasn't true, but from what she'd heard of James' father, it was entirely possible he felt that way. James craved approval he was never going to get, and the yearning was tearing him apart. "If your father could see what you've done here, he'd take back what he said in that letter."

James' shoulders sagged. "What have I done but get myself fired?"

"You succeeded in getting nine stubborn mining executives to fund a wooden pipeline to Mammoth."

A smile twitched at his lips. "That wasn't me. That was you. And your shotgun."

"You dug hundreds of feet of trenches to water my cherry trees."

"That was purely selfish. I'm hoping Alice will make me a cherry pie."

Jessie rolled her eyes. "You'll get your cherry

pie. You'll get so many cherry pies, you'll be sick of them, but if you think I believe you dug trenches just for a cherry pie, you are greatly mistaken. You also milk my cow at least once a day, and just look at Scully's new roof. He couldn't be happier."

He kicked the dirt at his feet. "But those aren't the important things or the kind of work that gets people's attention. That's just the everyday work that everybody does because they have to."

"You never had to do any of those things. You did them because you have a kind heart. Maybe those things aren't important to your father or the London Mining and Ore Company, but they're important to me. And to Scully. And to those men in Mammoth who won't have to pay ten cents for a gallon of water." She scolded him with her eyes. "Never underestimate the power of everyday work. It's what keeps the entire human race alive."

He smiled sadly and bowed his head. "But there's not a lot of money or glory in it."

"No, but money and glory aren't everything." She tilted her head to coax his gaze upward. "If only your father knew you spent seven days trying to find me."

"Seven panic-stricken days," he said.

"Seven hard, hot, exhausting days. Alice says you barely ate or slept. She and I will be grateful forever."

James' eyes went soft. "If everyone else in the world rejects me, I know I can count on Alice fixing me a warm dinner and finding me a place to sleep.

Jessie and James

She likes me."

"In case you forgot, I like you too. Sort of."

His smile made the lantern seem mighty dim. "I won't ever forget it."

Jessie slid the sparkling jar of wonders into her apron pocket and went around to the back of the house. James didn't see her. He was milking Lily Bell while humming a tune Jessie didn't recognize. She stood very still for a few minutes. It was a sad tune, and his voice was so beautiful, it almost made Jessie cry. Almost. She was too mad to get teary and too sad for such sentiment.

She didn't know what to say, or even how to talk to him. Pushing her sorrow down deep, she decided to show him her angry face, because if she showed him any weakness, she'd burst into tears. She wanted to bully James into submission, not make him feel sorry for her. She placed her hands on her hips and glared at where she estimated his head was, even though she couldn't see him and he couldn't see her because there was a cow between them. "James Kelsey, Alice says you're moving out."

He leaned to the side so his head appeared right behind Lily Bell's rump. What an appropriate place for him to be because he was behaving like a fool. "You heard right."

His head disappeared behind the cow, and when she realized he wasn't going to say more, the anger flared at the base of her throat. How dare he think he was going to just up and leave? Didn't he care about her family or the boarding house? They couldn't run the place without him. Didn't he care about Alice or Papa or Scully? Didn't he care about her?

The anger cracked, and her eyes stung with tears. Hadn't he spent seven days searching for her? Just last night he'd kissed her. Twice. Hadn't he told her he loved her? And now he was leaving?

Jessie swiped the tears from her eyes and let herself get good and angry. So what if he'd been fired by the London Mining and Ore Company. That didn't mean he had to leave her. That didn't mean anything had to change.

She marched to the other side of Lily Bell and kicked at James' milking stool. The stool didn't budge and neither did he, and he didn't even seem to notice. He just kept his head down and went right on milking, like she didn't even exist. Like he didn't care that he was breaking her heart. She wasn't about to put up with that. "Talk to me, James. Right now. Look at me and explain yourself. You can't hide behind Lily Bell forever."

"I can't stay here either," he said, without even a glance in her direction.

"Why not?"

"The company has cut me off. I don't have the money." He stood and set the bucket of milk on the

Jessie and James

back porch and knocked on the door. That was Alice's signal to come and get it. He untied Lily Bell from the post and walked her out to the orchard.

Jessie followed him because he was going to hear what she had to say, like it or not. "Who cares about the money? As far as I'm concerned, you can stay at the boarding house forever without paying us one more cent. Papa and Alice would be happy to let you stay. Your help is worth more than your board."

"I would never consider taking charity."

"It's not charity."

"Miss Jessie, that's exactly what it would be. I wouldn't be any kind of man if I lived off the kindness of your family." He slapped Lily Bell's rump to send her off then walked toward the house as if there was a fire.

She had to jog to keep up with his long stride. "There's still a chance the London Mining and Ore Company will hire you again once they know you've recovered the money."

He shook his head. "They've instructed me to send the money to Salt Lake City."

"Oh," Jessie said, her heart sinking.

He looked at her, his eyes filling with pain so profound, Jessie almost cried in sympathy. "Scully invited me to sleep in the stables with him until I earn enough money working the mines to buy my own tent."

"The mines?"

He reached out and smoothed his hand down her cheek. "The thought of not being near you is unbearable, but if I stay in Eureka, that means working the mines to support myself. I'm not afraid of the work, but I won't be good enough for you."

"You're already good enough. Better than good enough," Jessie said, dread growing like mold in her chest. Jessie didn't want James working the mines. It was grueling, unforgiving, dangerous work that wore down even the best of men.

"I'd barely make enough to get by, certainly not enough to give you the life you deserve. My father would be so ashamed, he'd probably pretend he doesn't have another son. Maybe he'd tell people I'm dead. That would be easier on him." He sat down on the porch step where they'd lingered many nights gazing at the stars. "I can't stay, Jessie. Maybe it's my pride, but I want to be someone my father can be proud of. I want to be someone you can be proud of."

"Me? What does that matter?"

"You know very well why it matters." He took her hand and pulled her to sit on the step. "I love you, Jessie. I want to be worthy of your love."

"You are worthy."

"No, I'm not. Not without an income or a home or a penny to my name." His voice cracked, and he fell silent.

Jessie had never seen any man so broken, as if

his life was over before it had even begun. Her heart hurt for him. She patted the little jar in her apron pocket and weighed her choices, but faced with losing James, her choice was as easy as falling down. She pulled the jar of gold flecks out of her pocket. "Alice says you found this in our water."

His brows rose in surprise. "I pulled it out of the well when I watered the trees."

"Why didn't you tell me?"

"Because I knew you'd think I was only interested in you for the gold on your land." He reached out and took a strand of her hair between his fingers. "The gold is the least reason I'm interested in you, Miss Jessie."

The way he looked at her sent a thrill of pleasure tripping down her spine. "How much gold is on our land?"

His expression was guarded. "Hard to tell. But from all indications, it's a rich vein, even better than what's on the Frenchman's claim."

She handed him the jar. "Then it's yours."

"What do you mean?"

She couldn't look at him for fear the pain in her eyes would betray her. "I want you to mine our claim. If there's as much gold as you think, we'll all be rich. You'll make your father proud." Her voice cracked. "And you won't have to leave."

James rolled the jar around in his hand. "The last thing you want on your property is a mine," he said softly. "You've told me so yourself, dozens of times."

"Losing you would be worse," she said, with great effort. Maybe it made her weak to say so, but raw honesty was all she had left to convince him. And she had to convince him. Losing him would break her.

He gazed at the jar as if it held the answer to every secret he'd ever wanted to know. "Miss Jessie, you love this farm. You love your house and your cow and your little flock of chickens. And your cherry trees. A mine might make you rich, but it would ruin the pretty little place you have here." He gave her a soft smile and shook the jar lightly. "And you know it."

"I don't…I couldn't bear it if you left." There. She'd said it. Let him laugh or poke fun or pity her for being so sentimental. She just had to convince him to stay, even if it meant giving up the peaceful, wonderful life they'd built here.

His gaze could have melted snow in January. He stood up and pulled her to her feet then wrapped his strong arms around her and kissed her as if nothing else mattered in the whole world. She was breathless when he pulled away. "You hate mining. You hate miners and prospectors and gold fever. You threaten claim jumpers with your gun, and you tore down the last headframe that was here."

"But I love you more," she said, and she didn't even flinch. As hard as it was to admit to any weakness like love, it was harder to think about life without James.

Jessie and James

He turned his face to the sky and laughed. "Do you know how long I've waited to hear that?"

"You would have been waiting a lot longer if you hadn't threatened to leave. I do irrational things when I'm desperate."

He kissed her, more slowly this time. She thought she might faint, and she wasn't the fainting type. "Oh, Jessie, I love you for offering to sacrifice your home and your farm for me. But you love this place. I wouldn't ruin it for any amount of money."

"But you'll leave otherwise."

"When I've made something of myself, I'll come back. Then I'll be truly worthy of you."

She swallowed past the lump in her throat. "I don't know why you think you're not worthy. There isn't a girl in all the Western territories who wouldn't marry you right now."

The look he gave her made her giddy. "It's you I want to marry, Jessie."

Her heart skipped a beat. "You do?"

"Oh, yes. More than anything. But I have to be able to look myself in the mirror. I have to know I can give you a good life. I have to know I am worthy of you."

She pulled away from him and rolled her eyes. "Enough with this worthy talk. I point my gun at people and let you do all my chores. I'm the one who's not worthy."

He chuckled. "Miss Jessie, I love you, and I promise that one day, I'll be worthy to make you my wife." Before she could protest, he took her in his arms and kissed her again. There was no way to argue with that.

They both started as the chicken feed pan that hung on the coop fence clattered to the ground and rolled about eight feet away. Jessie's gaze flew to the fence. Someone ducked behind the corner of the house.

"It's no good sneaking," James called. "We saw you."

Jessie gasped as Denny Waller crept around the corner of the house, looking as disheveled and grubby as ever, with a feral, panicked spark in his eyes.

He didn't seem especially threatening, at least not to Jessie, but James quickly pushed Jessie behind him and squared his shoulders. "You need something, mister?" He obviously didn't recognize Denny as the boy who'd captured Jessie last week or he probably would have started swinging.

Denny took off his hat and wrung it in his fists. "I need to talk to Miss Jessie."

"She isn't taking visitors right now," James said, which seemed a little silly, especially since Jessie was standing right behind him.

Jessie shoved James aside as forcefully as she could. It wasn't easy. He was as immovable as a tree stump when he put his mind to it. "Denny," she said. "How did you find me?"

Denny's eyes darted in James' direction.

"They give me directions at the land office."

James' eyes suddenly got as round as saucers. "You're one of them who kidnapped Jessie, aren't you?"

Denny wrung his hat beyond recognition and nodded. "We didn't never mean to do it. You was supposed to be by yourself."

James lashed out, grabbed Denny's collar, and yanked him forward. Denny squeaked in distress.

"Stop that," Jessie yelled. "Stop it, James. You'll hurt him."

"He should have thought of that before he kidnapped you," James growled.

"James, let go of him now." She said it with just enough schoolteacher authority to get his attention.

He hesitated for a moment then released Denny and shoved him backward. "Miss Jessie, I can't understand you."

Jessie raised an eyebrow. "Well, whose fault is that?"

He scowled at her, but she sensed frustration instead of the desire to murder anyone.

"James, this is Denny, and he's only fifteen years old. He's not going to hurt you."

James simply grunted and folded his arms across his wide chest.

Jessie tried to ignore his bad attitude. She reached out and smoothed a lock of hair from Denny's face. "How did you get here, Denny?"

"I ran as hard as I could until it hurt too much.

Then I walked."

Jessie tried not to think of how painful that must have been on his malformed foot. "You know it's not safe for you to be in town."

With wide eyes, Denny glanced at James and then back at Jessie. "I'm sorry to bother you, ma'am, but I didn't know where else to go. Anson's been shot."

Sixteen

It was full dark when they finally arrived at the little shack at the top of the mountain where Anson and Denny had held Jessie for seven days. They had ridden their horses as far up the mountain as they could go then tied them near a little brook halfway up the side of a hill. Then they'd hiked a treacherous trail for another two hours in the half light, and James held tight to Jessie's hand to keep her from tripping over a stone or falling off the edge of the precarious trail. It got later and later, and James had gotten madder and madder with every step. The two brothers had put Jessie's life in danger just making her walk up this trail in the first place. And they were going to get what was coming to them.

Jessie didn't know it, but she'd made a grave tactical error. She'd revealed the whereabouts of the enemy, and James wasn't going to let the opportunity pass.

When Denny had come to the boarding house, James had refused to let Jessie come up here by herself, and she'd made him promise not to hurt the brothers, but she hadn't made him promise he wouldn't send a posse tomorrow to bring them in.

Denny's limp had become more and more pronounced the farther they went up the mountain, and James had started to feel sorry for him. The poor kid was young and crippled and obviously in a great deal of pain, but he was concerned enough about his brother to keep going.

Anson and Denny lived in a shack hidden deep in the hills above Mammoth, and when they finally reached it, James didn't feel so bad for not being able to find this place. It was situated higher than he'd ever gone in his searches and so far out of the way, it was hard to believe that anyone could even survive here.

The trail came out on a flat area where sat an entrance to a mine. Denny led them past the mine up some stone steps to a small shack that looked as if it would blow over with a good stiff wind.

Jessie opened the door, and James and Denny followed after her. A dim lantern sat on a small table that looked to be the only piece of furniture in the room. James tensed when he saw a boy, not much older than Denny, lying on the floor pointing a six-shooter at Jessie. James roughly grabbed Jessie's elbow and dragged her behind him.

"Anson, it's me. Don't shoot," Jessie said. James tried to corral her behind him, but she pushed her way around him and knelt down on the floor next to Anson.

Anson let out a great sigh and lowered the gun to the floor. "Denny, what did you go and do that for?"

"I don't want you to die, Anson. Miss Jessie's our only friend. She can help."

These boys were in a bad way when their only friend was a woman they'd kidnapped not two weeks ago. James pressed his lips together. Jessie had said Denny was fifteen years old. His sister Abigail was fifteen. How would she have fared without money and without a mother?

Anson seemed to lose any fight he might have had in him. He winced, rolled onto his back, and closed his eyes, resting his head on a rolled-up blanket. "Is that the sheriff you brung with you, Miss Jessie?"

Jessie placed her hand on Anson's forehead. "Of course not. This is my friend, James Kelsey. He's here to help."

Actually, he was there to protect Jessie and shoot any boy who tried to hurt her. It was best Anson knew who he was dealing with. "I'm the one you pointed a gun at. I don't take kindly to men who kidnap women. Or men who try to kill me."

"Oh, James," Jessie said. "For goodness sake. We can talk about it later. Just keep your mouth shut, and help me." With an arch look, she reached out her hand to him. He grumbled quietly but gave her the pack of supplies they'd brought from the boarding house. He was as angry as a badger, but she was right. They could and would talk about it later. Right now, they needed to try to save a man's life.

It wasn't hard to tell where Anson had been wounded. A substantial circle of blood stained the right side of his shirt just below his ribcage, and a frayed hole showed where a single bullet had pierced his side. "Let's take a look," Jessie said, unbuttoning Anson's filthy shirt.

Anson winced when she peeled back the blood-stiff fabric from the nasty welt on his side. "There ain't no bullet left. It went right through the meat and out the other side. It stuck in the far wall of the cabin."

James was pretty sure Jessie didn't have any experience tending to gunshot wounds, or any other kind of wound for that matter, but she kept her head and acted as if Anson had a sliver in his finger rather than a hole in his side. That's what came of being so stubborn. She wasn't about to let a little blood get the better of her, and she wasn't about to frighten her patient by acting too concerned.

James swallowed hard past the lump in his throat. Jessie had every good quality a man could want in a woman. She was stubborn, headstrong, independent, and smart. She wasn't afraid to get her hands dirty and didn't mind enforcing her will with a shotgun when she had to. And it didn't hurt that she was the prettiest woman in the territories or any state in the Union.

Oh, boy, how he loved her. And someday, he'd be good enough for her.

Jessie lightly pressed her fingers around the wound crusted with dried blood. She huffed out a breath and pinned Anson with a stern look. "You didn't think to wash it?"

Anson draped his arm over his eyes. "It bleeds fresh every time I touch it."

"You've got to have more brains in your head, Anson. It's got to be washed, or you'll attract all sorts of dirt. Not to mention maggots." She turned to Denny. "I'm going to need a bucket of water."

Denny ran out the door almost before she finished her sentence.

"James," she said, "would you put more coal in the stove?"

At that moment, James would have walked through fire for Jessie. The way she talked to Anson, like she was his fierce and loyal big sister, just about made James' heart burst out of his chest. She got righteously indignant about the grungy miners that came to her father's service every Sunday, and she didn't suffer any kind of fool, but she was willing to help the boy who'd kidnapped her and treat him with kindness—even though her kindness came with exasperation and a lecture.

Anson opened his eyes. "We don't need a fire,

Miss Jessie. I'm sweating as it is."

Jessie frowned and wrapped her fingers around Anson's neck. She was checking for fever. "We need to warm up the water and a needle. But maybe we should move you to the mine. It's cooler in there, isn't it?"

Anson nodded. "Especially if you go down the ladder to the spring. But I don't think I can climb."

Jessie glanced at James, and he caught the worry in her eyes. "We'll do what we have to do to keep you from catching the fever."

James loaded coal and kindling into the stove, found a match on the shelf against the wall, and lit a fire. The shack would soon be unbearably hot. James didn't know what they'd find in the mine, but anywhere was better than a stuffy shack on top of a hill.

"All right, Anson," Jessie said. "Help me get this shirt off." With painful effort, Anson rolled to one side and then the other while Jessie eased him out of his shirt. "I think we should burn it."

"That's the only shirt I got, Miss Jessie," Anson said, trying to breath through the pain.

"You'll just have to go without one." She handed the shirt to James. "Didn't your mother teach you to always have two shirts, one for washing and one for wearing?"

"My mama taught me good, but I don't always measure up like I should."

Jessie patted his hand. "You're doing just fine.

You take good care of Denny, seeing that he's fed and clothed. Your mama would be proud."

Anson swiped his hand across his mouth. "You're wrong, Miss Jessie. There ain't much she'd be proud of."

Jessie shook her head. "Never tell a lady she's wrong. It's not good manners."

Denny came in the shack with a bucket of clear water. Where had he gotten that? These hills were so dry, the wind blew them away inch by inch every year. Denny poured half the water into a dented saucepan from the shelf, then put it on the coal stove to heat. He set the half empty bucket next to Jessie.

Jessie took a washcloth and a bar of soap from her pack. "We can wash with cold water first." She dipped the cloth into the bucket then rubbed it into the soap. Anson sucked in a harsh breath when Jessie dabbed the cloth at his wound. "Now," she said, "tell me how you got shot."

"It happened near about three days ago," Denny said.

"Three days ago?" Jessie pursed her lips and pinned Denny with a stern gaze. "It took you this long to fetch me?"

"Anson told me not to go cuz he didn't want me to get kilt. But then he got sicker, and I didn't want him to die."

Jessie sighed. "Three days ago. Tell me what happened."

Anson hissed when she pressed too hard. "He

came all the way up to get his money."

"Who came up?" Jessie said.

"The man what hired us to steal…"

"Borrow," Denny said.

"The man what hired us to borrow that fellow's money. He came up to settle with us. I don't know how he found us. He's never been here before. When he found out we done gave you back the money, he pulled his gun. I don't think he was meaning to shoot, but Denny jumped on his back and the gun went off. He run on out of here fast, and we never seen him again."

James drew his brows together. Where was Frank Roberts, and would they ever be able to bring him to justice?

Denny lowered his eyes. "I didn't mean to make him shoot. I thought he was going to kill you."

Anson winced in pain. "You done the right thing, Denny. It just didn't turn out right."

James studied Anson's face and saw him a little differently than he had just moments before. Anson was trying to make his brother feel better about something that was Denny's fault. How many brothers would be so kind? By the light of the lantern, Anson looked younger than he probably was. Younger and more vulnerable. It was what Jessie had seen, even if James hadn't wanted to believe it.

Jessie rinsed out her cloth in the bucket. "We think the man who shot you is Frank Roberts. The money you stole from James—"

"Borrowed," Denny said.

James' throat constricted. "Oh, you stole it all right."

Danny frowned. "We gave it back."

"Your brother put a gun to my head. You stole it."

Jessie raised her hand. "We are not going to talk about this right now. I won't have you upsetting Anson."

Anson's arm was draped over his eyes. "I ain't upset, but it's a good bet I'm going to pass out."

"Take deep breaths," Jessie said. "And I'll give you a cold rag to put on your forehead."

After Jessie washed and rinsed Anson's wound with warm water, she sewed up the hole, both front and back, with a needle and thread. Anson flinched and hissed, but he stayed conscious and didn't complain. It was obvious to James that Jessie was uncomfortable with a needle in her hand, but she stitched Anson up as if she was a trained doctor, and probably nobody looking would be able to tell the difference.

When she finished wrapping the wound with a bandage from her pack, the water was red with blood and Anson was shivering violently. Jessie's face was flushed, and James had sweat trickling down his neck. James helped Anson sit up, and Jessie gave him some water. "When is the last time you ate anything?" she said.

"I ain't ate nothing since I been shot."

Jessie grunted in exasperation. "It's a good thing I got here, or you'd die from being stupid."

"It hurts too much to eat."

She wiped her sleeve across her forehead. "We've got to get you out of here. Down to the mine where it's cool." She reached into the pack and pulled out a loaf of Alice's good bread and four eggs that she'd wrapped in paper. James widened his eyes. He hadn't seen her pack those. She glanced at him. "These boys live off hardtack and jerky. I knew they'd need something to eat." She rubbed her hand up and down Anson's arm. "I'm going to have James and Denny help you down into the mine where it's cool. Do you think you can climb down the ladder?"

Anson nodded. "I think I ain't got no choice."

"You're right."

James and Denny knelt on either side of Anson and hooked his arms around their necks. He groaned as James lifted his right arm, but there was no way to avoid the painful task. They rose at the same time Anson anchored his feet against the stone floor and pushed to standing. Anson suddenly went limp and his eyes rolled back into his head. James caught him around the chest and lowered him to the floor.

Jessie grabbed the tin cup of water and held it to his lips. "Anson, wake up."

Anson opened his eyes. "I ain't feeling too good."

Jessie tipped the cup and forced it between his

lips. "Drink," she said. He did as he was told, even though he didn't have all his wits about him. "I can see I got here just in time. I don't think you should try climbing down the ladder tonight, but I'm going to have Denny and James take you outside. It's too hot in the cabin, and I need the fire going. You can sleep under the stars."

"Okay," James said, grabbing Anson's arm. "Let's try this again."

Anson tried to shrug away from him. "Ain't no use. I'll pass out again." He pressed his palm to his forehead. "I'll crawl."

"Crawl?"

"Yeah. Get out of the way, and I'll crawl out the door. That's what I done when I had the fever last spring."

"I won't drop you," James said.

Anson raised his head and eyed James. "Maybe. But I'm going to crawl."

"Try it."

With a lot of groaning and grunting, Anson rolled to his hands and knees and slowly, painfully crawled to the door. James had to admit it was a good plan. Crawling wouldn't pop his stitches, and if he passed out again, he didn't have very far to fall. Denny jumped to open the door for him, and Anson crawled out the door and collapsed onto the stone ground. James and Denny rushed to help him, but he hadn't fainted, and he rolled onto his back without assistance.

Jessie grabbed the rolled-up blanket and

propped it under his head. "Let's just pray it doesn't rain."

Anson opened his eyes. "The sky's clear."

"At least it's cooler out here." Jessie propped her hands on her hips. "I'm going to fry some eggs, and we need more water. Anson needs to drink a gallon before daylight." She gave Anson one last look-over then ducked back into the shack.

"I'll fetch more water," Denny said.

James peered at Anson, who was in obvious pain but holding his own. "Mind if I come with you? Because if you aren't conjuring up water by magic, I'm mighty curious to know where it's coming from."

Denny grinned. "We got our very own spring. Ain't nobody knows about it but us. We discovered it."

Anson's eyes flew open, and he found enough strength to prop himself on his elbow. "You're not allowed down there, mister."

James tried not to react with hostility. "You need water, and I'm going to help Denny."

"It will be all right, Anson," Denny said. "He just wants to help."

Anson was breathing heavily, but he didn't back down. "He doesn't want to help. He wants to jump our claim."

James narrowed his eyes. "You kidnapped Jessie. You don't have any right to tell me what I can and cannot do."

"And you don't have any right to steal our

claim."

James bit his tongue on the reply that he could take whatever he wanted and Anson didn't have the power to stop him. "I don't want your claim, Anson."

"James wouldn't steal a penny," Jessie called from inside.

He nodded. "I wouldn't steal a penny, and I'm not going to steal your claim. I just want to see the water."

Anson glared at him. "Then swear to me."

"What?"

"Denny, go get the Bible." Denny raced into the shack once again and returned with a big black Bible. He set it in front of Anson who motioned for James to kneel next to him.

James didn't very much like the idea of making an oath to Anson, but if he didn't, Anson would probably try to stop him from going into the mine. It could get ugly. James put his hand on the Bible. "I swear and promise I won't steal your claim. Ever."

Drained of energy, Anson lay back, crossed his arms over his chest, and closed his eyes. "That's good enough then."

James couldn't help but be impressed. Anson was a robber and a kidnapper and a ruffian, but he was also a believer. It made no sense.

Denny knelt next to Anson. "It's going to be okay, Anson. We got to get you some water. You got to drink."

"Don't you start bossing me around. Miss Jessie is bad enough."

"I heard that," Jessie said from inside the shack.

Denny went inside and came out with the bucket of dirty water and a wooden pitcher. He tossed the dirty water into the juniper bushes and handed the bucket to James. "Come on then," he said, obviously thrilled to show James their very own spring. He led the way down the stone steps. James stepped carefully. It was dark, and the steps were anything but even. They came to the door James had seen when they first arrived.

"Is this your mine or one someone else abandoned?" he asked.

Denny opened the door, pulled a lantern off a hook inside, and lit it. "Oh, this here's our very own mine. It was my mama's claim till she died, then me and Anson got it. We dug every last inch of it ourselves." He held the lantern up to illuminate a single tunnel that angled slightly downward for about twenty feet then stopped at a shaft that likely went straight down. "We ain't got real far in our digging, but we hit a vein, and the silver is enough to feed us and keep us warm in the winter."

"Silver?" James said. "You found silver down here?"

Denny lifted the lantern higher. "Have a look." They went to the edge of the shaft, and Denny lowered his light so James could see the

Jessie and James

ladder. "I reckon I should go first with the light so's you don't fall."

With the bucket and the pitcher in one hand, Denny climbed down the ladder like a mountain goat. He'd probably done it thousands of times. James' nerves were on edge. He was a mining geologist, so he didn't mind small spaces or the darkness, but if Denny wanted to hit him over the head and dispose of his body, this was the place to do it. Of course, James had at least eighty pounds on the boy, and he was a trained fighter, but it was best to be vigilant.

Denny held the lantern high above his head so James could see where he was going. He came down on solid rock, which he expected, but he didn't expect the sound of dripping water that met his ears.

Denny handed James the lantern, pulled a match from his pocket, and lit a second lantern that hung on a spike in the wall. James gasped as the combined brightness of both lights illuminated a pool of clear water not four feet from where James was standing. Water dripped from half a dozen stalactites hanging from the ceiling into the pool. It was a pleasing and continuous symphony of drips, drops, and plops.

"This isn't a mine," James said. "It's a cave."

Denny nodded. "We dug down ten feet, then the whole ceiling just caved in and opened up here." He pointed to the right, which by James' calculations, led deeper into the mountain. "Then we started three tunnels down that way, but we're mostly working on the middle one cuz that's where we found silver."

James lifted his lantern. Three beginnings to tunnels stood too close to each other on the far side of the cave. Anson and Denny obviously didn't know anything about mining. "You can't dig tunnels willy-nilly like that or the whole thing will cave in on you."

Denny frowned. "How do you know?"

"I'm a geologist."

"What's a geologist?"

"I've gone to school to learn about mining and minerals. The London Mining and Ore Company sent me out here to set up a mining operation. If you dig all three of those tunnels as they are now, the rock won't be able to support what's above."

Denny eyed James doubtfully. "Okay. I'll tell Anson. Do you want to see our silver?"

James didn't especially want to go down any of the questionable tunnels, but they'd held up so far. They weren't likely to collapse in the next thirty minutes. "Lead the way," he said.

Denny led James down the middle tunnel, but it was a short walk. The tunnel ended not ten feet from the entrance. It was a lot of work digging through solid rock. Denny raised his lantern and pointed to the ceiling. "We got plenty of silver to last us for a year or two. Then we'll just dig out more rock."

James' heart leaped into his throat. A

glistening vein of silver ran from the ceiling to the floor of the tunnel then forked horizontally in three separate places like tributaries of a river. He held the lantern closer. The silver glistened like stars in a galaxy. He'd never seen anything so beautiful.

It was the most silver he'd ever seen in one place at a time.

The brothers didn't know it, but they were sitting on a fortune.

Seventeen

James was going to miss George Madsen's sermons. They were inspiring and sincere and not too long. The best preachers were always brief. After they'd sung "Rock of Ages" accompanied by Alice on her concertina, George pulled his chair forward to give the last sermon James would hear for what could be many months. He wasn't sure how long he'd be in Colorado. It might take him years to recover his reputation and make himself worthy of Jessie's love. He was determined to give her the life and the man she deserved.

George sat up in his chair and tapped his cane on the floor. "Today, it is with heavy heart that we say goodbye to our dear friend James Kelsey."

There was a bit of a stir in the dining room as the congregants put their heads together and whispered or craned their necks to look in James' direction. "Is he dead?" asked one of the miners.

Jessie and James

Campbell Tomlinson laughed out loud. "He's in the back there, fit as a fiddle." Every head turned to look at James. Two ladies twittered their amusement.

"He's not dead," George said, glancing at James and smiling. "That did sound like a funeral, didn't it? James will be leaving for Denver on Thursday."

The congregation laughed, but James couldn't find any humor in it. He felt as if he were dead, or at least going to die very young. He tilted his head to look at Jessie. She was sitting right up front, her arms folded, an angry pout on her lips. She was furious with him for leaving, but he couldn't see any other way. He loved her more than ever for offering to let him mine her claim, but he also loved her too much to ever take it from her. He would never let her make such a sacrifice for him. But he couldn't convince her that he was right. Needless to say, she was not going to give him a friendly send off when he rode out of town. She might never speak to him again.

I'll be back soon, my darling. Please wait for me.

They had stayed with Anson and Denny for three days until Jessie had been sure that Anson wouldn't die from neglect or foolishness. It had actually been three of the most glorious days of James' life. For two of those days, he'd spent almost every waking hour with Jessie, helping her with chores, watching her care for Anson and Denny, observing her kindness and compassion for two strangers who had treated her very badly. Just being in her presence was a healing balm to James' soul and obviously to Anson and Denny's too. Jessie was kind and bossy and unyielding when she thought herself to be right. The boys needed her firm hand and stubborn determination.

On the second day of their stay at Anson and Denny's shack, it had been obvious that the boys weren't going to make it into town for supplies anytime soon, and Jessie needed more to eat than biscuits and jerky. James had taken Jessie's shotgun and killed a wild turkey. Then he'd gone down into town and bought a chicken so they'd have a continuous supply of eggs, a bag of carrots, ten pounds of potatoes, and a few other supplies to tide them over. It had been no picnic getting everything back to the shack. No wonder the boys didn't venture into town very often.

James knew right where Anson and Denny's hideout was and exactly how to get there, but he had abandoned his plan to have the boys arrested. Like Jessie had said, they were young and not without hope of reformation, but he wouldn't turn them in mostly because Jessie would never forgive him if he did. And he'd do almost anything to make Jessie happy.

Except stay in Eureka.

The night after Jessie and James had returned to Eureka from the Waller brothers' place, Frank Roberts had come limping into town, dirty,

Jessie and James

hungry, and a bit disoriented. After shooting Anson, he had gotten lost on his way back down the trail and had spent a week wandering the hills, living off sego lily bulbs and the two rabbits he'd been able to shoot. James and Jessie had paid him a visit that very night, and James had slammed Frank against the wall and threatened him with all sorts of violence.

Unfortunately, Frank had been unrepentant. In fact, he'd laughed right in James' face, taking great pleasure in James' anger. Frank was sure he'd find investors for the mine he intended to put on the Frenchman's claim. He was as happy as a clam. Frank may have hired Anson and Denny to steal James' money, but they never actually gave him the money, and there was no proof tying him to the kidnapping unless Anson and Denny testified against him.

But if Anson and Denny testified, they'd go to prison, and Frank might very well go free anyway. It was incredibly frustrating, but there was nothing Jessie or James could do if they wanted to keep the Waller boys out of trouble. And helping Denny and Anson was more important to Jessie than getting revenge on Frank Roberts.

So James had socked Frank hard right between the eyes, giving him a bloody nose and, eventually, two shiners to remember him by. Frank had hurt Jessie and James in too many ways to count, but short of putting a bullet through his chest, there wasn't much James could do to exact recompense.

He wasn't going to hang for killing a snake like Frank. The revenge just wasn't worth forfeiting his life.

Frank would go free, work the mine that should have been the London Mining and Ore Company's, and grow obscenely rich by being a scoundrel. It wasn't fair or just or right, and James hated that sometimes life worked out that way.

James didn't bother singing the closing hymn. He just stared at Jessie, trying to drink in her features and memorize her face for the lonely days ahead. He wanted to stay so badly his bones ached. But he loved Jessie more, and whether she realized it or not, he was making the sacrifice for her.

After the last prayer, Jessie ducked into the kitchen before James could even catch her eye. She was mad at him, and she wasn't about to give him the chance to soften her up or try to convince her that he was right. James was about to follow her and make her see reason when Alice laid a hand on his arm. "You don't have to go, you know."

"Miss Alice, I hate to contradict a lady, but if I want to count as any sort of man, I have to go."

Alice made a face. "Oh, posh. Don't give me any nonsense about your manhood. You've proved your manhood time and time again. You've got nothing to prove to any of us, least of all Jessie." She pressed her lips together and huffed out a breath. "It's pride, pure and simple."

He didn't agree with her assessment of his

character, but he didn't argue with her either. Alice was fiercely loyal to Jessie, and that thought gave him great comfort. They would take care of each other until he returned. "I suppose it is pride, ma'am. But I still have to go."

Her eyes pooled with tears. "I fear you'll never come back, Mr. Kelsey, and I don't know what that would do to my Jessie. It seems awfully cruel, if you ask me."

"I assure you, Miss Alice, no one is going to suffer more than I am."

"Then why don't you stay?"

It was a fair question, but one he'd answered so many times in his head that there was no need for more discussion. He didn't want to be rude, but he didn't want to talk about it either. "I think I'll go look in on Jessie and see if she needs my help."

"She needs more than your help."

James ambled into the kitchen, eager to see Jessie but reluctant to be drawn into an argument. Couldn't they just enjoy their last few days together without fighting about whether or not he should go?

Jessie stood at the sink, dutifully and insistently washing the breakfast dishes. The air was charged with emotion, and if James had lit a match, he probably would have sparked a fire. He picked up a towel, but she pulled the clean plate out of the water and dried it herself as if he wasn't in the room, as if she didn't need him to help her with anything ever again.

"Why double your work?" he said. "I'm here to help."

She washed with increased fervor. "Not for much longer. I should get used to doing my own chores again."

"You might as well take advantage of my services while you have the chance."

She wouldn't look at him. "Yes, because you'll be gone soon enough." Without warning, she burst into tears even as she kept washing dishes, as if her tears were just an annoyance that weren't going to keep her from finishing her chores.

Heedless of her wet hands, he gathered her into his arms and pulled her tightly against his chest. "Hush, darling. It's going to be all right."

She snapped her head up to look at him, and fire flashed in her eyes. "How dare you tell me that? How dare you be all smug and noble, knowing full well I'm not going to be all right?" She balled her wet hands into fists and pounded on his chest. And he'd just washed that shirt. "Your words mean nothing, and your promises are meaningless."

"That's not true, Jessie. I love you."

She narrowed her eyes and stopped pounding. "I'm not a fool, James. Two weeks from now, you'll have found someone prettier and sweeter in Denver. Someone who carries an umbrella instead of a shotgun and wears fancy hats with feathers and beads. In three months, you'll be relieved you got out of Eureka when you

Jessie and James

did. In six months, you'll barely remember me."

"Jessie, that isn't going to happen."

A sob escaped her lips. "I don't know why I'm so upset. It's not like I didn't know this was coming. I shouldn't have let myself fall like I did."

He tightened his arms around her, even as his heart broke for his own pain. "I thought you knew me better than that. I won't forget you. It's not possible."

"I thought I knew Reuben well too. I agreed to marry him, remember?"

It shouldn't have surprised or upset him that Jessie didn't believe his reassurances. Why should she? All she knew was that James was leaving her, and she'd made up her own reasons why—the only reasons that made sense to her, because she couldn't comprehend that someone could love her like he did.

He laid a feather-soft kiss on her forehead. "Jessie, my love, my best reason for living, I know you don't understand. I know you've been hurt before. I know you don't trust my sincerity, but I'm leaving because I love you. I won't forsake you or abandon you for another girl. And unless I'm dead, I promise to come back and marry you, if you'll still have me. If you aren't too mad to let me in the house."

Her lips twitched. "I'll be too mad. We'll have to get married in the front yard. Either that or I'll be seventy years old, and I'll be married from my deathbed."

James frowned. "Do you have so little faith in me to think it will take me fifty years?"

She pushed away from him. "I've lost all faith in you, James Kelsey. You're leaving me, and just because you say you'll come back doesn't mean you will."

"I've always been a man of my word."

"Until someone prettier comes along."

He tried to hold her again, but she pulled back and shoved her hands in the water. He wanted to growl. She was being particularly stubborn today. Hadn't he already earned her trust in a thousand different ways? The irritation bubbled up inside him before the truth hit him squarely between the eyes. Jessie's mother had left her. Reuben had taken advantage of her. Frank Roberts and half a dozen other claim jumpers wanted her land. Jessie didn't believe she deserved James' love. She thought that the minute he met another girl, *any* other girl, he'd drop her like a hot potato. It wasn't that she didn't trust James. It was that she didn't understand her own exquisite value. That was the most painful thought of all.

"Will you walk outside with me for a minute?" he said.

"I've got to finish these dishes."

"The dishes can wait. I've got to show you something."

She scowled. "What if I don't want to see it?"

"Come anyway. It's the least you can do for the man who punched Frank Roberts in the nose."

Jessie and James

She didn't even flinch, determined not to let him behind that wall of hers. She wiped her hands on a towel and walked out the back door without waiting to see if he followed. "Let's get this over with," she said, which was as much encouragement as he was going to get.

He stepped out onto the back porch, took her hand without asking permission, and pulled her down the step. He pointed to the nearest cherry tree, which was brimming with ripe, red cherries. Hopefully, he'd get a chance to pick them before he left for Colorado. "We have hundreds of cherry trees in Massachusetts, but none are more beautiful than these ones standing in your backyard. In fact, these are the most beautiful cherry trees I've ever seen."

He tugged her arm and pulled her into his embrace. "Jessie," he said, "I've been to too many parties and events to count. I've seen girls in fancy dresses with perfectly curled hair and stylish hats. More than once, my mother schemed to marry me off to one of her friend's daughters. I've been to Denver and Philadelphia and Salt Lake City and lots of places in between. I've met scores of pretty girls in my travels, but none of them compare to you. I could go another twenty-seven years and never meet another girl who makes me feel like you do. You're the girl I want to spend the rest of my life with, the one who makes me irritated and happy and crazy all at the same time. I don't want another girl, Jessie. I'm not looking for something other than what I've found right here. You're feisty and temperamental and know how to use a shotgun. Why would I ever look for someone else? In fact, you've ruined all other women for me. After meeting you, none of them will ever be good enough. Why won't you believe that?" He kissed her with aching gentleness and felt the tears running down her face. He couldn't bear the thought that he was responsible for those tears.

"I don't want you to leave," she said, her voice a wisp of a breath against his neck.

"I have no right to ask, but will you wait for me?"

"Don't you dare keep me waiting too long, James Kelsey."

"Not a minute longer than I can bear."

She pressed her fist into his chest. "Oh, how I hate you right now."

"I don't like you very much either seeing as you're going to give me a bruise."

She rolled her eyes. "Don't tease me, or I'll pull out my shotgun and show you how mad I really am."

"As long as you'll wait for me, you can be as mad as you want."

Eighteen

On Wednesday night after dinner, Alice asked James to favor everybody with an informal concert since he'd be leaving the next day for Salt Lake City to return the London Mining and Ore Company's money and then on to Denver to start his new job.

Jessie's anger was a simmer instead of a boil, and she'd been able to at least be civil to James since Sunday. She had pretended to make peace about his leaving because it made him unhappy to see her upset. Pretending not to be devastated was the last gift she could give him.

James sang five or six songs then asked everyone to join in on several more songs that everybody knew. Besides Alice and Jessie, they were a house full of men since Ann Whitlock and her children had moved on to California. There was Papa, of course, and James, Campbell

Tomlinson, the three miners who rented the middle room, and Aden and Willis Spackman, father and son who were in the area looking into cattle grazing rights.

The group finished singing, "Home on the Range," and Alice passed a plate of cookies around. "James, I don't want to impose, but could you sing one more for us? We won't have the pleasure of hearing you sing for a long time."

"Anything for you, Miss Alice," James said, as charming as ever, even if it wasn't true. He said he'd do anything for Alice, but he wouldn't stay in Eureka.

And yet Jessie believed deep in her heart he'd come back because James truly was a man of his word. It was one of the reasons she loved him so desperately and was so desperately sad that he was leaving. How could she bear his absence? How could he truly love her and still want to be apart?

But she understood that too. James couldn't live with himself unless he thought he was worthy, unless he proved himself to his father and to himself. He would never take the easy road, and he would never settle for being less than the man he wanted to be. It was irritating and inspiring at the same time.

"What would you like me to sing, Miss Alice?"

"Oh, I don't know. You pick. You know more songs than I've ever heard of."

Jessie and James

James glanced at Jessie, smiled at Alice, and began to sing. "God be with you till we meet again. By His counsels guide uphold you. With His sheep securely fold you. God be with you till we meet again. Till we meet, till we meet. Till we meet at Jesus' feet. Till we meet, till we meet. God be with you till we meet again."

It was a good thing Jessie had determined to never, ever cry again, because that song would have sent her into hysterics only a few days ago. James' voice was low and beautiful, like the wind blowing through the cherry trees in her orchard or water tripping down the rocks in the river. At times like these, she wished she didn't love the sound of it so much.

Alice wiped tears from her eyes, as did most everyone else in the room. The men stood and shook James' hand in turn then went upstairs to retire for the evening. Jessie should have gone to bed too, but she wanted to savor every last minute she had with James. The time was so precious.

Alice grasped James' hand warmly. "Thank you for singing. Thank you for everything. I'll never forget all you've done for us."

"My pleasure, Miss Alice. Thank you for your cooking, your kindness, and your very good advice. God willing, we will see each other very soon."

"Yes, indeed," Alice said.

Papa gave James a strong handshake then strolled into the kitchen after Alice. Jessie and

James were alone in the great room. She folded her arms and cocked her eyebrow at him. "That last one was a funeral song."

He huffed in mock protest. "Not necessarily. It's more like a farewell song."

"It's a funeral song, and it better not bring either of us bad luck."

He pulled her into his arms. "It won't. We've both had our fair share of bad luck. There are only good things ahead."

"What a ridiculous thing to say when you're about to leave for who knows how long."

He laughed. "That's what I like about you. You always look on the bright side."

The boarding house door squeaked open, and a big man with a long, scraggly beard stepped into the dining room. James moved himself between Jessie and the stranger, though he probably didn't even realize he was doing it. "Can I help you?"

A thin layer of dust covered the man's face, and he was in sore need of a laundry. He wore a short-sleeve brown shirt open at the collar, revealing his bulging arms and thick neck. He was bigger than James, but James' body looked more like a sculptor had chiseled it out of stone, where this man was stockier and burly. "I'm looking for Mr. James Kelsey. They told me he's a staying here."

James squared his shoulders, as if expecting trouble. "I'm James Kelsey."

Holding a frown firmly in place, the man

Jessie and James

stepped forward and shook James' hand. "Alistair Simmons is the name. They say you know the Frenchman."

Jessie moved out from behind James because it was hard being a part of the conversation cowering behind James' wide shoulders.

Mr. Simmons took off his hat. "Ma'am."

"Do you mean Jean-Pierre Bonheur?" James said. "That Frenchman?"

His eyes lit up. "That's the one. Do you know where I can find him?"

"I'm sorry. I don't. He left town not four weeks ago. Said he was going to California."

Mr. Simmons scowled and let out a string of curse words. He glanced at Jessie. "Sorry, ma'am. I thought I had him this time, but he's as slippery as a snake." He eyed James. "You didn't buy anything from him, did you?"

"I was going to buy his claim in Mammoth, but the money got stolen, and he sold it right out from under me."

Mr. Simmons raised his eyebrows. "Well, mister, you may think that was a misfortune, but I'm telling you right now, you saved yerself from getting fleeced."

"Fleeced?"

"Last fall, the Frenchman sold me a claim in Idaho. It had veins of gold coming right out of the ground."

Jessie's gazed flicked to James' face. That was just how he'd described the Frenchman's claim.

Mr. Simmons swiped his hand across his mouth. "It turns out, the Frenchman salted the whole claim. It wasn't worth the ground it was sitting on."

James' frown could have been carved into his face. "He salted it?"

"What does that mean?" Jessie said.

Mr. Simmons nodded in Jessie's direction. "He bought a wagon load of high grade ore and spread it all over his claim. Then he took a shotgun, loaded the charge with gold dust, and blasted it onto the rock, making it seem like there was gold when there wasn't. I bought that claim for five hundred dollars, and it ain't worth a plug nickel."

The lines on James' face deepened. "That's what he did. He tried to sell me a salted claim. That's why he was in such a hurry to get out of town. He knew I'd find out when we started digging."

"I lost everything," Mr. Simmons said. "I'll make the Frenchman pay if it's the last thing I do."

James hung his head. "I should have known. I should have seen it. That gold on those rocks could only have been put there by a shotgun. I'm such a fool."

"Don't be too hard on yourself, mister. Them shysters are clever. There was a mining engineer in Boise they fooled with one gold nugget. You ain't the first, and you won't be the last. It's good news you didn't pay him any money."

A smile slowly grew on James' lips. "No, I

didn't."

Mr. Simmons returned his hat to his head. "I don't know that I can chase Mr. Bonheur all the way to California without more information. If you think of anything else, I'm staying at the hotel until tomorrow morning."

"I'm leaving in the morning as well," James said, sending a shard of glass right into Jessie's heart. She'd almost forgotten. "You riding up Salt Lake way? I'd be glad for the company."

Mr. Simmons nodded. "Yes, I am. At seven a.m."

"I'll pick you up on my way out of town."

They shook hands, and Mr. Simmons ambled out the door, with considerably less energy than he'd walked in with.

Jessie slumped her shoulders. "At least you won't have to go all that way by yourself. Just don't let him know you've got a thousand dollars in your saddle bag."

"I'm wrapping it under my shirt. I won't be so unfortunate as to have it stolen again."

Suddenly, Jessie couldn't contain a smile. "Maybe you're not as unlucky as you think."

They looked at each other, and both of them burst into laughter. James laughed so hard he no doubt disturbed the boarders who were trying to go to sleep. "I shouldn't laugh at another man's expense, but I can't help but think this is just what Frank Roberts deserves."

"Of course it is. If there ever was a blessing in

disguise, this is it."

James wrapped his arms around Jessie's waist. "Can you imagine how much worse things would have been for me and the company if I'd spent all that money and had nothing to show for it?"

"God truly does work in mysterious ways."

"Yes, He does."

They both jumped when someone tapped on the front window. The lanterns were lit inside so Jessie couldn't see anything outside. She went to press her face against the glass, but James held her back. "I'll look." He cupped his hands around his eyes, gazed out into the darkness, and groaned. "It's our favorite kidnappers."

Jessie's heart skipped a beat. "Anson and Denny?"

James nodded.

What were they doing here? Was Anson getting worse? Did they need more food?

James opened the door and stepped outside. "Stop lurking under people's windows and come in."

Jessie giggled. James still didn't know how he felt about Anson and Denny, but he didn't seem inclined to kill them or turn them in, so she wasn't worried.

Denny came in first, eyes wide and curious, followed by Anson who walked under his own power even though he favored his right side. It looked as if his recovery was coming along well enough. He wore the shirt James had bought for him when James had come to town to get supplies. It was the cleanest part of Anson's appearance. Anson gave James a furtive glance. "We don't want no trouble."

"Then you should stop spying in people's windows," James said.

Denny frowned. "We wasn't spying. We didn't dare knock on the door cuz we was afraid that big fellow was the sheriff."

Anson pressed his hand to his side and winced. Jessie pulled a chair out from the nearest table. "Sit down before you fall over. Didn't I tell you to stay in bed another week at least?"

Anson sat down and grimaced in pain. "We got something important to tell you."

"Couldn't it wait?" Jessie said, clucking and putting her hand on Anson's forehead. "At least there's no fever." She sighed and pinned Anson with a stern look. "What is so important that it couldn't wait?"

Denny pulled up a chair and sat next to Anson. "Frank Roberts came back to our place last night with two black eyes and a nose double the size of what it used to be."

Jessie grinned at James before setting her mind on more serious matters. "Did he hurt you?"

"No," Anson said. "Denny caught him sneaking just beyond the trees. He was taking a look at our claim, no doubt about it."

Denny nodded eagerly. "Anson says Frank

wants to steal our claim and run us off. He's not a good man, and we ain't smart enough to figure out what he's got planned."

Jessie pressed her lips together. She knew plenty about Frank sneaking around people's property. "Frank is getting ready to dig another mine, though it's not rich like he thinks it is. Maybe digging one mine will keep him busy enough that he won't think about stealing yours."

"Maybe," Anson said. "But he's a sly one, and we're worried."

Denny tapped his palm on the table. "What if he shoots Anson again?"

Jessie glanced at James. "Do you think he will try to get these two arrested? If they're out of the picture, he could jump the claim, and no one would be the wiser."

James shrugged. "You never know with Frank."

She patted Anson's hand. "We'll do our best to keep an eye on him. I don't know what else we can do. We don't want to stir up any more trouble for the two of you." Jessie's heart sank. James wouldn't be here. She would have to do her best to keep an eye on Frank without James' help.

James must have realized the same thing. His eyes darkened like a gathering storm. "Stay far away from Frank Roberts, Jessie. I won't have you putting yourself in danger, not even for Anson and Denny."

"We don't want that neither," Denny said.

Jessie and James

The anger pressed into Jessie's chest. "You won't be here, James. You have no say in what I do or do not decide to do."

James, it seemed, could get just as angry. "I don't care if I go halfway across the world. You're not to tussle with Frank Roberts."

Anson looked from James to Jessie and back again. "That don't matter. We've got another plan." He pointed to James. "You work for a big mining company."

James spread his feet and folded his arms, his irritation with Jessie still simmering under the surface. "Used to."

"We want you to make our mine a big operation. We'll split the profits half and half. If you get it up and running, Frank won't be able to touch it, and Denny can get his operation."

Denny nodded. "I want to learn how to read too."

Jessie's heart lurched. Would such an arrangement even be possible? James wouldn't be able to do it without a huge outlay of money, money he didn't have, but maybe money he could get.

James knit his brows together and fell silent.

Denny was more than eager to prime the pump. "We've got our own water. You said that was the best thing about our mine."

James nodded slowly. "The water is good."

Anson brightened, though he wasn't inclined to smile. "Water is very good, and you seen how much ore we got."

"Yes," James said, deep in thought. "You've got a fortune in silver up there."

Denny nudged Jessie's elbow. "I told you we was rich."

James sat down at the table with the rest of them. "But you can't even get a horse up there. Transporting ore down the mountain might be too expensive to make it worth the trouble."

Denny thought very hard about that. "I suppose so, but if you get us one of them mining carts, we can wheel the ore down the mountain one load at a time. Anson and I will do it by ourselves."

"No," James said, suddenly getting very animated. "But there might be another way." He reached over to the other table and grabbed a salt shaker. He excitedly unscrewed the lid and dumped the salt in a big pile on the table. Denny's eyes got big. Jessie had no idea what he was doing, but she hadn't seen him this worked up since he'd come up with a way to water her cherries.

James smoothed the salt with his hand and traced the shape of a mountain in the grains with his finger. "A man named John Roebling invented continuous wire rope cable that some mines in Colorado and California are using to transport ore by tram."

"What's a tram?" Denny asked.

With his finger, he traced out a square mining car connected to a line that went up the mountain.

"It's a car that hangs on a cable in the air. You could run a cable from your mine to the base of the mountain, and you wouldn't have to take the ore down the trail. It could fly overhead."

Anson studied James' salt drawing. "I think that might work."

James nodded. "I know it would work. I've seen it. It's relatively cheap and makes the transportation go ten times faster."

"So will you help us?" Anson said.

James threw up his hands. "I don't have any money, I don't even like you boys, and I'm supposed to be in Denver next week."

Anson squinted one eye as if to get a better look at James. "Is that a yes?"

James gazed at Jessie, his eyes aglow with happiness. "It looks like I'll be staying after all."

Nineteen

Jessie stepped outside and swung the empty milk bucket back and forth while humming the song James was always singing. He said it was called, "Little Jessie," but he might have changed the lyrics because he wanted to sing about her instead of some other girl named Mary or Ethel. A chilly breeze teased wisps of hair from her bun as she strolled to the milking post and tapped the bucket. Lily Bell perked up her ears and ambled toward Jessie as if she was happy to see her, even though Jessie wasn't Lily Bell's favorite person and she didn't sing while she milked.

  October was a beautiful time of year in Eureka. The fallen leaves of her cherry trees made a golden-orange blanket on the ground that glowed in the afternoon sun. The air was chilly, but crisp and tart like a red delicious apple, much nicer sleeping weather than in the middle of July, especially for James, who had suffered every weekend in the sweltering attic.

"Miss Jessie," Anson said, coming up behind her from out of nowhere and taking the bucket from her hand. "You wasn't planning on milking that cow the night before your wedding, was you?"

She grinned at him. "You're back."

"And just in the nick of time, I reckon."

Jessie's heart did a dance on her ribs. If Anson was here, it was a good bet James and his family were back too. "Where is—"

"James?" Anson said. He pressed his hand to his chest. "Why, Miss Jessie, it hurts my heart that you're always more excited to see Mr. Kelsey than you are to see me. But I won't take it too hard, what since he's your bridegroom."

"I am hoping the bridegroom isn't stuck on the mountain or you might have to take his place tomorrow."

Anson chuckled, something he'd done a lot more of in the last few weeks. "It would be my pleasure, Miss Jessie, only Mr. Kelsey would shoot me where I stand if you married me instead of him. I'd rather not give him an excuse. He's been itching to shoot me for months."

Jessie smiled. "Yes, he has."

Alice poked her head out the back door with a towel draped over her shoulder and a pair of scissors in her hand. "Anson, you're going to have to let Jessie milk the cow. I need to cut your hair so you look presentable tomorrow."

Anson groaned. "Aw, Miss Alice. I don't need a haircut. There's going to be a hundred guests. No one will notice if my hair ain't cut."

Alice propped her hand on her hip. "I'll notice, and I won't have a slouch at my daughter's wedding, especially not a member of the family."

"Cut Denny's hair first so I can milk."

"I cut Denny's hair yesterday morning, and now he looks like a fine, educated young man."

"That traitor," Anson said under his breath. He pinched his lips together in disgust. "He got one look at James' sister and lost his head. He's even cleaned out the dirt from under his fingernails."

Jessie laughed. "If you cleaned your fingernails once in a while, Clara Parker would be more inclined to look at you."

Anson grunted. "Miss Clara's a darn sight too uppity for me. I can't even read, and she can recite poems off the top of her head."

"You're learning how to read, and soon you'll be one of the richest men in town. Clara won't be so uppity after that."

Anson looked at the ground and shook his head. "I don't want no woman who only loves me for my money."

"You're right," Jessie said. "But don't worry. I'll make sure to keep the gold diggers away from you." She took back her bucket. "Go. I'll milk the cow. You know you can't argue with Alice."

Anson's mouth curled upward on one side. "She said I'm part of the family."

"Of course you are, and you must uphold the family name."

From the night she'd met them, Alice had taken Anson and Denny into her heart like they were her prodigal sons back from a far country. First she'd given them a stern lecture about the evils of kidnapping people. Then she'd sat them down and fed them the rest of the stew from dinner and every last cookie in the house. That first night, she had let them sleep on the floor in the great room. After that, while they made plans with James, the boys had stayed in the stables with Scully and taken all their meals at the boarding house. Jessie had never seen two boys enjoy food as much as Anson and Denny did, eating anything Alice cooked for them. There was nothing more satisfactory to Alice than an appreciative eater.

Jessie tied Lily Bell to the post and pulled the milking stool next to the cow. Even though she was forced to milk the cow the day before her wedding, Jessie had never been happier. She didn't know there was this much happiness to be had in a lifetime. It turned out the London Mining and Ore Company wasn't so foolish as to pass up a sure thing and a good, honest man. James had sent them a telegram the morning after Denny and Anson had offered him half their claim, and the company told James to keep the thousand dollars and use it to develop Anson and Denny's mine.

James and the boys had started pulling ore from the ground the very next day.

Anson and Denny named the mine Lady June, after their mother, and they worked it as hard as the twenty other miners they'd hired to help.

James, Anson, and Denny left Eureka on Monday mornings, stayed at the mine all week, and came home on Saturday nights to spend the Sabbath with the family. Jessie hated being away from James that many days in a row, but he'd spent his time well and successfully.

They'd erected the tram in early September, and ore was pouring from the mine like rain from a storm cloud. Digging four hundred feet farther down, they'd found another rich vein of silver and one of gold. James, Anson, Denny, and the London Mining and Ore Company were going to be very wealthy. Of course, Jessie didn't care all that much about the money except that it meant James didn't have to leave her and that she could spend the rest of her life showing him how much she loved him.

"Why is my bride-to-be milking the cow the night before her wedding?"

Jessie caught her breath. James stood on the back step, grinning like an idiot, with his sleeves rolled up clear past his elbows and his hat slightly askew on his head. Jessie jumped from the milking stool and threw herself into James' arms. He lifted her off the ground and twirled her around, laughing as if he never wanted to stop. He set her on her feet, tightened his arms around her, and kissed her like a man starved for something sweet. "Oh, Jessie," he said when he finally relaxed his grip. "I don't deserve to be this happy."

"*You* don't deserve it? I'm the one who points shotguns at people and can't make a decent cherry pie."

"I've tasted your cherry pie, and it's delicious."

"You only think it's delicious because you've been blinded by love."

He chuckled. "If this is blindness, may I never see again." His kiss made her feel so light, she might have floated off the ground for a fraction of a second. "How are plans for the wedding? Anything I can help with besides taking a bath so I don't smell bad for the wedding guests?"

Jessie lost her ability to breathe at the thought of James standing at the front of the church, freshly bathed and shaven with slightly damp hair and a boyish grin on his lips. Her heart beat an unruly rhythm. Oh, how she loved him! She loved his sense of honor, his desire to always do the right thing, his yearning to make his father proud. She loved how he frowned when he was working out a problem in his head. She loved how he smiled when he looked at her, as if she was the only woman in the world and that was enough for him. She loved that he had chosen her to be his wife. She promised herself that she would never make him regret it. He was her world, her life, her everything. He was her home.

Jessie caressed the stubble on James' face. "How did your parents and sister like the mine?"

His eyes glowed at the mention of his family. James' mother, father, and sister Abigail had arrived two days ago for the wedding, having spent more than a week and hundreds of dollars to get here to witness the happy event. It was a sure sign that James' father didn't wish James was dead and that he truly cared about his son. His father had even used the word "proud" in his last letter. James couldn't have asked for a better wedding present.

James' sister Abigail was as petite as James was solid, and she had the same yellow hair James had. Denny and Abigail were the same age, and Denny had been immediately smitten with her, pulling chairs out for her even when she didn't need to sit, giving her the last piece of cake even when she wasn't hungry, opening doors for her even when she didn't need to go out. Jessie found it incredibly endearing, even if James acted annoyed that anyone might be interested in his sister.

James' mother, Sophronia, was reserved and a little bit nervous, but she seemed ready and eager to love any woman who loved her son. Jessie could tell they were going to be friends because though Sophronia was quiet, she had an accepting and open way about her. She was happy to love Jessie because she could see how happy Jessie made James. Alice, who had a heart to love everybody, immediately took to Sophronia, welcoming her into her home and her kitchen, teaching her how to make bread and cherry tarts, because Sophronia didn't know how to cook a thing.

Jessie had been a little apprehensive to meet James' family, but her nervousness had been overshadowed by her annoyance at James' father, Marcus, for how he'd treated James over the years. But if Denny and Anson deserved a second chance, so did James' father. He'd brought his wife and youngest daughter across the country for James' wedding, and even if he was a stern, austere man, Jessie was inclined to forgive him. She'd even made some attempts to pull Marcus Kelsey into conversations, and Marcus seemed pleased that she was interested in the shipping business. Jessie smiled to herself. Anything to make James happy.

"They loved the mine, my dad especially." James squeezed her tighter. "I didn't take them all the way to the top, but I showed them the tram and our transportation system. My father thought the tram was a genius idea."

"Of course he did."

"He was even talking about investing some money in the mine."

"That should make you happy," Jessie said. "He wouldn't invest in your mine if he didn't trust your abilities."

James' smile put the sun to shame. "I suppose not."

"Where is your family now?"

"Father is in the dining room talking to Campbell about the railroad. Mother and Abigail are in the kitchen with Alice. She said something about whipping up a batch of wedding cookies. Denny is sticking to Abigail's heels like a puppy. Abigail doesn't know what to make of him."

Jessie giggled. "Denny is smitten. Abigail is a pretty little thing."

James frowned in mock annoyance. "Denny Waller is not allowed to take a shine to my sister. She's my sister, and he's a kidnapper."

"They're just children, and Denny is the sweetest boy I've ever met. He'd make any girl a fine husband, but if you're worried about it, tell him to come out and milk the cow."

"I will. He needs to quit bothering Abigail, and you shouldn't be milking the cow today of all days. I'd do it, but I really need to take a bath and do some laundry."

She nodded. "I hate to think what the wedding guests would say if you came to your own wedding smelling like a cow carcass wearing that hat and those filthy trousers."

James drew his brows together and grunted. "What's wrong with my hat?"

She giggled and kissed him. "Nothing. I love you in spite of what you look like or how you smell."

"I'm glad, because after tomorrow, you're stuck with me."

She slumped her shoulders dejectedly. "I

guess I still have time to change my mind."

"Don't even think about it. I've half a mind to sleep in front of your door tonight just to make sure you don't run off."

Jessie slung her arm around his neck and kissed him again. "I would never run off. You're the one who's going to be stuck with me. And my shotgun."

"I wouldn't have it any other way." He pointed to the north beyond Jessie's cherry trees. "In the spring, I'm going to build you a house right there."

She shook her head and pointed west. "I like it better over there."

"Too sunny. We'll cook like a pair of quails in the oven."

"Well, you can't build it to the north. You'd have to cut down at least three cherry trees."

"No, I wouldn't," James said. "There's plenty of room for a house beyond the cherry trees."

Jessie turned up her nose. "I look forward to winning that argument."

He smiled. "I think you mean you look forward to losing that argument."

"I don't plan on losing, especially not to you."

James laughed as if he was the happiest man alive. "I look forward to spending many nights out on this porch arguing with you about anything you want to argue about. I might even let you win sometimes."

She tried to give him the evil eye, but it was

kind of hard staring down the man she loved with her whole soul. "Don't do me any favors. I don't need your help to win anything. Admit it, I'm better at arguing."

"Miss Jessie, I wouldn't be any kind of man if I didn't let you win all the arguments."

She let her mouth fall open. "Where's the fun in that?"

"The fun is in seeing you get all riled up. I love the way your eyes flash when you're mad at me."

"You can plan on seeing them flash a lot when we're married. You're just too aggravating for me to keep my temper."

He tipped his hat. "I'm glad I can be of assistance."

Jessie giggled. "Assistance? For sure and certain you're going to assist me off a cliff one of these days."

James reached out and smoothed a lock of hair from Jessie's face. "But can I help with anything else tonight? I want you to have the wedding you always dreamed of."

"I will have the wedding I've always dreamed of because I'm marrying the man of my dreams. You can't do anything to help but take a bath. Alice killed four chickens this morning and is roasting a whole bag of potatoes, several ears of sweet corn, and a pan of yams. Emmaline Johns is bringing two chickens, three cakes, and four pies. Merilee Parker is in charge of the cornbread, and some of the other neighbors are bringing more food. It's going to be a feast."

"I won't be able to eat a thing," James said. "I'm not going to be able to do anything but stare at you and try to resist pulling all the pins out of your hair."

Jessie brushed her lips across his. He trembled. "Don't even think about touching my hair. I'm wearing my shotgun to the wedding."

Dear Readers,

I hope you enjoyed *Jessie and James*. I had such a wonderful time writing it.

If you liked *Jessie and James*, could you help spread the word about it? Reviews on **Amazon**, **Goodreads**, and **Bookbub** not only help us writers but help other readers find our books. Thank you so much. And please, tell your friends if you liked my book. Word of mouth is invaluable!

For updates on new releases, giveaways, and my other books, please sign up for my email newsletter at JenSpencerAuthor.com. And be sure to join my Facebook group: Jen Spencer's Ten-minute Book Club, where I do an interview every week with a sweet romantic fiction author. You might just discover a new favorite author!

Also be sure to stop by my Facebook page and

check out all the news and posts there. I have a great group of readers, and we have a lot of fun!

Thank you for being such amazing readers and fans. I wouldn't be where I am without you!

Jen Spencer

Books by Jen Spencer

Dandelion Meadows Series
Dandelion Meadows (coming 2022)

The Cowboys of Butterfly Ranch
Jessie and James
Anson and Abigail (coming 2022)
Rachel and Riley (coming 2022)
Max and Maggie (coming 2023)

Made in the USA
Coppell, TX
14 June 2021